That
White Girl

ALSO BY JLOVE

We Got Issues! A Young Woman's Guide to a Bold, Courageous, and Empowered Life with Rha Goddess

That White Girl

[A NOVEL]

JLove

ATRIA BOOKS
New York London Toronto Sydney

ATRIA BOOKS

A Division of Simon & Schuster, Inc.
1230 Avenue of the Americas
New York, NY 10020

First Atria Books trade paperback edition August 2007

ATRIA BOOKS and colophon are trademarks
of Simon & Schuster, Inc.

For information regarding special discounts for bulk purchases,
please contact Simon & Schuster Special Sales at
1-800-456-6798 or business@simonandschuster.com.

Designed by Jaime Putorti

Manufactured in the United States of America

1   3   5   7   9   10   8   6   4   2

Library of Congress Cataloging-in-Publication Data

JLove.
That white girl: a novel / by JLove. — 1st Atria Books trade paperback ed.
p.   cm.
1. Teenage girls—Fiction.   2. Female gang members—Fiction.   I. Title.
PS3610.L68T47   2007
813'.6—dc22   2007022384

ISBN-13: 978-0-7432-8781-4

The life sentences in this book are dedicated to the hip-hop generation fighting for global liberation, and to the founders of this great culture in whom our faith is built and from whom our vision springs: Bambaataa, Flash, and Kool Herc.

For white girls, who understand the pain and joy when moving beyond the color lines.

For people of color who put the hue in human, as Talib would say; your struggle has defined our humanity. Thank you for putting up with us while we learn what it means to be allies.

Truth.Love.Freedom.

That White Girl

Prologue

he sound of the shot vibrated through my body and I froze. Everything happened in slow motion after that. I heard the shot, saw his body fall, and felt my life change. Blood was gushing out of his chest, seeping into the red-soaked ground. Amidst the shouts of confusion, police sirens, and screams of pain, the shell I had built around my body cracked open. For the first time, I understood I was in way too deep; the life I was leading would bring me nothing but broken promises. I had paved a path of destruction, a dangerous line between illusion and reality.

I ran and I ran, away from a world where I didn't belong, but had chosen; others had no choice.

I ran.

One

HIGH SCHOOL, FRESHMAN YEAR, LATE 80S

I could hardly believe it, so I went over it again and again in my mind:

Week One: Permission granted to meet some of the fellas.

Week Two: The distinct honor of being seen with the crew in public.

Week Three: My first Crip party!

Week Four: Juan reported that things were looking good. They had been talking about me all month, debating how things would play out. A couple even placed a wager on if I would get in or not. The biggest thing going for me, Juan said, was their curiosity: Could a white girl really get down?

A burning pride swirled through my body. Over the past month I'd gone from a kinda cool, hip-hop loving teenager to a girl on her way to chillin' with the notorious Crips. The mere thought of being affiliated with them put a smile on my face, which Juan would immediately want to slap off; I had to look hard. I considered Juan an expert on coolness: He was the only Latino in the Rollin' 30s; mad chicks dug him; plus he was brilliant. *Don't fuck things up* became my silent mantra.

After an endless day of lectures the bell rang and the hallways swirled with student chitchat. Juan and I were finally free. The sun shone brilliantly and the reflection bounced off the sidewalk, causing me to squint.

"So what we gettin' into today, Juan?" I asked, hoping he'd say something adventurous. We started walking our usual route up Jackson Street. The urban neighborhood was alive with kids on every corner hanging out, just getting home from school. There was a mix of small Victorian houses, apartments, and the brick projects, or the "pj's" as everyone called them. Three o'clock became the time of the great divide: bused-in whites went home, blacks and Mexicans remained.

We turned the corner and ran into an older black man walking a dog. He was light-skinned, and a jagged scar danced around his chinline, cutting across his handsome face. A blue rag hung from his back pocket.

"What up, cuzz?" he said to Juan. They exchanged some kind of handshake, followed by three pounds and hitting their knuckles together. I watched, and committed it to memory.

"This is my homegirl Amber. Amber, this is T-Dog," Juan said. T-Dog acknowledged me with a slight nod.

"When you coming through, Juan? It's been a minute," T-Dog said.

"Maybe *we'll* come through this weekend, if that's cool," Juan said. T-Dog eyed my white skin and long sandy-brown hair before he spoke. Until now, his dog paid me no mind, but he turned to me as if on cue, sniffing my legs. I was too scared to push him away—I didn't want to offend T-Dog, or get bitten.

"If you sure about that, come on," T-Dog said. "I gotta get back to the rest of my pups. Stay up, cuzz." He gave Juan a pound and nodded at me. "C'mon, sugar," he commanded, pulling the leash. Relief washed over my body.

"That right there is an O.G., but not just any O.G.," Juan told me as we resumed walking. "He's from Chicago and down here he runs the Rollin' 30s Crips."

"O.G.?" I looked at Juan.

"Original gangsta." He nodded with pride.

"*He's* the leader of the Crips?" I asked, surprised.

"Why you say it like that for?" Juan frowned and quickened his pace. Falling slightly behind, I spotted my favorite tattoo just below his jet-black hair. It was an intricate Japanese dragon that swirled around from the back of his neck to the side. Its mouth shot out bright orange fire, and in the middle of the flames it read "30s 4 vida," 30s for life. He got tatted up in celebration of his initiation. As always, Juan carried his large black backpack for his piece book and art supplies.

"He looks so regular. He doesn't even look mean." Trying to keep up.

"What's wrong with you white girls?" Juan said, shaking his head. "You're so ditzy sometimes. Tell me, what *do* gang leaders look like?"

Juan gave me the silent treatment; I felt like a fool. When my punishment was up, he put me on to the whole Denver Crip scene: the Rollin' 60s and the younger generation of Crips, the Rollin' 30s. Death and prison had left only a handful of O.G.s on the streets of the city.

Tyrone, aka T-Dog, was running things in Denver. Juan said he was known for his business savvy and skills in negotiating gang territory. T-Dog was cool, a laid-back type. He knew the game well, but didn't have an ego, just a staunch code of ethics. He learned early in life that an inflated ego can get you killed; his older brother's bravado ended with a fatal bullet to the chest. So while others were quick to fight or bark on someone, T-Dog picked his battles wisely. The only thing that got his temper flaring was disrespect. Then his fury would unleash and someone was bound to get hurt.

Juan and I ended up sitting in the park for a while before I headed home. He gave me a pound before we parted.

"So," he started, "are you gonna come with me to—"

"Of course," I said. "I'm there."

My family had dinner together every night; one-sided conversations, my mom asking about school or telling us family news. Occasionally, it was stuff that I really wanted to hear, but most of the time it was just random, useless information. "Well, your aunt Annie is just *so* upset about the continuous noise from the neighbors that she told Shirley from church she may have to move out of that house." Did Mom really think we cared?

We were sitting in our sunlit kitchen waiting to eat one of my mom's specialties, hamburger pie with green beans on the side. I watched as she cooked. She was as beautiful now as she was in our family albums, looking fly with her 60s-style platinum beehive hair and supershort miniskirts. As a little girl I thought she looked like a movie star. Now brown hair replaced the platinum.

I took off my mom's ID tag from her blouse. She worked in the cookware department at Sears.

"Amber, grab me some water while you're up." My older brother TJ's eyes were red and puffy, somewhat hidden under the long brown hair hanging in his face. He probably had cotton mouth, I thought. I shot him a quick look with attitude.

"Please?" TJ asked. He gave me a half smile.

I decided to be nice. How could my mom not know he was high all the time? Maybe she just didn't *want* to know. She was already struggling to pay the mortgage and raise us by herself. My father walked out years ago. We saw him when it was convenient for him, but he never seemed to have any money to spare. Mom was on her own in that department.

"Okay, sit down. It's time for dinner," my mom said, and we prayed.

My stomach was tingling, hot and uneasy.

"Amber, why aren't you eating?" Mom asked with a pleasant smile. "I made your favorite."

My mind flashed to the new crew I was hanging out with, which I knew Mom wouldn't approve of. Here I was so safe. Everything in this house was so . . . *regular.*

"I'm just not hungry, Mom."

I watched my mom and brother as the conversation buzzed in my ears. I knew I loved them, and believed they loved me too. But would they still love me if they knew who I really was? If everything went according to my plan and I rocked a blue rag?

I wished I could talk to my best friend Carmen about this, but would she understand?

Nobody knows who I really am, I thought. Sometimes not even me.

Two weeks later, I was finally going to T-Dog's crib. I went through five different outfits and several lies to make it out of the house.

"Amber." My mom grabbed me before I could hit the door. "Please use your head tonight." She hugged me tight and reminded me to be home by midnight. It seemed like she could tell when I was lying to her.

"Relax, Amber." Juan gave me last-minute instructions as we headed to Five Points, the black section in Denver. "Be cool. And try not to talk too much." Twenty minutes later we were at our stop. Juan led the way up to the middle of the block. We approached the side of a small white house in serious need of a paint job. The yard was mostly dirt, with patches of grass struggling to grow. I was both nervous and excited, but no matter what, I knew that Juan wouldn't let anything happen to me.

Juan led me downstairs and I clung to his arm as my eyes adjusted to the darkness. The room was packed, the stereo was pumpin' LL Cool J's tape, "Rock the Bells." Usually that song got me hyped, but as Juan and I sat on the small itchy couch I obsessed over my skirt. Everyone was in jeans or dickies and I felt overdressed.

I wondered who all the people were and, as if he knew what I was thinking, Juan whispered in my ear, "Just chill, let them get used to you. They all down with the Rollin' 30s." I nodded.

I drank a forty by myself and stuck to Juan's side. T-Dog came and kicked it with us for a while, I guess he was feeling me out, making sure I was straight. When we left hours later I relaxed; I could finally let my guard down.

But as the weeks went on, the more I kicked it with the Crips, the more I was able to slowly allow part of myself to come out. My first couple of encounters with them were crazy. We'd all get drunk and high and they'd make me do the Crip walk, or flash Crip signs I had just learned.

"Yo, Amber, you just threw up a Westside sign, that ain't our hood—you lost or somethin'?"

Most of them were having a blast making fun of me. But I couldn't escape the look on a couple of Crips' faces who didn't find anything funny.

"You sure she ain't no cop?" Ray-Ray asked Juan once.

"Nigga, please. I don't chill with no narcs. Get outta here with that shit!" Juan snapped.

"I don't trust that bitch, cuzz," he continued. "Does she really think she can get down wit' us?"

A lot of pressure fell on Juan, whose assurances allowed me to stay. But by no means was my trial period up.

Two

My daily marathon began when the lunch bell rang.

First, I met Carmen in the lobby. We headed to the pizzeria across the parkway. She hated cafeteria food, and I loved getting away from school for a while. Carmen dropped a twenty on the counter and told the guy, "Let me get a slice with anchovies and extra cheese and a Coke." She looked over at me.

"I'm not having anything," I said, putting my hand on my stomach. "I had a huge breakfast."

I checked my watch. Another ten minutes to shoot the shit with her before I had to leave. Carmen's dark brown eyes sparkled as she joked about some of the girls in our class. But they saddened when we compared our test scores from English class. She had been struggling with her grades ever since she hit high school.

I grabbed her hand. "Don't worry, Carmen, I'll help you study this weekend. We'll get your scores up." I hated seeing her so upset.

She wiped a tear off her cheek. "I just hate feeling stupid in class, especially with Mr. Henry. It's like he enjoys embarrassing me when I don't know the answer. I can't stand him!"

We talked about the dreaded Mr. Henry until the time came for me to leave. I stood up and put on my jacket. "Where you going this time?" Carmen had become used to my early departures.

"I gotta talk to Juan about something before lunch is up."

Carmen sighed. "You know I hate eating alone," she said.

"Sorry, Carmen, but it's really important," I replied, and headed for the door. "I'll check ya later." I could feel her staring at me as I left, but I didn't have time to care; my itinerary was tight.

On the way back to the school, I made my usual stop at a small, dingy lunch spot, *Uncle Charlie's,* where Juan and his graffiti homies would be. Leaning on the counter, I plunked down a bill and said, "Yo, hook me up with the chicken deluxe." I immediately saw Juan and Diablo sitting at a small brown table pushed up against the wall. I kicked it with them and waited for my order. Skinny-ass Diablo with his XXL baggy pants had his piece book out and was working on a sketch of a crazy dope bunny character throwing up a peace sign.

"Amber, you hear about the beef between Zen and Chaos?" Juan said, after giving me a pound.

"Yeah, I heard something about Zen being pissed 'cause he thinks Chaos bit from that piece he did on Colfax," I answered.

"He did," muttered Diablo.

"So you know what Zen did?" Juan said. "He went down to the train yard and tagged up all over Chaos's new shit." He laughed.

"That's what homeboy gets for bitin'," Diablo added.

"Word," I said.

The counter guy summoned me over to get my order. I checked my bag to make sure that he got it right. Wrapped in white paper was my chicken sandwich. Next to it, wrapped up in a napkin, was the deluxe—a fat joint.

"Zen and Chaos need to squash that shit before it goes too far," Juan continued. "We need unity in our crew."

I took the weed from the napkin. "I gotta break out," I said as I opened the door. "Juan, you want to roll with me? I'm going to check Chavez."

"Nah, I got some business to handle with a certain chick." He winked at me. "But I'll call you later. I may need to call a Writers' Meeting this weekend 'cause of this shit." Juan saw my eyes light up immediately.

"Members only, cuzz," he said, shaking his head. "Sorry."

"Whatever."

I hustled toward the school, checked my watch. Lunch was half over and I had two more stops to make. Next up: the bleachers.

Chavez was the first one to notice me. "What's up, Amber?" He ran toward me and tried to reach for my bag. "Yo, what you got in there?"

He knew what I had in there. That was exactly why he was asking. *"No te importa,"* I said in my best Spanish.

"Ah, you funny!"

I shared my blunt with all of them like I always did. With ten minutes left till my next class, I hurried to the cafeteria, where the black kids hung out. I only got to kick it with Keisha for a minute before the bell signaled us back to class. I knew Keisha from way back. We met in church, our first communion class, and remained tight ever since.

In front of my friends, I rolled my eyes when the bell rang, but secretly I loved hearing it. It meant my marathon was over.

My school, Five Points High, had a good reputation for our athletic teams, but a bad reputation for gang violence and dropout rates. The school was officially integrated, but you couldn't tell that by walking through the halls. We had whites, blacks, Mexicans, and some Asians all mixed up at the same school, but come lunchtime, parties, or events, people hung out with their own. That was just the way it was, and not many people chose to question it. Except, for some strange reason, me.

During that lunchtime race I was a chameleon, speaking a common language with each group to communicate a degree of sameness, or at least enough to be considered friend, or *blanquita,* or that white girl.

After lunch, I spotted Darnell, our school's favorite hip-hop fans, standing in the doorway as I walked down the corridor to my English class. When he saw me, he dashed back into the classroom yelling, "Yo, she's coming!"

Each afternoon I walked to class with a mixture of pride and nerves. They had tested me every day for the past three months, and so far I had passed every single time. I was proud because they had yet to trip me up, and nervous about what would happen when the day came that they did catch me out there, not knowing my shit.

I stepped into the classroom. As usual Darnell, Tony, and the others were crowded around my desk. Tony didn't even let me sit down before he fired the first question. "Amber, check it." He cleared his throat and put his palms against his chest like he always did before he started to rhyme.

"I'm the authentic poet to get lyrical . . ." he started.

"I know this," I said. "Hold up, lemme just think for a minute." I hummed to myself as I thought about it, and they tittered and nudged each other, thinking they had snagged me. But I did know it. The lyrics came to me as I ran the rhythm through my head. Then I finished, "For you to beat me, it's gonna take a miracle." Tony almost caught me out there with "Ain't No Half Steppin'" because he started in the middle of Big Daddy Kane's verse.

"Aw, man!" Tony groaned, letting me know I had gotten it right.

Keisha clapped, and her girl Maxi gave me five. They always rooted for me. But the others hovered around my desk like vultures over a corpse. Another hater named Tammy yelled to get everyone's attention. "Bet she don't know this." She gave me a hard look, then said, "With knowledge of self, there's nothing I can't solve . . ."

". . . At three hundred sixty degrees, I revolve." They all roared. Stupid-ass Tammy. That Rakim joint was the shit. Who the fuck wouldn't know that? But I knew to keep that thought to myself, because I wasn't trying to have her waiting for me after the bell.

"I got it, I got it." Darnell hushed everyone. He parked himself on my desk and put his finger in my face as he rhymed. "You know I'm proud to be . . ."

And just like that, this daily quiz of theirs had taken a new direction. It was an easy song. I mean, *everyone* knew these words, it was a classic. But was Darnell trying to get me to say them to clown me?

"She don't know it!" Tammy yelled. "Amber don't know it." She laughed in triumph and gave Darnell a pound.

And that pushed me past my fear over how they would react. "I do too know it." Even though it might have cost me my ass, I had to say it to shut her up. I jumped out of my seat and pumped my finger back in Darnell's face as I rhymed.

"You know I'm proud to be black, y'all, and that's a fact, y'all, and if you try to take what's mine, I'll take it back, y'all!" It was quiet for minute after I finished. I waited, tense.

"Oh, shit!" Then they all laughed and clapped, even Darnell and Tammy. Darnell said, "This is one weird-ass white girl." I took it as a compliment.

Dear Diary

My new crush: Brian, a senior on the basketball team.

My favorite outfit: my new Lee's with the red satin roller skate on the back.

TV show of the week: CHiPs! Ponch is so cute!

Listen, things are a little mixed up right now. It used to be that I hung out mostly with white people, and had some black friends. Now, I hang out mostly with black people and only have a couple of white friends. I went to a party and started talking to Evan. He said he missed the REAL Amber! He said I used to be so fun, happy, and exciting. I miss being happy too. He said people could always depend on me to cheer them up. I don't know why things suck so bad in my house, but it really fucks me up inside.

I know I've changed but it feels good to me. I love hangin' out with the Crips, even though sometimes I wonder if it's good or bad. It's hard to talk to Carmen about it. She doesn't understand, and she thinks it is pulling us apart because we don't hang out as much. I don't tell Keisha anything, because I know she would be against all of it. Should I change back? I need to know! The me right now—the way I'm acting—is this the real me? Am I who I want to be? Or should be? I need answers!

After I proved to Darnell my love for rap music, he started putting me on to what he called "real hip-hop," like KRS-One of Boogie Down Productions and Eric B. and Rakim. Instead of trying to clown me, he looked out for me, hooking me up with mix tapes. He lived by Five Points High, but had cousins in Forestville, so he was in my neighborhood all the time. An added plus, he had his own car.

The weekend rolled around, and I was reading a new novel my mom picked up for me when someone's bass started rattling our windows. I looked outside and saw Darnell's clean, black car with shiny rims in the front. I ran out and hopped in the front seat.

"Yo Amber, lemme put you on to some new shit. You ain't gonna hear this on the radio, 'cause this be talkin' about black people loving themselves." Darnell was handsome; he rocked a flattop and loved Drakkar Noir cologne—he put it on a little too heavy, though. He hated that the only radio station catering to the black community played mostly R&B and party music. "We need to hear some lyrics with knowledge in them. Jungle Brothers, KRS, Public Enemy, Public Enemy, man, I'll even take LL Cool J."

"I don't even understand everything KRS is sayin'," I confessed.

"KRS-One always kicks knowledge. Especially to black people—he wants us to elevate—give up the ignorant shit, like that gang shit." He looked at me. "What are you doing hangin' out with Crips, anyways?"

"Why do you care who I hang out with?" I asked.

"'Cause you being real stupid about it, Amber. I mean, you're cool with me and all, but you think this is all a game. Look at your house, where you live."

I looked over at my house, and saw what Darnell was talking about. There was no getting around it. I had a house in a neighborhood lined with trees and backyards. Darnell kept talking.

"You don't have no reason to be bangin'. My people in the

hood ain't got no choice. They bang to survive. You bang to be cool. It's not a popularity contest. People are dying over colors, Amber."

I crossed my arms and remained quiet. Darnell was right in many ways. I thought back to when the idea first entered my mind. Juan and I were kickin' it downtown one afternoon, just messing around. He had his Walkman on, which he never left the house without, and at one point he started moving his hands—his fingers dancing. I asked him what he was doing, and he told me about the Crips, and that his fingers had been telling a story. Once he taught me some basic Crip signs, I became enthralled. On the bus home that day we sat apart and practiced communicating through our fingers.

I loved learning new things, and I felt like something was missing in my life. Even though I couldn't place what it was, my urge was to fill the void.

"Anyway," Darnell said, "back to KRS, he just wants us to be successful, and that's what his music is all about, which is why they call him the Teacher."

"It seems like they should be playin' him on the radio," I said, happy we were off the subject of me.

"Well, you know the reason they don't, right?" He saw by the look on my face that I wasn't following. He laughed.

"You're a nice chick, Amber, but you're real naïve. I know you kick it with us black people and everything, but you obviously don't really understand our struggle."

I wasn't sure what he was talking about, but I could tell it was important.

"I'll put you on another time. I gotta break out. I'll see you at school."

"Cool. Are you gonna come around next week?"

"No doubt."

Darnell and I started having weekly "listening parties" in his fully loaded car. The sound system pumped bass into my body until it became my addiction. I felt a pull, a web of energy, beats pulsating and rhymes drawing me in. Every song had something that spoke to me—I had to have it in my life. Growing up, we had all kinds of music in my house. TJ was into classic rock and heavy metal, while my parents liked classical music. When I started kicking it in different circles, I got put on other kinds of music, from Bob Marley and Menudo to Whodini and Levert.

It was under the tutelage of my homies that my fate as a hip-hop junkie was sealed. Sometimes I wondered what I'd be like if it weren't for hip-hop. In school, at church, in my neighborhood, I looked at other white kids who didn't know anything about the music or the culture. I felt sorry for them, even though it was they who viewed me with indignation. And what if my homies, like Juan and Darnell, got tired of "teaching" me? Could I follow this path, this new cultural awakening, by myself? Sitting in Darnell's car, listening in appreciation, I hoped I never had to find out.

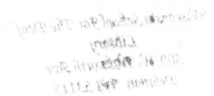

Three

The scent of weed rose to greet us as we hustled down the dark staircase to T-Dog's basement. Juan and I got there late. I'd been waiting for him to come back from the Writer's Meeting, where they'd been debating the recent drama between Zen and Chaos. I got passed a forty. I took a swig, then surveyed the scene.

There were about fifteen of us, most of whom I knew. I was cool with a few of the Rollin' 30s by now, especially T-Dog, Lil D, and Rodney.

"Come on, Amber, lemme hear you sing our new theme song!" Lil D said. He was the youngest of the Rollin' 30s, and he liked me from the beginning. I started laughing as he did the Crip walk singing "blue is the color of the Crips." He always made me smile with his cute dimples and long eyelashes—he looked so innocent. He was so young, just thirteen. I wondered what kind of initiation he had to do at that age.

"You buggin', man, I can't sing!" I laughed. But my laughter came to an abrupt halt when I saw the scowls of two guys whom I didn't trust, Ray-Ray and Killa. Ray-Ray never liked me. He had come from New York, and even though he was only sixteen he had dropped out of high school and spent his time running the streets. He was forever rockin' T-shirts that said NEW YORK; I guess that made him feel like we should be scared or something. I never liked being around him.

Then there was Killa who grilled me with that crazy look he always had. I needed to remember to check myself and not get too carried away. Killa was a good reminder of that. He had a 'fro that was never combed, and didn't care how sloppy his clothes looked.

Blunts passed from one to the next, causing a haze of smoke to rise to the ceiling. The blue lightbulb supplied minimal lighting and cast eerie shadows everywhere.

"Yo, we out of drink, who got some ends?" T-Dog yelled above the music, looking around at everyone. Lil D stopped dancing and everyone started checking their backpacks, going in their pockets and coming up with, if we were lucky, some lint.

"We all broke, man. You know niggas ain't got no dough round here." Rodney chuckled. Rodney's appearance was a top priority. He always dressed with the crispest creases, Jheri curl with just enough activator, and hat always tilted at the exact same angle.

"So let's roll up on 7-Eleven and get what we need," T-Dog announced. Everybody started talking at once, I looked around and waited, unsure of what all the fuss was about.

"I'm down. You down?" Lil D set it off. It was like a ritual to ask the question. It went around the room, one Crip at a time. Everyone said yes.

"Yo, Amber, you been kickin' it with us for a minute, how

much heart you *really* got?" T-Dog asked. The whole room got quiet with all eyes on me. "If you wanna rep with us, you gotta get your hands dirty."

My heart was pounding. Was I getting jumped in tonight? I glanced around, and realized that I was the only female in the room. How could I have not noticed that before? I had heard rumors of what gangs did to initiate females. Where was Juan? In my panic, I couldn't spot him, couldn't see his eyes telling me it would be okay. Had he gone outside? Had he known this was coming? My mind was racing. I felt like I was going to throw up. The time for indecision was over.

As if on cue the music stopped, engulfing the room in complete silence as I made one of the most pivotal decisions of my life. I had to give T-Dog an answer, though it wasn't clear if I even had a choice anymore. Not sure what I should say, or how I got the guts to say it, I heard the voice as if it wasn't even mine.

"I'm down," I said. "I got heart."

"We'll see about that," T-Dog said, and I heard a couple of people laugh.

What was I gonna have to do tonight to prove my loyalty?

It was dark when we walked out of the house fifteen minutes later. Lil D passed by me and gave me a "you'll be aight" nod. T-Dog was by my side. Juan was ahead of us, staying out of the way of what was clearly the leader's domain.

"We're hittin' the 7-Eleven on Fillmore Street," T-Dog commanded. "They ain't installed a security camera in that one yet."

We headed toward the store, all of us fucked up from the alcohol and weed. The young white clerk looked worried as soon as we walked in. His eyes questioned me, trying to make sense of what he was seeing. He was alone and there were fourteen or fifteen of us. He paced behind the counter.

The guys sauntered over to where the beer was kept on the far side of the store. I wandered up and down the aisles, acting like I was looking for something. I didn't know what the hell I was supposed to be doing. I heard the guys laughing and carelessly talking shit. I turned down another aisle and ran into Juan, who looked surprised when he saw I didn't have anything in my hands.

"Take whatever you want!" Juan said. The thought hadn't crossed my mind that it was that easy. "Yo, hurry up!"

Looking up I saw the guys walking toward the counter—they had so much stuff in their arms: beer, chips, and cigarettes. With my heart racing and my head buzzin' from the alcohol, I grabbed a whole box of king-size Snickers and Juan yelled, "Let's go!" As I walked toward the door to leave, T-Dog put his hand on my arm, signaling me to wait. Without hesitating he pulled a gat out of his jacket.

"Cover us," he said in a low voice. "Do what you gotta do." He paused a moment to look me dead in my eyes, then put the cold piece of steel in my hands and strolled out of the store with his head held high.

I was terrified.

Juan came behind me and whispered, "Yo, point that shit at him before he calls the cops!" I looked at him for help. "This is what you've been waiting for, right?" He turned his back on me and ran to meet T-Dog outside.

I wasn't prepared for the flood of feelings I got when I raised the gun, pointing it straight at the clerk's face. He looked freaked out. Behind him, taped on the wall, was a picture of a cute little girl—maybe his daughter? I felt sorry for him and prayed nobody would get hurt. The rest of the Crips walked out with all their shit. Lil D put a handful of pennies on the counter and said, "Thanks, man."

"Don't hurt me, please!" He was staring at *me*. "I have a family, I have a daughter!" He was stuttering and shaking. "Take what you want and go! Please don't shoot!" His hands were up, and the tears started streaming down his face mixed with his sweat. I simultaneously felt detached and stunned, knowing I could cause someone's complete and total fear.

Now I was alone in the 7-Eleven with the clerk. It felt so weird, me and this white guy—who looked like an older version of my brother. Neither of us knew quite what to do. His expression was a mixture of fear and anger, still and questioning.

Without the Crips with me I lost focus, and my mom's face kept popping into my mind. *I gotta get out of here.* I counted to three in my head to calm my nerves, and then sprinted out the door, running as fast as I could. My adrenaline kicked in, I felt powerful. The liquor, the gun, and my fear collided. I was out of control.

We met back at the house in the basement; everybody was celebrating and laughing and giving each other daps. T-Dog walked over to me and without a word held out his hand for the gun. I handed it over, happy to be free of it.

We put all the stuff we had stolen in the middle of the room. The rest of the night was spent drinking, smoking, eating, and telling stories about our mobbin' success. I waited for someone to mention what I did, but nobody said anything. After a while I relaxed, wondering if I had passed the first test. Was that my initiation?

"Yo, T-Dog," Ray-Ray called out.

"What up?" T-Dog asked, looking over at Ray-Ray, who was sitting on the couch.

"I'm sure everyone want to know," he said.

"Know what, cuzz?"

"You really gonna let a white bitch into our crew?" Everyone looked from Ray-Ray to T-Dog to me.

"Yo, cuzz, you think you in charge?" T-Dog stood up and started walking toward Ray-Ray. "You ain't runnin' this shit, nigga."

Ray-Ray stood up, and put his hand behind his back. Did he have a gun? Would he use it? The room got quiet—all of the earlier fun was gone.

"Chill out, cuzz," Lil D said. Everyone knew Lil D was the only one who could talk sense into T-Dog. Lil D was planted in front of him, his hands pressing against T-Dog's shoulders. T-Dog was moving forward, his strength causing Lil D to stumble backward.

"T, c'mon man. He ain't worth it, cuzz. Let's drink another forty and chill, cuzz," he pleaded. Even though Lil D was a Crip, I could tell that he really didn't like violence. He was the peacekeeper.

"Cuzz, we fam, right?" Juan said. "We don't need this between us." He started approaching T-Dog from the side. Ray-Ray was standing strong and silent, his hand still frozen behind his back, his jaw clenching.

T-Dog was grilling Ray-Ray. Lil D was talking to him in a low voice so I couldn't hear what he was saying. I looked at Juan and saw him messing with the old radio. Suddenly music filled the space.

Lil D let go of T-Dog and started being silly, doing the Crip walk, and hollering, "Rollin' 30s, cuzz!" Ray-Ray put his hand down, but remained standing, still watching T-Dog. We were all waiting to see if T-Dog would back down.

"Get outta my way, cuzz!" T-Dog yelled, and pushed Lil D away from him. He looked straight at Ray-Ray and said, "The white bitch is in!" Then he turned around and returned to his big black chair. "Now somebody get me a fuckin' blunt," he growled.

The whole room breathed a collective sigh.

A couple of days later, Carmen and I walked out of school, giggling about boys. She had met a new guy named Kyle at a party and was all wrapped up in how cute he was. We were on our way to her house to hang out. When we hit the corner bus stop, Juan was there, waiting for me.

"Come on, cuzz, let's roll to T-Dog's," he said, without acknowledging Carmen. I had been reluctant to see them ever since Ray-Ray called me out. I felt like I only got in because T-Dog was proving his leadership to not just Ray-Ray, but all the Rollin' 30s.

"You just said you were coming to my house, Amber." Carmen looked at me, waiting for my answer.

"I know, but can I get a rain check? I'll make it up to you, promise," I said, hoping she would understand. Juan sighed impatiently.

"Whatever. Do what you want. I guess I'll just see you tomorrow." She flipped her black hair back and turned toward the bus stop.

I was preoccupied about Carmen. I could tell she was upset. But as soon as Juan grabbed my arm and told me to hurry up, the source of my anxiety changed.

"I don't want to go to T-Dog's," I began. "What if Ray-Ray is there? I don't want any problems."

"You can't be scared of that fool. He ain't gonna do nothing to you, 'cause none of us will let him. He don't like you 'cause you're white but who gives a fuck? T-Dog got love for you for some reason. You got no idea how fuckin' lucky you are."

"But that wasn't cool, how he called me out like that!" I said.

"What the fuck, Amber. Do you have any idea how easy your initiation was? You barely had to do shit to get in the baddest gang in Colorado." Juan walked faster; I struggled to keep up.

"But—" I started.

"No, shut up for a minute. Instead of whining about Ray-Ray said this and I had to do that, why don't you open your eyes and look the fuck around! You *lucky* to be chillin' with the notorious 30s, do you get that? Damn, you don't even know what other motherfuckers had to do to get in this shit. You didn't even get jumped in!" Juan shook his head. "You know what Amber, I don't even feel like kickin' it with you today. I'm tired of schoolin' you and havin' to get your back all the time. Sometimes you just gotta let things go, and just be down." He stopped and looked at me with pity in his eyes. "I'll check you later, cuzz." He left me standing there.

I walked back to the bus stop in a daze, hoping Carmen was still there, but she was already gone. I spent the whole trip home swearing to myself I would never be that soft again. Here I was complaining about somebody being mean to me. Think about it, I said to myself. I'm talking about the Crips! My upbringing was going against me, no question about that. I was raised with my parents always talking about college, tons of books in my house, church every weekend; I was sheltered to a certain extent. I didn't have what it took to be down. At the same time, I felt the sting of being told I wasn't good enough by my mentor. Didn't he know how hard I was trying? I started wondering what the hell I was doing in the middle of all this.

I couldn't deny the fact that I was drawn to the Crips. I couldn't deny how good it felt to see the look of surprise on people's faces when they saw me getting pounds from Rollin' 30s in the school hallway. But I also couldn't deny my whiteness.

Four

The whole school was hyped for the pep rally that week but me. Our football team was playing a major home game determining whether we were going to the state championship. As soon as I hit the gym, the dreaded decision was inevitable; which clique would I represent? At least the Crips weren't here—those who even bothered to go to school cut whenever they could, and the rally provided the perfect opportunity. Carmen cut as well. She was probably at the park having fun chillin' with Kyle. I should have gone with her when I had the chance.

"Amber, come sit over here!" Michelle, who I sat next to in science class, called me over. She was surrounded by a bunch of preppy white kids. I saw Chavez and his homies sitting behind them on the bleachers. Keisha was on the gym floor with the student council members. I caught her eye and she waved at me. At the other side of the gym were the jocks, the cheerleaders, and some rowdy juniors and seniors.

Just then Chavez and his girl, Shelia, spotted me. "Yo, *blan-quita!* Come chill with us. We got a spot for ya." I gave a nod, and started walking toward the bleachers, trying to figure a way out of this mess. No matter who I sat next to, the other group would feel dissed. If I sat with Michelle and her friends, I was going to be seen as a regular white girl, even worse, a prep. I couldn't lose cool points in front of Chavez and his girl. I'd just started kickin' it with them a couple of weeks back. I was wearing blue jeans, sneakers, and the blue Gucci sweat-shirt I had stolen from Juan. Well, at least I wasn't rocking anything that was embarrassing. But still, what would they think if I sat with the preps instead of them? Fuck this, I thought. Why is this so damn complicated?

Michelle waved to me desperately. "Come on, Amber, I saved a seat for you!" She started making people move over so that I could sit next to her. I wished she wouldn't be so nice to me, it just made things that much harder. I walked over to where she was and sat down, without looking back at Chavez.

"*Chica!*" Chavez yelled to me, making everyone turn and look at him. "What up, homie, come sit with your peeps, not them corny *gringas!*"

Chavez didn't like too many white people. Ever since busing started, his school was flooded with white kids who had money, or at least more money than his family. Some kids drove to school in their BMWs and sat next to kids on welfare. Some white parents, upset over the new laws, even pulled their kids out of public school and sent them to Catholic school. Chavez was one of only a handful of Mexicans in the accelerated classes. He often complained that the teachers ignored him and focused on the white students.

Michelle turned to me, red in the face. "I can't believe he just called me that! Why do you hang out with *him*? He's such an asshole!"

Before I could reply, the pep rally started, the screaming echoing off the gym walls. Michelle kept talking at me, and finally just turned away, my silence speaking louder than words.

I got up, squeezing past people to get to Chavez. I knew that my decision would cause waves, but as he and his girl gave me approving smiles, I felt like it was worth it. After the rally I said my good-byes and slipped out of the gym, avoiding confrontation.

After that day, things got progressively worse between Michelle's buddies and me. Rolling their eyes when I walked by, starting stupid rumors about me, someone even wrote "Amber is a bitch" on the bathroom wall.

"I'm just so sick of those fuckin' girls, man," I said to Carmen. "I didn't do shit to her!" We were walking to the bus stop after school.

"Well, it was kinda mean that she made room for you and then you split for some other friends. I might get upset too." I could tell Carmen was thinking back to the other day when I left *her* so I could be with Juan.

"But I had already made plans to sit with Chavez," I protested, which wasn't entirely true.

"The thing is, Amber, you're starting to do that a lot more, now that you have new friends," she said.

"But who cares about that? I don't get mad when Michelle hangs out with someone else. Shit, every other day she has a new best friend," I said.

"I don't think it's just that. I think it's *who* you're hanging out with that matters. Those girls think they're the shit, but they know they don't run things at this school. They don't like seeing a white girl who is accepted by everyone, because they aren't. They don't like that blacks and Mexicans talk to you and stuff."

"It really doesn't need to be like this. Michelle makes it like a competition and shit," I said.

"Don't get caught up in what's cool and what's not. Be yourself and the right people will be around you—like me!" Carmen said, bumping me with her hip, smiling. Guilt stabbed my heart. Why had I been putting Juan in front of my best friend? She had stood by me my whole life. Me and Carmen had been through a lot—perverts flashing us, our brothers beating us up, experimenting with alcohol and weed in middle school. It wasn't until high school that things started changing, and I began gravitating to other friends.

"You have always been different," I said. And it was true. Carmen refused to be a follower. She'd dealt with some crazy shit while growing up. Even though she was half Chicana, half white, many of the Mexican students didn't accept her because she was raised by her white mom. The white cliques, well, sometimes they were nice to her, but they could get mean when they wanted to. In elementary school they would call her names, but we had always stuck together. I knew that with our friendship, Carmen would always be in my life.

Dear Diary,

Song that makes me happy: "Ribbon in the Sky" by Stevie Wonder

New Crush: the tennis player Andre Agassi, his long hair is so sexy!

The truth is that I grew up how many other white kids grew up. My early childhood was nothing special, dodging blows from my brother who liked to pick on me, bringing sanity to my mom, drama to my dad's girlfriends. I was into sports and I loved the one knockoff Barbie I owned. I blamed my cavities and knack for getting lost all the time on my mom. From my father I learned that I

would never be good enough. Whether it was my grades,
my appearance, or my friends.

I just want to feel normal. Or maybe not. Maybe what
I really want is to feel special, feel different . . . not sure,
still trying to figure it all out.

The following day, I was surprised when I saw Juan at my front
door. He walked straight to my bedroom.

"Get a bag 'cause you 'bout to throw a lot of shit away. You
can't be caught wearin' no slob colors," he said.

The night at the 7-Eleven, the gun, the clerk, even the
drama with Ray-Ray . . . I got what I wanted. I was accepted,
not necessarily as a Crip, but as an associate, which meant that
I could hang around them, learn crew codes, and use my
association to secure my rep. Juan looked inside my closet and
started taking out anything that was red and throwing it on
the bed.

"Listen and listen good. There is an important order to colors and their significance." He broke it down.

"We reppin' Parkside Hoods set of the Rollin' 30s. We can
wear blue and black. White and gray accents are okay. Buy or
steal Raiders stuff—everything Raiders. The biggest thing is *no
red!*" He paused from making a pile of clothes on my bed and
looked at me. "Red represents the Bloods. From now on, anytime you write or wear a 'B' you have to cross it out. So if you
get those fresh British Knight shoes you been wantin', you
gotta get a black Sharpie and put an 'X' over the 'B'—are
you getting all this?" Juan was in prime teacher mode. I was
hanging on to his every word but I was also getting nervous
because it was almost six and my mom would be getting home
from work soon.

Before Juan left I learned the entire Crip wardrobe—

everything from shoes whose laces had to be done in a certain design to hats, which could be blue or black but had to be rocked to the side or the back. As headlines in the *Denver Post* revealed, in certain parts of town the wrong color could end up getting you in a lot of trouble.

Five

SOPHOMORE YEAR

Juan was considered one of Denver's first and finest graffiti artists, and on top of that, he was a Crip. You couldn't beat those credentials.

"I wish I could paint like you," I said to Juan, looking at his latest masterpiece in the alley behind a grocery store.

"Vapors" was spray-painted in computer rock, his favorite style, with two characters on either side wearing name belts, fat laces, and a blue rag. "Dedicated to my homegirl Amber, Always Keep the Faith! Graffiti is Art Design Not Street Crime!" It was the first time somebody had dedicated a piece to me. I was glowing inside.

"What are you talkin' about, girl? Like you can't do what I do. It just takes practice and dedication. I mean look, I got you into the Crips, right? Hell, if you serious about being a graff writer, I'll teach you. You can be my student." He paused. "And you know what, I even know what name I would give you." He had a smile on his face and shook up his spray paint.

"What name?"

"Corazón."

"What does that mean?" I had never heard that word before.

"It's Spanish for heart." Juan put his arm around me, his eyes warm. "'Cause you got heart for a white girl."

That day began our ritual of "How to Be Down 101" for the white girl from Forestville, including painting, tagging lessons, and most important, graffiti writer etiquette. My days and nights became filled with the smell of fresh spray paint, multi-colored fingertips, and a marker or two always hidden in my pockets.

A couple of weeks later, we sat in the park drawing in each other's piece books, just hanging out by ourselves.

"Man, Amber, people been writin' on walls since the beginning of time," Juan started, rubbing his goatee as he spoke. "Back in the day, Egyptians were writing their tribes' histories on the walls, some ancient-type shit, fo' real. We're carrying on the traditions of the people that came before us."

Juan blew me away with his ongoing graffiti storytelling, dropping gems on me daily. He had me studying up on O.G. graff artists, paying close attention to the female artists, like Lady Pink. She was a New York legend, who got much respect on the street because she threw down as hard, if not harder, than the guys.

"Did you do your homework?" Juan's question snapped me back into reality. In my backpack among my schoolbooks was an envelope full of cartoon characters, which Juan made me draw until I had that shit down.

"Yeah, check this out. Pretty cool, right?"

My favorite was Betty Boop. She had style for a cartoon

character. I showed Juan her picture in my piece book, a writer's most prized possession. Each writer's book contains drawings, tags, ideas, or sketches; whatever inspires them. When writers meet other writers they respect, they'll ask them to hit up their book. My book was becoming part of my identity.

"Graffiti isn't for suckers—it's not *only* about your skills with a spray can," Juan said, taking off his new black-and-blue plaid button-down he lifted from a store downtown. I could always tell how long a lecture would be based on how engrossed he was in his work. When sketching out a real elaborate piece, he really got into it. "Dope hand style is a must. Speed and accuracy in busting out your piece from start to finish is critical." He searched for his markers and started adding color to his pencil sketch.

"You know I'm getting faster, Juan . . ." He put his hand up to stop me from saying more. "Last is your physical abilities. If you can't run from the cops, building owners, crazy junkies, or stick-up kids, you'll either be in jail, get a hellafied beat down, or both. The result?" He looked up at me. "Devastating. An incomplete piece come sunrise, and you'll be marked as a complete toy by lunchtime. "

Juan and I first met in middle school, where we stumbled upon our mutual love of the written word in English class. We'd quote poetry to each other during school, passing notes across the room with a verse from Edgar Allan Poe or fantasizing about our "royal" families. He laid claim to Spanish royalty, while I whispered fleeting thoughts of kings of Ireland. His reality was far worse than mine. His father was out of the picture, and his mother was having her own troubles, so she sent him away to live with her older sister. Sometimes he'd come to my house after school. He loved waiting until my mom got home from work because she'd always cook something for us, and Juan loved talking to her. She listened to him and made him feel special. But that was middle school. I watched him evolve from sweet poetic schoolboy to angry, defiant rebel. Once he found others similar to him, there was nothing to stop him from becoming a straight-up gangsta by the time we got to high school.

"Nobody gives a fuck about me, Amber, except you and the Rollin' 30s," he told me one afternoon, right after we graduated from eighth grade. "My moms barely even calls the house. My *tia* is so old-school. She has no clue how hard shit is for me. I mean, she tries, but . . ." He shook his head.

From then on we rolled everywhere together. Neither of us cared everyone gossiped about us being a couple. We knew we were best friends. As we strolled across Forest Park, Juan would school me on street life. He taught me how to say things right, what was cool, what was dorky, and put me on to things that I otherwise wouldn't have learned.

After spending a couple months studying graffiti under Juan, he announced his master plan and swore me to secrecy. I spent a tireless amount of time and effort to make it happen. Late nights pretending to do homework but instead tracing an intricate design; almost breaking my neck climbing up trains in the yard to get the optimal tag; hitting up spots when I was with my family without them even noticing.

Finally, the plan succeeded; the name "Corazón" besieged the city, tagged on every conceivable flat surface.

People commented how the writer came out of nowhere and marked territory meticulously as a dog. "Yo, how'd he hit that highway sign?" they asked one another. Questions circulated on whether he was new in town, maybe from the East Coast coming to infiltrate Denver's graffiti scene. Friend or foe? Something about the curve of the "C" intrigued them. Every writer in Denver was trying to figure it out. Who is Corazón?

We met up after school to hang out with Diablo, Zap, and some other cats from his graffiti crew. Zap was a really dope graffiti artist, top in the game, and cute too, with a short 'fro and Black Power pick sticking out. We gave pounds all around and they started talking. I was hanging in the background listening, trying to act like nothing they said was important—you know, *cool.*

And then he said it.

"Yo, I been meanin' to ask you. Who the fuck is this Corazón kid?" Zap asked.

"You don't know who that is?" Juan smirked.

"Nah, man," Zap said.

My heart was about to fall out my chest. I found myself wishing I had on that cool Raiders hat Juan had gotten me. Be calm, I kept telling myself.

"This right here is Corazón. She's my protégée." Juan put his arm around me.

"Word?! That's *you?*" Zap turned to me, smiling incredulously.

"Yep," was all I managed to say. But inside, a new flame of confidence had been born.

For the next two weeks, those types of moments were the norm as word got out that Corazón had been identified. It created a buzz, which was nice, but then it was all about living up to the name I had created, forcing me to work much harder than before. The pressure was on, not so much because I was white, but because I was a girl. No one knew of any other female tagger in all of Denver.

Three weeks later I was sitting in my history class when I noticed Juan looking at me through the little window in the door. He motioned me to come out.

"Mr. Henry, can I go to the bathroom?" I asked my teacher.

"Hurry up," he said, without looking up from the newspaper on his desk. I was glad he didn't embarrass me in front of the class like he did to other students.

"What's up, Juan?" He usually didn't come to my class—we always met up after school.

"Writers' Corner is what's up. We gotta go—now."

"But how am I gonna get out of class? My backpack is still there."

"Damn, girl," Juan said with disdain. "Tell him you have your period or somethin'."

I rolled my eyes at him. "That's so gross, Juan. Can't this wait until school's out? This class is important," I said, feeling like a nerd. My classes were much harder than when I was a freshman.

"You care too much about this school shit. We got some bidness to handle. If I leave here without you consider yourself mentorless. The choice is yours." He crossed his arms, scowling.

"*Mentorless,* Juan? That ain't no word!" I laughed, trying to lighten the mood.

"Whatever, cuzz," he said, without smiling.

This was serious. "Just give me a minute, okay?" He nodded putting his arm out to usher me toward the door.

My stomach was doing flips as I walked back in the class. I didn't want to get in trouble because Mr. Henry would not hesitate to call my mom.

"Mr. Henry?" He looked up at me from behind the desk. "I have a little problem." I waited for him to say something but he just kept looking at me, annoyed. "I need to leave class and go to the nurse's office. It's, um, personal." I prayed he wouldn't ask me any questions. I felt like everyone in the class was looking at me.

"Well, go, then. What are you waiting for, an escort?" he asked.

I started blushing, went to my seat, grabbed my bag, and practically ran out of the room. Juan was waiting for me in the stairwell to avoid our hall monitor.

"See, that wasn't so bad, was it?" He smiled at me. "It'll be worth it. I promise."

When we showed up at Writers' Corner, Zap, Diablo, Chaos, and Zen from Juan's crew were waiting for us. Chaos and Zen had squashed their beef for the good of the crew.

"What up, y'all," Juan said, giving them pounds.

"Peace, Corazón," Chaos said, busy drawing in his piece book.

"What up, what up, party people!" Zap was picking out his 'fro and had a big smile on his face; he gave me hugs instead of pounds. Zen gave me a nod, barely making eye contact. We sat down on the tagged-up cement bench. Juan hadn't told me anything about a meeting today, so I wondered why his crew was here.

"Corazón, do you remember the first time I brought you here and you put down your first tag?" Juan asked me.

"Yeah, of course," I said, remembering how nervous I was that day. Juan explained why the Corner was so important to graffiti artists, as a place to pay homage to our art and come together and paint. He told me to tag my name, but I kept hesitating, afraid I wouldn't do it right. Finally I put the marker to the wall and wrote my name. It seemed so long ago now.

"Shit, man," Zen said, and I followed his eyes to the street. A squad car was creeping down Colfax in our direction, the cops looking at us hard.

"Yo, don't even sweat them, man. It's too early for them to be fuckin' with us. They like to wait until it's dark," Zap said, digging his hands deep in his pockets and turning his face away from the cops. Chaos didn't even bother looking up, still engrossed in his work. The cop car finally drove away.

"Damn pigs," Zap said, spitting on the ground.

"Anyways, like I was sayin'," Juan said, reclaiming our attention. "You put in mad work since then. You paid your dues and got up all over this city. From this day forth, whenever you tag up your name, put "RTS" on that bitch. Now you're officially down with Runnin' The Streets crew."

My mouth about hit the ground. Nobody from the crew had let on that I was being inducted today. Juan continued, "And remember, graffiti is about respect. In this world we don't get no respect, 'cause we poor, we young, and we ain't white." He looked at me intently. I held my breath hoping he wasn't going to say something about me being white. "Writing your name on the wall tells the world you can't ignore us no more—even with all your money and your laws and dirty cops—we still here. Our names on the wall prove it."

"Word up. We're here to make *history*, Corazón!" Zap said.

"Here, this is a piece I did for you today, to celebrate," Chaos said, and tore out a page of his book. It said: "To Corazón, the all-by-yourself bomber." "I know you are gonna be judged out there because you're a chick—but don't let nobody fuck witchu; you got in this crew strictly 'cause of your skills," he said, shooting me a quick smile.

"Thank you," I said, admiring the contrasting hues in the piece he had drawn. I got chills just looking at it, knowing it was specially done for me.

"You the first female in our cipher," Zen said, after being quiet the whole time. "But don't get it twisted—we gonna treat you like a dude. So you better represent. Don't front on us or you'll be out." I knew he wasn't totally cool with me getting down with the crew because he didn't think girls could rep. He'd given me drama since I first started kickin' it with them. At times I wanted to get my Crip homies to set him straight, but Juan reminded me to remain humble, told me to just keep paying dues.

"You know I ain't gonna do that. I got love for this crew and I'll show that love every time I hit up. You'll see," I replied.

"All right then. Since this was the first place you tagged up, this is the first place you'll put your crew affiliation. Go do your thing." Juan motioned for me to come to the bench. My first tag had long since been buffed, but I remembered clearly where the spot was. I broke out my black Sharpie marker and tagged up *Corazón-Uno, RTS* with pride.

Dear Diary
    I'm listening to Lisa Lisa & Cult Jam "I wonder if I take you home . . ."
    New crush: Joe the soccer player. He's so cute.

    Guess what? I'm in two crews now, the Crips and RTS—an official graffiti crew! We tag every day and I love it, even though it's against the law. We bust graffiti all over—now I'm "up" so I can be down—there's a writers' convention on Thursday—I decided to tell Carmen— she thinks I'm kinda crazy. At home I have to hide all of my markers so my mom doesn't find them. It feels weird driving down Colfax seeing Corazón all over the bus stops. And to think my mom has no idea that that is me! It's a whole other world my family doesn't have a clue about.
    Another thing is I love my brother TJ but I think he has a drug problem. It scares me a lot. He hates my music, but more than that, I feel like he hates me. Ever since he got into high school he's changed, but one day I walked

in on him sniffing coke, and that freaked me out. Now the pain of constant conflicts in my house bubbles up inside of me. He will never realize how much I care about him, even though we fight all the time. It hurts me so much. I don't want him to mess up his life. He never talks to me anymore. I feel like he doesn't give a damn. I really want him to care. Our whole family is falling apart but I can't do shit about it.

Mom was trying to raise two teenagers who were in high school while working full time. Our family had been so close before, but now things were becoming more and more strained. I wanted to be out more with my friends and craved my own identity. She was pulling back inside herself, struggling with the daily battles with us, my father, life. TJ and I were arguing a lot, cursing at each other. Every time there was a problem between us, she would go in her room, close the door, and sometimes not come out until the next day.

We weren't always like this. Was everything fucked up because my parents split up? No, that's way too simple. I mean, yeah, it did hurt and I felt like my dad and I weren't close, but a lot of my friends had even worse situations than mine, and they seemed fine. I surveyed my bedroom walls—my Bobby Brown poster, pictures of all my friends, the smile on my mom's face in our family portrait. She looked happy then.

More and more I was relying on friends to help me get through the ups and downs. Juan was there for me, flat-out. I could rely on him as I expanded into a new and more complicated life. And slowly, I began to feel like I could rely on the crews I was now a part of.

Six

"Yo," Juan's raspy voice growled over the phone. "You got plans?"

"No. I'm just chillin' right now," I said, stretching the phone cord to get into my room so I could shut the door.

"Meet me downtown in one hour. Writers' Corner. We got some business to handle."

"Cool, I'll be there. Peace."

It was easy for Juan to hang out whenever he wanted because his *tia* couldn't control him. With me, it was harder. I had to scheme in order to get my tag on, creating elaborate lies to tell my protective mom. First I called Carmen, to let her know I was using her as my excuse. Her parents didn't really care if Carmen had friends over, they let her do whatever she wanted. Then I had to sell my mom the plan. I found her smoking a cigarette at the kitchen table, her checkbook out, her blue box overflowing with bills. Damn, bad timing.

"Mom, can I go to Carmen's house?"

"I don't know, Amber, you spend so much time there. Why don't you stay here and do your homework?" She took a puff of her cigarette and tapped her pen against the table.

"But, Mom, you always let TJ go to his friend's house," I complained.

"What are you going to do over there?"

"Just hang around, talk, and study a little bit for a test in history coming up. I'll get all my homework done, I promise."

"Are her parents home?"

"Yes! God, Mom, why are you making this so hard? I just want to go to a friend's house!"

"Lower your voice, young lady, or you aren't going anywhere! And do not use God's name unless you are praying to him!" She pursed her lips and raised her chin slightly. I held my breath.

"Please?"

She took another plug from her cigarette, slowly exhaled the smoke. "Okay, you can go. But be home by nine."

"Thanks." I breathed a sigh of relief as I grabbed my backpack and walked out the door. If she found out I wasn't going to Carmen's after all that . . . I shook the thought from my mind as I hustled up to Colfax and jumped on the bus, walking all the way to the back. I practiced my cool look: one leg extended, arms crossed, slight scowl on my face. Juan always told me I couldn't look like a vic or I risked getting jacked by someone.

It took a long time to get downtown, what with the bus stopping every other block. By the time I got there I was late, so I hustled to our meeting spot. I was wearing my favorite jeans, a regular blue baggy T-shirt, and a light jacket, where my markers were hidden. My eyes searched for my mentor. Damn, I thought, maybe he bounced, but then I saw his Jheri curl, Raiders hat, and saggin' jeans.

"What up, cuzz?" he said as I approached. "You late."

"My bad. The bus, you know," I said, smiling at my homie's fresh style. We gave each other a pound.

"Let's go do some damage and give people somethin' to talk about tomorrow." Juan started walking toward the heart of downtown.

Juan and I were no joke. Writers strived to be up more than any of their competitors. Crew affiliation was also important, along with location. A tagger got mad respect for hitting up places heavily watched, or where extreme measures had to be taken in order to fulfill the mission. Hitting up a highway sign was definitely a bonus. From the moment I started tagging, my eyes opened to all the flat surfaces available. I had an intense pull to put my name up wherever and whenever I could. All I wanted to achieve: the perfect tag.

"Word up. Let's do this," I said.

"All right, let's hit up from here down to the trains. I got left, you got right. Don't forget: smooth—never lift your marker until it's done. We need to represent down here so don't fuck up with some weak-ass tags."

Juan needed to protect his rep, and since I was his protégée and in his crew he would have to answer to any wackness on my part. We had double pressure because we repped for both the graff scene *and* the Crip scene. But I knew that; he didn't have to remind me. All that accomplished was to make me more nervous. Sometimes he could be a real asshole, but I think it had to do with the fact that he was a dude, and dudes encourage each other differently than girls do. Whatever, the important thing was I had the ability to show and prove.

Juan tagged up while I watched his back; downtown was full of cops, so we had to be really careful. Then it was my turn to do my thing. The main targets included bus stops, street signs, and other metal surfaces. As we worked our way toward the trains it started getting darker. I quickened my pace to match my homie's stride. After winding our way through downtown and the train station, we crossed what seemed like miles of tracks and finally reached an abandoned warehouse.

"Walk to the other side of the building," Juan said in a low voice, even though no one seemed to be around. He started moving in the opposite direction.

I jumped as I heard a distant train whistle. Juan always warned me about the yards—it was far more dangerous than street taggin' because of the crazy junkies and the private security companies that kept watch on the trains. For me, the desolation of the yards at night always freaked me out. My heart beat rapidly as I ran around to meet him, blood racing through my body, adrenaline pumping. A million feelings flooded my body; like going down a roller coaster for the first time. Excitement, fun, and terror combined for the ultimate rush. As we met up on the other side, Juan dropped his bag and quickly pulled out a bunch of spray paint cans.

"Watch my back," he whispered. He began to work. After painting the complicated outline of his latest tag name, iRoniC, he ordered me to fill in the spaces. "No drips!" he added. Hastily I threw on gloves and tried to calm my nerves so I wouldn't go outside the lines. Juan finished what he was doing and waited for me so he could complete the final touches. He started on the dedication. Juan was known as much for his unique dedications as his incredible talent. Most graff artists shouted out their girl, their crew, or their moms and although Juan did that too, he preferred philosophers.

He started painting: "All the praise afforded to me is but of no consequence if within myself I feel I have failed . . ."

About ten spray cans later, I stood back to watch the master at work. All was silent except for the steady stream of the paint hitting the wall, and the occasional clicking as Juan shook the can. It was only when I turned to throw a can away that I saw flashing lights.

I yelled "Five-o! Five-o!" but they were already on us. I panicked. All I saw was red-and-blue lights, and then the sirens started.

Through the noise I could hear Juan shout, "Run!"

I sprinted around the corner of the warehouse, where I leaned against the wall, trying to catch my breath. I looked around the corner and saw one cop who seemed to be looking for me, but then turned back to join the others. Juan was lying on the ground, surrounded by cops, his legs curled up tight and his arms trying to protect his face. Shit, what could I do? I heard the steady thud of the billy clubs coming down on him time and time again, and his muffled grunts of pain. They picked him off the ground, some of the cops cursing at him, others laughing. They handcuffed him, dragged him to the cop car, and threw him in. He didn't even look conscious. One by one the cars drove away.

So I wouldn't attract any unnecessary attention to myself, I didn't run—a lesson Juan had drilled into me. The walk back to the bus stop seemed to take forever; I jumped at every little sound. The lonely back streets cried out, "Danger!" and I found myself looking over my shoulder. Once I saw the bus I started running for it. My mind was crowded with images of Juan's limp body in the hands of the police.

I wondered if they'd beat me as bad if I got caught.

The next week of school was horrible for me. With my mentor beat down and locked up, I felt very alone, even though I was surrounded by people. Juan used his one call from jail to warn me about opening my mouth.

"Don't say shit, Amber. If word gets out that I'm locked up, other crews are gonna try to take over my walls. You gotta play it cool. Act like I'm laid up with a chick or something. And you need to be out bombin'." Juan only wanted to talk about business. "You can tell T-Dog and Lil D that I'm locked up, but that's it."

When I asked if he was okay he laughed and said, "I'll live. I've been through plenty of beat downs, girl. They can't stop me. They just make me work harder."

Seven

Juan was hyped to go bombin' the same day he got out of jail, especially when I told him some buster had written *Toy* across one of his pieces downtown. He wanted revenge.

"Wanna roll wit' me, homie?" He flashed me that grin I loved so much.

He didn't expect me to say no, especially since he just got out of juvie. He looked at me sideways when I told him I couldn't, because of basketball tryouts. He mumbled something about priorities, and said, "I'll check you later, cuzz." He left abruptly, armed with a bag of spray cans.

But I didn't have time to dwell. I was the only white girl trying out for the team and had already gotten some looks from older girls. Some of my white classmates warned me the basketball team was only for "black people." When I asked Carmen for advice, she told me to go for it. Luckily Keisha the ultimate athlete, who played volleyball, basketball, and ran track, came to tryouts with me, so at least I had some company.

"What's up with Joe?" Keisha was on the floor, stretching out her legs. "Did you talk to him yet, or what?" Sometimes I wished my mouth wasn't so big. Last week I mentioned to Carmen and Keisha that I thought Joe was a cutie.

"Not yet, Keisha, you know it's hard for me to approach guys." I rolled a basketball her way. "Come on, let's warm up," I said, changing the subject.

Ten minutes into our warmup, a big girl who played varsity stepped to me, hand on her hip. "So is it true?"

"What?" I snapped, throwing the ball back to Keisha.

"I heard you gave crabs to all the Crips." She looked at me, waiting to see my reaction.

"What?"

"You heard me, crabs . . . Crips. Do I need to spell it out for you?" As her voice got louder Keisha walked over to us.

"That ain't true. I ain't no ho." My face was burning with humiliation. "Who told you that?"

"Girl, it's all around the school by now. You betta watch out 'cause someone don't like you!" She walked back to the court, yelling, "We don't want no ho on our team!"

Everyone stared at me. Keisha grabbed my arm and led me to the drinking fountain at the back of the gym.

"What was that all about, Amber?" she asked me.

"Hell if I know!" I was trying hard not to cry. "I can't believe this! Why is this happening to me?"

"I don't know. But ever since your new friends came into your life you've been having problems." Keisha knew only what she saw, because I never felt comfortable talking to her about what I was going through. I had introduced her to Juan a couple of times and they got along fine. But I didn't take her out with me when I chilled with all the Crips. She was straight-laced and had very strict parents.

The coach blew the whistle for tryouts to begin. I tried to get my mind off of what happened the rest of the afternoon, but that was hard to do.

I called Juan as soon as I got home. He wasn't there, probably still out bombin'. The rage that filled me had no release. I went into my room, closed the door, put on The Police super loud.

Sometimes I still played the music TJ raised me on. I remembered when we were young and he would play the Beatles on my dad's beat-up tape deck, over and over again. We would sing together, and even my mom would join in, telling us endless stories about how her parents thought it was devil music. TJ was my teacher and DJ when it came to rock music. From the Rolling Stones and the Who, to Jimi Hendrix and Led Zeppelin, he schooled me about classic rock and taught me all the lyrics. That was when we were really close. The Police evoked memories of days less complicated.

I was singing "Every Breath You Take," and I couldn't stop the tears.

Dear Diary
I am so sick of life right now. It's official. I've diagnosed myself with multiple personality disorder. I walk into my house and become a regular high school girl—I talk on the phone, eat dinner with my family, and do my homework. Once I leave the house the transformation begins: my language, style, and attitude—it all adjusts to fit the environment I'm in. I'm a master at hiding things from people like Carmen and Keisha, but the hardest is my mom. Deep down inside I know how much it would hurt

her if she found out; she's struggling so hard to keep it all together. I have so much love for her, but at the same time I feel our worlds drifting apart. She can't understand what I'm going through. I'm overcome by these mixed feelings of wanting things to be the same, yet knowing that it is impossible.

I have to be me.

Instead I play the role she needs to see. There are a lot of "Ambers," each expressing something important to me, but at the same time in conflict with one another. It isn't always easy. I have to maintain.

I don't know what has happened, but I don't seem to fit in anymore. At parties, I don't have fun and people hate me! I get totally depressed and don't know what to do, my whole black and white conflict; the Crips, the crews I'm in. I feel real shitty. FUCK THIS!!

I stopped writing and called Juan for the tenth time. He finally answered.

"Juan, someone's talking shit about me, spreading mad rumors!" I tried not to but I started crying again. I hoped he couldn't hear me. "I bet it's that sorry motherfucker Ray-Ray!"

"All right, girl, slow down, chill out, and tell me what happened. What's the rumor?"

I told Juan what had happened during tryouts.

"Damn, girl, that's fucked up, for real. I'm gonna make some calls. I'll hit you back."

The day I found out I made the basketball team, Juan learned Ray-Ray started the rumor. Ray-Ray spouted hate from his eyes every time he looked at me. Maybe because at the end of the day I got into my mom's car and left the hood to go to the safer side, while he had to stay. Sometimes I thought about what

Darnell said to me in the car that day about not understanding, but then I'd just push it away. I didn't want to deal with that.

Ray-Ray had been down with the Crips for a long time. He was considered fam. I was a visitor, at best. I couldn't make a big deal out of the rumor, so instead I just tried to stay out of his way. I realized that bangin' was a choice for me. I wasn't forced into it because it went way back in my family, or because in my hood you had to have protection or your ass would get jumped. I was bangin' because Juan was bangin' and that was the naked truth. I had choices. My skin color and neighborhood protected me from something that was a necessity for many people, which made it more important for me to be more down than the others. Crazier and wilder, anything that would help me hide from the reality of my choice.

Ray-Ray had started a rumor about me. It was just a rumor, just words. If I couldn't handle words, how was I going to handle some of the other shit that was bound to come down? I hardened myself once again. I felt like I was having to do that all the time now. Maybe someday I'd just become one giant body of steel—no heart, no soul, just cold, hard steel.

Eight

The blood seeped out and I cried out in relief. The pain tickled me. I put the razor down and sat on top of the toilet seat. It was a small cut, on my upper thigh where no one could see. I watched a trickle of red roll down, but caught it with tissue before it messed up my mom's white seat cover.

Sadness had overcome me. The daily decisions about who to hang out with, my family situation, staying on top of the graff game—everything. Today, two weeks after the rumor dropped, was no different. When it got really bad, when writing in my diary didn't help, when the emotional pain became unbearable I caused physical pain.

I put a Band-Aid on my cut, washed my razor, and went into my room to hide it in my closet.

My mom wasn't home from work yet, so I took advantage and left a note for her, then headed to Carmen's house, a block away. She'd make me feel better. We were dying to see each other. While I had been busy with Juan she and Kyle had started going pretty strong. Her parents were out of town and she was throwing one of her infamous parties later that night.

As soon as I got there she gave me a big hug and took me into the kitchen.

"Amber, I invited Joe to the party! I hope you finally get over this shy shit and make out with him already," Carmen said.

"Get me drunk and we'll see," I said. Carmen had left some weed out on the table in anticipation of my visit.

"Roll us up a fatty," she told me.

"Carmen, you remember the first time we did this together? How old were we?" I hit my expertly rolled joint. I loved smoking pot. Most people couldn't roll a good joint to save their life. They distributed the weed unevenly or they licked the damn rolling paper too much, which yielded a lumpy, unprofessional result. I was a pro. Carmen admired my latest example of this as she toked up.

"Of course I remember!" She was kicking back, wearing a turquoise silk blouse that flattered her tan skin and faded jeans that hugged her hips, showing off her curves. Her black hair had grown almost to her hips. She inhaled deeply and we both giggled.

"Do you have the lighter?" Carmen said. We were in the alley behind her house. She'd found some weed that her older sister Brenda had left in the basement and felt it was time to give it a try. I agreed. We were thirteen, after all, and in eighth grade.

"Check," I said.

"Coke can?"

"Check."

"What about the scissors to poke holes?"

"Check."

"You start working on the Coke can and then I'll put it on top, okay?"

Very carefully, I did what Carmen had instructed me to do. I wanted this experience to be perfect. First I gently stepped on the side of the can to make a place for the weed and keep it from falling off. Then I poked about ten holes in the can with the scissors. What I was making was considered the "poor people's pipe," but from what we had been told, it worked just as well.

"Okay, ready?"

"Yeah." I giggled.

Carmen put the weed on the Coke can. "You light it for me while I inhale." She put the opening of the can to her mouth and I put the lighter on the weed while she breathed in. She coughed and then put her lips together a couple times to see if she tasted anything.

"I don't think it worked. I think you have to leave the lighter on the weed longer. Let's try it again."

So this time I really left the fire on the weed, until it started getting orange and smoke was coming out of it. This time Carmen inhaled and coughed violently, with smoke coming out from her mouth and nose. We both started laughing.

"Wow, I really felt that! It hurt my throat!"

"How do you feel?" I asked.

"Hmmm, I don't feel anything. Why don't you try and then I'll go again." She handed it to me. "Remember to breathe in all the way."

I put the can to my mouth, feeling awkward, but glad I was trying this with my best friend instead of at some party with people I didn't know.

"Ready?" My moment of truth was about to happen. She put the lighter over the weed.

The first thing that I noticed was that the lighter was really close to my face. The thought crossed my mind that my nose hairs could catch on fire, but I tossed that thought aside and inhaled as deep as I could. The burn hit me immediately. My throat felt hot and I began to cough uncontrollably. Carmen started laughing at me, and then I started laughing too because it was funny, plus I felt a little light-headed. We practiced a couple more times each, until we both started laughing hysterically, feeling the effects. I guess we actually laughed a little too loud, because before we knew it Brenda came out into the alley.

"Did you steal my weed, you little shit?" She started yelling at both of us, saying how stupid we were for getting high in the alley. "The neighbors can see you out of their windows! Do you want to get arrested and have Mom and Dad come pick you up from jail?"

Our first-time high was definitely dwindling. I felt bad because she was screaming at Carmen.

"Go inside, both of you," she ordered, "and go to the basement until your high wears off. I don't want to get in trouble because of your mistakes! What if Amber's mom finds out about this?" I saw tears come to Carmen's eyes.

"Let's go," I said, and we walked into her house together and went downstairs to the back room. Carmen was bawling, her sister was still cursing us out, and I was just trying to make sense of it all. The back room was small, dark, and full of cat hair, which I was allergic to. I felt my eyes start to itch.

After a while her tears were dry, and we were giggling softly, amazed that we had actually "done it." A couple hours later, when the high wore off, I headed for home. Okay, what would my story be for my mom? I needed to be nonchalant, give some kind of answer to the "Did you have fun? What did you do?" questions. Enough information to not give it away, but not too much where I would have to go on describing an elaborate lie. I felt tired and groggy, but it was worth it. In fact, a small part of me felt like I had accomplished something on that day; one step closer to being a real teenager.

At the party, I ran over to where Carmen was and whispered loudly into her ear, "We kissed, we kissed!" She hugged me with delight. Joe and I had finally hooked up.

Joe was a junior and played on the soccer team. We flirted all the time, and after our kiss he became my first high school boyfriend. I liked him because even though he was cool with the white kids he didn't care that I hung out with blacks and Mexicans. In fact, he defended me if people talked shit about it. We spoke on the phone as much as possible, and sometimes he would pick me up on the weekends. Joe knew how close Juan and I were, and he really wanted to meet him. But I wasn't sure if I wanted that to happen.

Juan and I were kickin' it after school while I waited for Joe to get done with practice. We were sitting on the steps with our piece books open, sketching out some new material.

"What's up with your white boyfriend?" Juan asked me. I glanced up and saw Joe walking toward us, looking sweaty and dirty, but still cute.

"He's cool, Juan. And he really likes me so leave it alone. Just because you're lonely and shit." I stood up, laughing.

"Please, girl. I can't even keep track of all the hoochies I got on lockdown. Just let me know when you get bored with the white Boy Wonder," Juan looked up at me, smiled, and then gave me a pound. "And don't forget about the homies, cuzz."

"Never that, baby, never that," I replied.

The next day at school, Tania from Spanish class came up to me as I was getting my books out of my locker.

"Hey Amber, can I talk to you for a minute?" Everybody

liked her because she was so pretty with her caramel skin and almond shaped eyes. On top of that she was really sweet, and one of our best cheerleaders.

"Hey girl, what's up?" I said.

"Well, some of the girls from the squad were talking about new recruits, and your name came up. We all like you, and we know you got *some* rhythm, so we wanted to ask you to try out for the cheerleading team."

She was smiling as she put her hand on my shoulder. I was in shock. I had never thought about joining the cheerleading team, not only because I was a tomboy and into sports, but the cheerleaders were the super-fly girls—and unlike me, they all had perfect bodies and fly dance moves.

One problem that really fucked with my self-esteem was my lack of assets. My ass, to be exact. Most of the white boys I knew liked skinny girls with big boobs and an ass that was small and tight to complete the package. Black guys, however, liked a little more cushion on the backside, a little something to hold on to; super-skinny wasn't their idea of sexy. As I began growing and developing, I became really self-conscious of my ass. I went through periods of wearing long shirts just to cover my shortcoming. I wondered if I could really be a cheerleader. Would I look okay in those little skirts?

"Wow, that's cool. But I don't know if I can do it, 'cause I made the basketball team," I said.

Tania smiled and pulled out a paper from her book bag. "See? Amber, I got you covered, girl." She showed me the school's practice schedules. "I already checked and you could do cheerleading right after school and then hit basketball at four; what do you think?"

"Let me think about it." My mind was whirling—thoughts of being in front of the whole school, workin' it to the hottest songs. I was gassed!

"Okay, but let me know as soon as you can, 'kay?"

As I walked to class, excitement was bubbling up inside of me. I would need to practice and get a routine together. I knew I could ask Darnell to teach me some moves; he was always poppin' and doing some crazy dances and he already taught me the Centipede. By the end of the day I had a whole plan worked out in my head. I was rushing to see if I could find Darnell before he left when I ran into Lil D and Juan.

"What up, cuzz?" Juan said, and gave me a pound. "Where you headed?"

"Hey Amber." Lil D smiled, showing his dimple. "Let's go hang out. Juan promised a blunt for both of us."

I opened my mouth to tell them the good news. But as quickly as I opened it, I shut it, unsure. They had already laughed when I told them about basketball. Not only did they think I was too short, all they saw me do was tag up and get fucked up. They thought I had no game on the court. "How 'bout if I catch up with y'all later—where you chillin' at, T-Dog's?" I asked.

"Yup. Catch up with us, cuzz," Juan said, and shot me a look. "Let's go, Lil D." Juan hated it when I didn't chill with them. Sometimes he acted like my man, always wanting to know where I was and who I was kickin' it with. I knew it was because we were so tight, and I liked it. Most of the time.

As I got closer to the lunchroom I heard music. Sure enough, Darnell was there with all his homeboys who danced together.

"I wanna rock right now, I'm Rob Base and I came to get down . . ." Darnell was singing the song blastin' on the boom box, as his boy got busy. When he saw me he turned down the music.

"What's up, Amber? What are *you* doin' here? I thought all the white people jetted *home* after school!" He joked with me as he gave me a pound.

"Why you always playin', Darnell?" I smiled. "For real, I need a favor."

"What's that, baby girl?" he said, as he did the wave with his arms, and passed it off to his friend.

"I need you to teach me some moves," I said tentatively.

"Damn, another white person who can't dance! Y'all come to me for the latest mix tapes, for dance moves, even the latest slang—I should start chargin', man, fo' real."

"Yo, have I ever asked anything from you before?" I said defensively. "I never *asked* you for the mix tapes, you just be givin' them to me. Look, the only reason I'm comin' to you is 'cause Tania asked me to try out for the cheerleading team. You know that's a big deal! I got some rhythm, I promise, I just need a couple of extra moves to take it over the top, that's all." How was he gonna put me in the same category as all those other white fools who couldn't even do the snake?

He sighed and signaled to his boy to come over to where we were standing. "Okay, Amber, I hear you, but you owe me. I may need to call in a favor."

I smiled. "Yeah Darnell, whatever you need. So who's this?" I asked, nodding to the dancer standing next to us.

"This is my newest recruit, Smooth. He's dope, and with a little training I know he could make it. I'm gonna have him help you get ready for tryouts. How long we got?"

"Tania told me tryouts are in two weeks. I can stay after school a couple days."

Darnell turned up the music. "This is the song I played for you last week in my ride. I remember you liked that funky beat."

When I got home that night after two hours of practice, I called Joe to tell him my big plans. He got excited with the possibility of me cheerleading while he did his thing on the soccer field. Things were finally looking up.

The next two weeks were spent working with Darnell and Smooth, and after that hanging out with Juan before heading home. Joe was busy with soccer practice so we only saw each other on the weekends. The more I put into this routine, the more excited I got about the possibility of making the squad—except when I went to T-Dog's with Juan and kicked it with the Crips. Then I couldn't even bring it up. Cheerleading? They would laugh. And then they would probably kick me out.

The day before tryouts I was in the lunchroom for my last practice with Darnell. Two girls from the cheerleading squad and Tiny, a girl from my class, happened to walk by and see us in there, so they stopped and watched us.

"You looking good, Amber!" Tiny said when I took a break. "But I'm surprised you agreed to try out."

"Why wouldn't I? You don't think I got the skills?"

"No, it's not that. I just didn't think you'd be down with filling a quota," Tiny said, crossing her arms.

The two cheerleaders glared at her. "Can you shut your mouth, please?"

"What are you talking about?" I demanded.

The cheerleaders turned and started walking away. "Come on, Tiny, we gotta bounce!"

"You don't know?" Tiny said, as they were pulling her away.

"Know what?" I said.

Tiny grabbed her arm free as the cheerleaders huffed away. "Look, I don't know you that well, but you seem cool to me, so I'm just gonna tell you straight up. They need at least one white girl or else the school will make them forfeit the squad." She looked at me and shrugged. "They only want you 'cause you're white." She turned and hustled off to catch up with her friends.

Darnell called me to finish practicing. Luckily he hadn't heard what just happened.

"Darnell, I gotta bounce. I feel good about everything, though—thanks for all your help."

"No doubt girl. I'm sure you're gonna knock it out the box tomorrow! And don't forget—you owe me!"

I turned and walked out of the lunchroom, got my stuff from my locker, and headed out to the bus.

The next day during cheerleading tryouts I was at T-Dog's smoking a blunt and drinking a forty.

Nine

Latest trend: ear pierces—now I got two on one side and three on the other!

Relationship: Joe's nice, I guess I'm happy—not sure.

Dear Diary,
Last night was cool. Me and Carmen had tickets to a concert, Keisha's mom wouldn't let her go. I put on my fresh white miniskirt, silver shoes, and black shirt I stole. We got dropped off at Mammoth Concert Hall where Kool Moe Dee and DJ Jazzy Jeff and the Fresh Prince were performing. The concert was sweet. Afterward we waited outside in a crowd of girls, all trying to be picked by the performers, who were looking at us from inside their fly ride. Kool Moe Dee's bodyguard signaled us and as the car door opened we jumped excitedly into the car. They were all freestylin', it was so cool, I wished Darnell could

have heard it. So we went to their hotel rooms and I messed around with a guy but wouldn't sleep with him. I had fun, but afterward I felt used.

They had to go back to Philly so they gave us ten dollars for a cab. We went to Breezin's and tried to ditch the cab but the cab driver caught us and got the money, so we were stranded. We met three guys and a girl and had to go with them to get out of that neighborhood. We went to a gas station and the car broke down. So we walked to one of the guys' apartments and got high, then we called everyone we knew until someone came and got us and took us home. It was a pretty fun night, some parts were messed up, but the rest was cool! After all, I love to have fun!

"Shotgun, cuzz!" Lil D hollered and started running to my car. Joe wanted to go out and was disappointed when I told him I had other plans. But I just saw him the other night.

I'd borrowed my mom's car and picked up Juan and Lil D to go meet up with a bunch of Crips at a park near Five Points High to drink and smoke. Juan and I were planning on breaking out at some point to get our tag on.

"Fool, get outta here with that noise. I don't care about no 'shotgun.' If I want the front, cuzz, I'll take the front!" Juan replied, walking up to the car. Juan always played with Lil D like that. Lil D, of course, ended up in the front seat.

My life felt like one big party, which was nothing new. I had been drinking alcohol since I was twelve. My dad was a bartender in college who was proud of passing down all he learned about alcohol. And then there were the times with my crazy rebel cousin who gave my brother and me an early introduction to what it meant to party when he was supposed to be babysitting. Once my mom was out the door, he'd invite all his friends over; drinking games replaced board games, until I was carried up to my bed, exhausted from a combination of drinking, dancing in my red cotton nightgown, and being up way past my bedtime.

"What up, cuzz?" Lil D smiled at me. "Let's roll!"

"Corazón, you heard how everyone's talkin' about us, cuzz?" Juan asked.

"Nah—"

"Yep. Zap told me that kids can't shut up about that 'Fight the Power' piece we did by the school; they're feelin' it."

"Word up," I said, and put my fist to the backseat to give Juan a pound.

By the time we got to the park it was already dark out, and we were chillin' on the swing set just talking shit, smoking blunts, and drinking forties. A lot of people were there, but we sat with T-Dog and Rodney. It was chilly out, so I wore my Raiders jacket and matching hat, which I put on backward. I wore a new pair of sneakers that my mom had bought me. I had just finished tagging my name on a bench when Juan started bugging out.

"So Amber, why is it that white people ain't got no rhythm?" he asked, trying to provide humor for the night. His comment brought back what happened with the cheerleading squad. When I didn't show up for tryouts that day, Tania had to scramble around and find a white girl for the squad, and they did. It was Michelle. The first time we saw each other after she had made the squad, she was walking with some of the other cheerleaders. She said, "Who's the cool girl, now?" and kept going.

Tania wasn't upset with me because she got what she wanted. The only person I had to make it up to was Darnell, who was pissed because he had spent so much time with me rehearsing.

T-Dog was laughing and shaking his head at Juan.

"Why you gotta bring shit like that up?" Lil D asked. Lil D

and I had gotten closer. I felt like his big sister, and he, in turn, looked out for me in his own little ways.

"Don't worry 'bout it, Lil D, I know Juan is just curious." I turned and said to Juan. "We just born like that Juan, didn't you hear about the gene study they did? We can't help it."

He loved talking shit whenever he started getting fucked up. He brought up my whiteness, while I was always trying to push it down.

"Yo, Amber—"

But before Juan could finish his sentence, we heard a weird whizzing sound, and it was getting louder and louder.

"What the hell is that?" Juan asked. Ten seconds later we found out; at least eight or nine cop cars descended upon us, driving into the park from every direction without their headlights on.

"Oh shit, it's five-o!" yelled T-Dog, throwing his forty to the ground.

I jumped up and screamed, "What do we do?!"

"Come on, we gotta bounce—now!" Juan said, grabbing me. "Come on. Let's go! Run! Run!"

T-Dog and Rodney ran one way, and me, Juan, and Lil D started running to the car—I could barely get the keys out 'cause I was shaking so much. I heard car doors slamming and cops yelling, "Take left, take right, get 'em, get 'em!"

I opened the doors and we all jumped in—I got in the front and Juan and Lil D got in the back and ducked down to the floor in hopes that the cops wouldn't see them. By then, the sirens were on and the flashing lights were everywhere. As we drove away we saw some of the cops on foot, and some still in their cars driving through the park chasing guys. I prayed T-Dog and Rodney got away.

"Where should I go?" I asked.

"Just get us outta here first and then we'll figure it out," Juan said. "What the fuck happened, man?"

"We just got vamped on by the *po*-lice, that's what happened!" Lil D said.

One minute we were just kickin' it, the next we were scrambling from the cops. I was worried about Lil D, thirteen years old and already running from the law.

"Lil D, where do you want to go from here? Your house?" I asked.

"Nah, man, that's not a good idea. Five-o may be right around the corner and I can't bring no drama to my house. Just drop me off at my cousin's." I looked over at him, concerned. "Don't worry, Amber, my cousin is good peoples." He gave me directions and I pulled up to an apartment building. Lil D got out.

"Stay up, cuzz." He gave me and Juan a pound, looked up and down the street, and then ran to the building. We waited until someone opened the door and let him in.

"That ain't right what they did to us. We weren't even doing anything wrong! They send the whole police force for a little drinkin' and taggin' on a park bench? Who do you think they were after, Juan?" I said.

"They were after all of us, any of us—don't matter to them," Juan mumbled. "We Crips. That's what we did wrong."

"Yeah, that's true, but still, did you see all those cops? They overdid it, for real. I'm just glad we got out in time. I hope nobody got hurt," I said.

Although we were slightly elated for ditching the cops, what we didn't speak about was the feeling of *this shit is real*— we were hanging out with gangstas, and five-o rolling up on us was part of the game, no matter what position we were playing.

Dear Diary

Things are getting crazier and crazier with the Crips. I hope we don't get caught and go to jail for all the shit we're doing. Anyways, I love Lil D and Juan—they are so cool.

Joe and I are still together. He's so cute, with cool-ass blue eyes, light brown hair, and best of all a big tribal tattoo on his back! So the big news is I had sex for the first time ever. The experience is still fresh in my mind. It hurt a whole lot, but was nice. I felt guilty about it, because of my mom—she wanted me to wait until I was married. But I did it anyway 'cause I really really like Joe—this has brought us even closer to each other! I look forward to another night with him.

Ten

Weeks later, I was hanging out at Carmen's house in her kitchen. She was making me one of her famous quesadillas with her homemade guacamole and telling me about last night's date with Kyle. "Hey Amber, you wanna go on a double date? You can bring Joe."

"I don't know, Carmen," I said. "I'm not sure what to do with him. I like him and everything, but I kinda feel bored. It's hard to explain. I used to really look forward to seeing him, and now it's like it doesn't even matter if he's there or not."

I had been with Joe for a while now. At first things were incredible, and I made the huge decision of losing my virginity to him. Now the relationship was weighing on me. He became needy and insecure. He was forever asking me if I really loved him, and always made me promise not to leave him.

"That's weird, Amber. He really likes you and he's a good

guy. What are you looking for, anyway? Maybe you're just feeling that way now and things will go back to feeling exciting again. How's the sex?" Carmen asked, smiling at me mischievously as she handed me a plate.

"The sex is fine. I love kissing him and he definitely treats me right. I wish I still liked him. I don't know what to do," I said, biting into the quesadilla. "Damn, this is good."

"Of course. What did you expect from *moi*? Anyway, let's go out this weekend and party. We need to have some fun."

"That's cool. I heard there are a lot of parties happening. One of us has to get the car!" I said. Carmen sat down at the table with me and we chatted the afternoon away.

Joe and I did go on the double date with Carmen and Kyle, and in the weeks that followed the suffocation became unbearable. I decided to end it with him before summer hit.

I spent the next couple of weeks feeling guilty, hearing all his friends call me a bitch and watching Joe sulk in the hallways. The guilt was killing me; I couldn't stand even looking at Joe. I was so happy school was about to be out.

Summertime was a blast—hanging out with my friends during the day, and hitting the parties at night. I made money by babysitting here and there. With Mom working overtime and coming home late, I had more independence.

Forestville had its fair share of nice and expensive houses, but then just five blocks north it changed; each block, the houses got smaller, the neighborhood dicier. That's where it became Blood territory.

I decided to invite Juan and Lil D to a house party a friend of mine was throwing. Even though it was in Blood Ville, as some referred to it, this wasn't supposed to be the type of party where gangbangers would catch beef. I was going with Carmen and Kyle. The plan was to meet up with Juan and them at the party.

As we drove up, it was clear that the place was packed because there was no place to park. After driving around for a while, we found a place a few blocks up.

It was a kegger. Three bucks got you all you could drink 'til it was gone. The crowd was a mixture of our hood, white, black, Mexican, rich, and poor kids all together, for better or for worse. The object was to get as fucked up as possible on beer bongs, Everclear, shots of "mystery punch."

Tonight was my type of party. I knew most of the people there. The house was locked because the dude's parents were out of town (hence the party spot), so we were all hanging out in the backyard, drinking, smoking, and talking.

Suddenly a bunch of Crips came crashing through the bushes with crowbars and gats, bandanas covering their faces, yelling, "This is Crip, fool!"

The Bloods who were at the party started yelling, "What up, Blood?"

Pop! Pop! Gunshots screamed through the night, and everyone started running, trying to get out of the yard. I couldn't find Juan or Lil D anywhere.

"Come on, Amber, let's get out of here!" Carmen grabbed my arm; we found Kyle and ran out of the yard. As we were running down the block toward the car, we heard more shots. We got in the car, and Kyle made a quick turn and headed down the alley. Out of nowhere, Killa jumped in front of the car, forcing us to stop.

"Open the door, let me in!" He started banging on Carmen's window.

I was sitting in the backseat of the four-door, so I opened the door and he threw himself next to me. That was when we all saw the blood.

"Go! Go! Go! Get me outta here," he said, holding his neck to try and stop the blood from spurting out. Kyle was driving fast, sirens were blaring, and my head was spinning.

"Don't take me to the hospital, just take me to my house," Killa said, moaning in pain.

"Man, you're hurt, you need to see a doctor." Kyle was looking back at Killa while trying to drive at the same time.

"Kyle, watch out!" I yelled, as he came close to hitting a parked car.

"Shit!" Carmen screamed. "Be careful! You're gonna crash!"

"No, I can't, they'll arrest me and I can't go to jail, cuzz!" Killa said.

"You sure, man?" Kyle asked.

"Yeah, just take me to my house, go down MLK!" As he said this he started fading.

"You guys, there's so much blood," I said. Even though I tried to stop it with my hand it kept gushing out.

"He said he doesn't want to go," Carmen said. She looked horrified when she turned and saw the amount of blood dripping from Killa's neck.

Kyle was driving in the direction of MLK. "We could get arrested if we take him to the hospital—do you understand that?" he said, looking at me through the rearview mirror. "I'm drunk, man! I shouldn't even be driving right now."

Killa fell in and out of consciousness, mumbling his address to me. "Okay," I said, "just take him home—hurry!"

We took him home. Kyle helped him out of the car and into the house, then he ran back to the car and we took off.

We were all silent for a while. I wanted to talk to Juan so badly, but I knew he wouldn't be home, and there was no way I could get in touch with him. I just wanted to make sure he was all right.

"Kyle, man, I'm so sorry about how everything went down. I had no idea it was gonna be like that."

"It's cool. I just wasn't sure what to do, you know? It's like, I don't want that dude to die, but it's not like he's my friend. I mean, if we got stopped by cops we'd be headin' to jail, you know?"

"I know, I know. Thanks for being so cool about it."

"The thing is, Amber, I just like to party and have fun—I'm not into gangs and graffiti and stuff. That's your thing. And I don't want you to bring it around me, 'cause I don't want trouble." He was almost apologetic in how he said it, but I knew that it was me who should be sorry.

"I hear you," I said softly.

Carmen was quietly crying.

They dropped me off, and I told Kyle he needed to wash the inside of his car, because there was blood all over it. I went in my house through the back, and walked quietly into the bathroom to scrub the blood off of my hands. When I turned on the light and looked in the mirror I saw that there was more blood all over my shirt. I worked to clean my hands off as much as possible—there was even blood underneath my fingernails. Then I tore off my shirt, carefully tiptoeing down the hallway, because the floor creaked in front of my mom's room. I put my shirt in a plastic bag, and threw on a sweatshirt. I ran outside to the alley where all the trash cans were. I looked to see if anyone was around. Seeing nobody, I walked two houses down and shoved the bloody shirt in their garbage.

Back in the house, I went into my room and sat on my bed. I hated the feeling that I could cause innocent people like Carmen or Kyle to get hurt. It was because of me that Killa got in Kyle's car, and who knew how things were going to play out.

I called Juan all day on Sunday for some news. "Listen, homie, he's alive," Juan whispered into the phone. I heard a girl's voice in the background. He said he had to go, and hung up. I called Carmen to let her know, and thanked God that Killa didn't die.

Eleven

When we gonna go bombin'?" I asked Juan the first week of school. It was lunchtime and we were eating at Uncle Charlie's, which got a fresh coat of paint over the summer. "Let's hang out because my mom is visiting my aunt tonight, I won't have any explaining to do." All summer Juan worked to get my art to the next level, which meant hours of drawing and then taking to the streets.

"Aight, bet. Meet me after school," he said.

"Do you want to walk back to school with me? Lunch period's almost over," I asked him as I got up to leave.

"Nah, I don't feel like going back to class today. I'ma chill here and wait for you."

After school we met up and walked to Forest Park. We sat on a bench facing the lake. It was my favorite park in Denver with beautiful trees and flowers everywhere. The park was full of people: joggers, mothers pushing strollers, and the homeless people, gathering around their possessions, talking, some even fishing.

From our view we could see the entire Denver skyline and with the blue sky and white clouds it was the perfect kind of afternoon. We were switching the headphones back and forth, so that we both got to hear one of Juan's favorite songs, U.T.F.O.'s "Ya Could Wanna Be with Me," and sketching out our next piece. Happiness overcame me.

I watched Juan's different arm muscles flex as he drew. "There we go, baby, I'm done. This piece is funky fresh, cuzz." He smiled in satisfaction. In front of us a mother and young son walked by, holding hands and laughing. I saw Juan watching them. "You know what, Corazón?" Juan looked over at me. "Your mom is so nice. You have the best mom in the world, man. All my family is good for is disappointing me."

He started drawing again. I wasn't sure what to say. Juan's family came in and out of his life, his mother never accepting the full responsibility of raising him. When his older sister came around, she'd hang out for an afternoon getting high, and then split for a couple of months, calling Juan sporadically. I wish I could take his pain away.

"So, are you down, Juan? Are we gonna get our tag on tonight?" I fiddled with the grass and waited for him to speak.

"I'm always down, Corazón. I got no choice." He grabbed the headphones from me, put them on, and finished his drawing in silence.

That night Juan and I packed his duffel bag. "Corazón, we need to rack some more paint and markers, so let's do that first."

We took the bus downtown and got off by an art store. Juan and I had an understanding. He always boosted the spray cans and I lifted the markers. Our routine was for me to distract the person working there while Juan got the spray cans. Then I would stuff the markers up my sleeves, buy something really cheap, and leave. We were successful, as usual.

We spent the next couple of hours behind an old warehouse. Juan had three characters representing his graffiti crew, with "FRESH" in the middle. Each of his characters had different color Adidas sweatshirts, baggy jeans with detailed creases, and gold dookey chains. The sneakers were big and exaggerated, rockin' two different colors of fat laces, laced in an intricate pattern. Juan's character was playing with a yo-yo, with a smirk on his face, representing Juan to the fullest.

"Corazón, tonight you can paint the crowns and the wizard on top of the E. Here's the paint you'll need. Hook it up quick, so we can make it to T-Dog's 'n shit."

We got lost in a zone. I did my thing on one side while he put the finishing touches on the other. When we finally finished we took a step back to look at it. "It needs one more thing," Juan walked up to the piece, shaking the last of the black paint.

He wrote above the characters: *"We Are the Crew That Is the Best . . . We Are Runnin' The Streets and We Are FRESH . . ."* He paced back and forth. It wasn't complete for him, but I couldn't tell what was missing.

Then he bent down, beneath the characters, and started painting again. *"If God can give life, and man can take life away, who is in power?"* Finally, after switching colors from black to red, he wrote, *"My mom told me to stay home. Did I listen to her? Hell No!"*

"Fuck!" he yelled, throwing the spray can against a fence. It made a loud noise as metal hit metal.

I walked over and put my arms around Juan. He stiffened at first, but as I kept holding him he loosened up, and at one point he locked his arms around me, pulling me tighter.

The daily grind took over my life for a while. Carmen was with Kyle all the time, and Juan had his ladies. I saw Keisha at basketball practice, but that was about it. I started getting low again, sometimes itching to use my razor to take away the numbness that invaded my mind, even though I knew it was bad. Instead I wouldn't eat, and moped around in my room.

It was Friday night, and once again Juan was nowhere to be found. I hated when he put his hoochies in front of me. I had resigned myself to another dull weekend, when Darnell called. He invited me to a new teen club. At first I thought about saying no, but something made me change my mind. Fuck that, instead of staying home feeling upset, I'm going out.

I cleared everything with my mom, and was dressed and waiting on Darnell, when the phone rang again: Darnell calling to tell me his ride broke down. He was staying behind, but one of his friends, a cutie I had met before, got on the phone.

"Do you still want to go? We might have fun, you never know," he said.

After all I went through to get ready for the night, I wasn't about to stay home, so I said yes. He picked me up an hour later. His name was Jamal and from what I had heard about him from the cool girls at Five Points he was a playa. The more I learned about him that night, the more I understood why; light-skinned, hazel eyes, and really built, to begin with. If that wasn't enough, he played basketball and was the star on the varsity baseball team at Excel Academy.

At the club we chilled together, talking, feeling each other out. From the conversation, I learned that he was smart, talented, and sexy. He was going somewhere in life. I felt a passion in him that was missing from Joe. Jamal was attentive to me, listening to my every word. Taking me in with his eyes. Flirting cautiously. At one point, I excused myself to the bathroom to check to make sure I was looking okay. I overheard two girls talking.

"Did you see his hazel eyes? He is *fine!*"

I knew immediately they were talking about Jamal, and when I walked by one of them asked me if that was my man.

"No way," I said, defensively, "he's just a friend."

Even then I knew what I was up against. But somehow, when that slow song by Luther Vandross played and he pulled me on the dance floor, I found myself entranced. Our bodies fell in sync with each other, the cologne on his neck softly accentuating his smell. As the song came to an end, he gently lifted my face to his and with a kiss sealed our commitment.

Dear Diary

Best concert: Fat Boys, Salt-N-Pepa, Dana Dane, and U.T.F.O.!

New outfit: A white satin Raiders jacket that Jamal bought me. It's inscribed "Amber" on the pocket. I wear it with my BKs. Juan loves it when I wear this out with him—he says 'cause I'm representing the set proper!

I haven't written in so long. Well, Jamal is my first black boyfriend. I wonder if it will be different than dating Joe. I've made up my mind to get on the pill. I wish I could talk to my mom about it, but she is so against sex before marriage. Getting pregnant is a huge fear of mine. It would ruin me and Jamal's life. So I'm going to start at the end of the month. Jamal said he'll pay for them 'cause it costs twenty dollars a month at the clinic.

Me and Carmen planned a trip to the mountains with our boyfriends. I told my mom I was going with Carmen's parents. We packed food and wine, and brought up a mix of our favorite music. Carmen loved rocking out to Led Zeppelin, Steely Dan, and Joan Armatrading. Kyle brought the Beastie Boys and some Fishbone.

Of course my man had Levert to serenade me with.

We made love on a blanket, deep in the woods, under a tree right next to a river. I could have sworn I heard him whisper, "I love you." Everything was just perfect.

Twelve

"Why is Dad taking only me out to dinner?" I asked my mom. My brother and I started spending every other weekend with him. Now my mom was telling me that TJ wasn't going.

"He wants to spend some time with you, Amber. He's picking you up in a half hour, so you should get ready."

I went into my bedroom and sifted through the clothes in my closet. The more I thought about it, the more excited I was. I loved going to fancy dinners with my dad, where everyone knew and liked him. I found my favorite pair of black pants and a matching top. I was growing my hair out, and now it reached the middle of my back; I brushed it out, deciding to leave it down, and then put on some eyeliner, mascara, and lipstick for the occasion.

"Amber, he's here. Come on, honey," my mom yelled from the front door.

"'Bye, Mom, love you," I said, and kissed her on her cheek. She hugged me back, holding tightly.

At the restaurant, my dad flirted with the young, pretty waitress and ordered a bottle of wine. She didn't mind flirting back, even with his teenage daughter giving her the evil eye. I was used to it by now. He was always a hit because of his good looks. He had a nice tan, blond hair, and blue eyes. He was also very fit. When asked his age, he always joked, "Somewhere between Robert Redford and Richard Gere."

"What are you thinking about ordering?" he asked me.

"Maybe the pasta primavera," I replied, my head buried in the menu.

"That's pretty heavy—the sauce is really fattening. What about a salad, or the swordfish?"

"Dad, why don't you just order for me?" I didn't want to disappoint him on our special night out. Although he never outright said I was overweight, I felt like I couldn't measure up to what he wanted me to look like. I tried to please him, but felt like I fell short every time.

I was on my second glass of wine, feeling nice. Serving wine to me was never a problem because my dad was cool with all the restaurant owners and waiters. We ordered dinner, talked about school, caught up on things. I was doing better this year, somehow balancing my time between bombin', bangin', sports, and studying.

"Amber, I want to talk to you about something," my dad said, after the waitress poured him another glass of wine.

"What, Dad?"

"I want to talk to you about who your friends are, and the guys you are dating." My stomach dropped. "I'm worried about you dating black guys. I don't have a problem with it, but I'm afraid if you date blacks, then white guys won't be interested in you."

I couldn't believe what I was hearing. At first I was happy

that he didn't know about the graffiti and the Crips. But after I got over that, I was furious. I felt betrayed by my mother, who must have told him something. How else would he know? I looked down at my plate.

"Is it that you only like black guys?" he continued softly, leaning in.

I felt sick to my stomach, confused and angry. My mom and dad both stood firm in their desire for me and my brother to be in a diverse neighborhood. In fact, they went against their families' traditions by sending us to public school instead of Catholic school, like all my cousins.

"I don't *just* like black guys!" I whispered back, barely able to get my voice past the lump in my throat. I hated what he was saying to me, but I knew what he was talking about. Ever since I started dating Jamal, white guys didn't even really flirt with me anymore. It was weird and it hurt. But I would never tell my dad this, not after what he said to me. Tears started streaming down my cheeks.

"Amber, if you don't change who you spend time with and who you date, I will take you out of Five Points and put you in a Catholic school."

On the verge of hysteria, I ran from the table into the bathroom, went into a stall, shut the door, and started bawling. I could barely breathe.

I don't know how long I stayed in there, but finally my dad sent a waitress in after me, who told me he was worried and wanted me to come back to the table. I emerged and walked right past him, straight to the parking lot, where I stood by his car. He came out and opened the door for me, not saying a word. I got in and stared straight ahead the whole drive home. He tried to talk to me but I would not speak to him.

I ran into my room and slammed the door, hoping my

mom would hear. She must have been in on this too. How could she?

Dear Diary
   Song I dedicate to my dad: DJ Jazzy Jeff/Fresh Prince—
"Parents Just Don't Understand!" For real.

   Tonight my dad took me out to dinner. He thinks I'm getting into a rut, only being with black people, and with people who don't seem to care about the future. I don't know. Right now I don't have any emotions, but I was crying a lot at the restaurant! I'm happy until people like my dad start talking to me like this! I hate it! I am so confused. I know that my dad doesn't have a problem with black people, because he always told me that blacks and whites were equal. But now I'm beginning to question this. So why can't I have a black boyfriend?
   All I want to know is how much can I take before I collapse? I cut myself twice tonight. I need help—I really really do. DEATH SEEMS POSSIBLE!

That weekend I wanted to get out of my house so badly. I was still angry with my mom for setting me up, my dad for all the things he said, and myself for allowing his words to raise questions. I didn't want to talk about anything with Jamal—it would only hurt him, and then bring up problems in our relationship. I called Juan at his *tia's*, but she said he wasn't there. When was he ever there except to shower and change clothes? The next best place to find him was T-Dog's.

   My mom needed the car to go grocery shopping, so I headed to Five Points on the bus. I popped Mantronix in my Walkman attempting to tune out the noise going on in my head. I got to T-Dog's, went around back, opened up the screen door, and knocked. To my surprise, a Crip named Omar opened up the door instead of T-Dog. I had met him a couple of times, and I knew Omar was tight with Juan and Lil D, but he wasn't around much. Juan told me he was enrolled in our school, but I never saw him there.

"Hey, what up?" he said. He was light-skinned, with big brown eyes and long eyelashes. He was really cute. Omar was rockin' beige dickies, pressed white T-shirt, and a blue rag hangin' out the back of his pocket. The only thing that stood out was the pencil behind his ear. It made me smile.

"Hey. Is T-Dog or Juan here?" I asked.

"They'll be back, they went to handle some bidness downtown," Omar said. "You want to come in and wait for them?"

I hesitated, not sure what I should do. What I really wanted was someone to talk to, and I didn't know Omar very well at all. I looked up at Omar and he smiled at me. "Come on, just come in the house already—whatcha scared of?" He opened the door wider for me.

I didn't really have anyplace else to go. "Okay, I'll come in and wait for a minute," and followed him down to the basement. "You here by yourself?" I asked.

"Yeah, I am. And I'm so glad 'cause I got some peace up in here!" he replied.

He walked over to where he was sitting, a makeshift little table made with two crates and a record cover. Resting on top was a composition book and a bunch of colored pencils.

"What are you doing with all that?" I asked.

"I'm writing a poem for my mom, it's her birthday next week."

I moved closer and looked down at the paper. On it was drawn a red rose wrapped delicately around a heart, and inside the heart was a poem. At the bottom it read, "To the most special lady on the planet—my Mom!"

"I didn't know you wrote poetry, Omar! Where did you learn?"

"That right there is a long story!" Omar said, adding more color to the heart.

"I got some time." I looked at him and smiled.

T-Dog and Juan never came back that afternoon. I honestly don't know what happened to us down there in the dark, dingy basement, but it was as if we were in a different time and space. Our normal inhibitions were shed and all that could come out of us was realness. We spent hours and hours talking to each other. He shared his story, which in a way helped to take away some of the pain I was feeling from my family.

Unfortunately for Omar, his closest friends and many of his cousins were Crips. So, as far as the Bloods were concerned, Omar was down by association. After dodging numerous beat downs and bullets, Omar decided he would be better off joining the 30s. At least then he would have some protection. It was a decision he felt he had no choice but to make.

Most of his life he had had to fend for himself. His father had moved to New Orleans when he was a baby. His mother worked hard to keep them off welfare because she didn't want to take anything from the government. There was rarely any food in the refrigerator, so he had to bring in his own money in order to eat. His life was so different than mine. It was hard to hear it because it made me reflect on how unfair life was, and how easy I had it by comparison.

After I left T-Dog's I was trying to fight it, but I couldn't get Omar out of my mind.

Thirteen

Dear Diary

Song of the week: U2, "I still haven't found what I'm looking for."

Ain't that the truth!

Recently, all the black guys are going for the white girls and the white girls are loving the attention. The black girls are mad! It's funny 'cause the preppy white girls ask my advice—'cause I have more experience with black guys than they do. Now everybody likes me 'cause I know what I'm talking about. It's stupid and it pisses me off. What I hate most is that the white girls are doing this just to experience something "new." I know because that's how they talk about it; like it's a fuckin' science experiment. It makes me mad the black guys don't see they are being used, especially my friends. I guess because black guys haven't been able to date white girls it's new to them

too. I don't know, some of the so-called interracial rela-
tionships seem fake to me, like a fad or something, but I
know what I have with Jamal is real.

I rushed into our school bathroom after the last-period bell to check my appearance before I saw Jamal, who picked me up every Friday. I ran right into the prep squad; all I saw was pink and white Izod shirts, and Top-Siders. Six white girls gathered around the mirror talking and putting on lipstick. Michelle was with them, but she barely acknowledged me except to roll her eyes.

One of the girls, a tall blonde, stopped talking midsentence. "Oh, hi, Amber, we were just talking about you."

"What's up?" I asked, really wanting nothing more than to have the mirror to myself for a minute and be out. I was preoccupied with a rumor floating around that this girl named Leslie was trying to steal my man, and I wanted to see if she was outside so I could step to her.

"Stephanie?" the blonde said, and everyone turned to a small girl wearing a pink Izod shirt with the collar up.

"Why do I always have to do everything? Why don't *you* ask her, Heather?" Stephanie asked.

"Fine, jeez, you don't have to get all prissy on me," Heather replied, and then turned her gaze to me, clearing her throat. "We were wondering something. Is it true that black guys have huge dicks?" They all started giggling. "I mean, we're, like, asking you because you have more experience than we do. I mean, not like we don't have any experience, but, like, just not with black guys."

"And," added a pretty brunette I had seen around, "we also heard that they like big butts."

Samantha from my math class came around to stand closer.

"Do you date black guys just to get back at your parents?" she asked, her eyebrows arching, waiting patiently for an answer.

"Yeah, because my parents forbade me to date blacks," a girl named Jenna added.

I let out an audible sigh. I felt torn. These were the "popular" girls, and even though they were superficial and rude, part of me loved the attention. Here they were, waiting to hear what knowledge I would bestow upon them.

"Ladies, all that crap about skinny being considered pretty, you gotta throw all that out the window. That's what white boys like." I paused. They all looked at me expectantly. "Black guys like more cushion for the pushin'."

"That's it?" Heather the blonde ringleader asked.

"Oh, no. One other thing," I paused and took some time to look at each of them. "Think about your decision long and hard, because it's true what they say. Once you go black, you'll never go back."

They didn't know how to react to this. Some giggled while others just started babbling about something else.

I ran outside to find Jamal.

I stepped outside of the school into the sunlight. There was already a crowd around him. Dudes admiring his ride, a lot of females up in his grill. I looked around for Leslie, but didn't see her. But there were plenty of other girls near Jamal. I hated the feeling in my stomach when I saw him smiling at some girl. Did she have something I didn't? The only thing that made me feel better was the fact that I was the one rockin' his high school letter jacket, which proved to the world *I* was his girl. But damn, he could be such a flirt sometimes.

"Hey, baby girl," Jamal said when he spotted me, smiling at me with his beautiful hazel eyes and perfect teeth. His passion, after sports, was stereo systems, so you could hear him coming from five blocks away because of the bass in his souped-up black truck.

I was happy in the relationship for the most part, but I noticed something new I didn't like: jealousy. I knew Jamal was a catch—girls went out of their way to let me know that. It didn't help that black girls were getting mad as hell because I had "taken" one of the best.

"Can we just get out of here?" I asked, annoyed. He gave a nod good-bye to folks like he was the president or something. I got in the car and slammed the door.

"Ease up on the door, baby, c'mon, I spent a lot of money on this shit!" Jamal said to me, leaning over as if to examine the door for damage. Instead he brushed his hand against my breast and then gave it a squeeze.

"I missed you girl," he whispered in my ear, then lingered at my neck and kissed it delicately. How could I stay mad now?

"Jamal, you need to stop flirtin' with those girls, you know I hate that shit!" I said, as he continued to caress and kiss me. Luckily the windows were tinted, and by now not many people were around, so nobody could see us.

"You know that you're my one and only," he whispered and continued kissing me. I started getting hot, my body responding to his touch. "Why you think I let you wear my letter jacket? Only Jamal's girl is allowed to wear it, and that's you. C'mon, let's go to my place, I want to feel your body against mine." He took my chin in his hand and led our mouths together. "I need you," he whispered. After we kissed, he turned up the music so loud it was impossible to talk. He sped down side streets to get to his house. The bass, the speed, and Jamal, igniting all my desires.

We spent the rest of the afternoon in bed.

Dear Diary

Quote: Love Is Letting Go of Fear! —Corazón

News: Carmen and Kyle broke up, so Carmen's depressed.

Song: Janet Jackson, "Let's Wait a While" . . . ummm I LOVE this song!

I'm so in love with Jamal that lately I noticed that I have a problem with fear. Letting go of fear is very hard for me. I don't usually let a guy have control over me, or feel that I have to depend on him for my happiness. I'm an independent chick, always have been. I think it's because of my older brother. Even though we don't get along anymore, I can't deny the good things he did for me. He taught me to fend for myself. Like when it comes to sports, he made me play super-hard and told me not to play like a girl. He told me I have to play to win, especially if I'm playing with boys. So I feel like with Jamal, he is making me weaker because I like him so much, and I think about him all the time. We got in a little fight today when I told him I was scared. He yelled at me and said I don't trust him. When I started crying, he put his arms around me and professed his love for me, saying we will always be together. I want that so bad, he means so much to me! He said he's even gonna get a tattoo of my name on his arm.

After Jamal gave me his letter jacket it was official. He was my man and now everybody knew it. Soon after, I was chillin' with Felisha. She was a certified Crippette, one of my closest girl-friends from my Crip family. She was a big girl, with a dark brown complexion, pretty face, and silky long hair. Felisha got down with the Crips because her older brother was bangin', but he was in a different set than her because he lived across town with his dad. We were sitting on top of a park table, talking shit about guys while we waited for the fellas.

She started messing with my hair. "You should do some braids in here, Amber. Every time I see you, you look exactly the same. Do something different."

"I don't know, Felisha. Do you think braids would look good on me?" I asked.

She turned me toward her and pushed my hair away from my face. "Yeah, 'cause you got a pretty face," she said, dropping my hair back down. "Did you know I did hair?"

"No," I said. "But, the thing is, I don't know if my man would like it. He likes my hair long. At least, that's what he tells me all the time."

"Yeah, whatever. Who cares what he wants? He probably tells all his bitches that. You should always be looking your best so you can get other prospects happening." She smiled at my surprised expression.

"But I have a boyfriend," I started.

She shook her head. "You always have to have a nigga on the side. That way, if he ever cheats on you, you have someone to fall back on and you never truly get played."

I was used to hearing the word "nigga" from the people I hung out with. Even Juan said it sometimes. But he warned me white people were never allowed to say it. "It's different when white people say it 'cause of slavery 'n shit," he told me. I always listened to Juan.

Felisha's words brought me back.

I understood Felisha's advice, but I didn't feel it applied to my relationship. Jamal and I made a commitment, and even though he was a flirt and had a rep as a playa, I knew that we loved each other. But I did listen; relationships were still some-what new to me and I didn't want to be the fool.

"My man tells me he loves me all the time," I said. "I don't think he's gonna cheat on me."

"Girl, please. All men cheat. The girls who say their men don't cheat just haven't caught them yet."

She obviously didn't understand my relationship with Jamal; we were in *love*. But I had been hearing rumors lately. Jamal had been seen several times with Leslie. I pushed the thought away.

"Felisha, what about you? Do you got a man?" I asked. She hung out with all the Rollin' 30s but I never saw her with one of them.

"Not now. I thought I had a good man, but he turned out to be nothin' but a punk bitch." Her face turned into a scowl; she looked away from me and didn't say anything else.

Juan mentioned to me that she had hung out with a Rollin' 30, but the whole story of how she had got jumped in was a forbidden topic. I had always been curious about it since she was the only Crippette I knew well. Juan told me that she had to beat somebody down in order to be certified. She elected a chick from the neighborhood that she had problems with, jumped her, and fucked her up in front of the guys. Later that night some other shit went down to complete her initiation, but Juan claimed he didn't know anything about that. I just think he didn't want me to know. Even though Juan got me in the Crips, there were things he still protected me from. I knew that Juan and them did a lot of dirt, because I would hear about it; beat downs, armed robberies, all of that. Juan made it clear that certain things were off-limits to me.

"Yo, here they come now." Felisha nodded toward the other side of the park. I looked over and saw Juan, Lil D, T-Dog, and

Omar coming toward us. A rush went through my body when I saw Omar. "I hope them niggas brought us something to eat, I'm hungry!" Felisha said, and added, "Don't forget what I told you today, Amber. You gotta watch your back. I don't want to see you cryin' over some dude who played you."

The fellas arrived and our conversation about men was over.

Fourteen

Jamal was trying to make up with me because we had gotten into a really bad fight. I had found a note from Leslie in his bedroom, threw a fit, and broke up with him. But he won me back two days later.

"I want to see you Amber. I got plans for you, girl." His silky low voice turned me on.

"What about tomorrow, Jamal? I'm doing a piece with Juan tonight," I replied, wondering if I should cancel my plans and get my groove on instead.

"Oh, you're hangin' out with your little Crip friends tonight?" he joked. I didn't like to tell Jamal when I was kickin' it with Juan, Lil D, and Omar. He wasn't down with any gang. It wasn't his style. He was against the drinking and drugs. Sports came first, just like Keisha. When I tried to explain to Jamal why the guys *had* to bang, he laughed at me over the phone.

"We all grew up the same way, Amber, don't make excuses for them."

"Yeah, but you had both your parents!"

"Why does that matter, if they were both working all the time? Me and my brother Deshawn have been on our own since elementary school. I remember coming home from second grade with a key to the house 'cause Moms and Pops were working double shifts to pay the bills. I didn't end up robbin' no stores or joining a gang! So don't give me that shit!"

"You just don't understand, Jamal. I don't even want to talk about this anymore."

"No, the problem is, Amber, you *think* you understand, but you really don't. I know you feel sorry for your homeboys, but I don't. They're makin' a choice, nobody is forcin' them into nothin'. I just hope you learn your lesson before it's too late. You don't have no business hangin' out with them."

"But they're my friends. Are you trying to tell me who I can and can't hang out with? You're starting to sound like my dad!"

I heard Jamal sigh on the phone. "Just be careful, baby. I love you and I don't want nothin' to happen to you."

I remained silent.

"And next weekend you're mine," he said before he hung up.

I thought about what he said while Juan and I did a new piece that night. I dedicated it to Jamal.

I wanted to have a girls night out. I hollered at Carmen, but she was having some drama with her man and was caught up. So I talked Keisha into going to a new hip-hop club on Downing Street that was supposed to be all that.

Juan called and said the fellas were planning on meeting up with us.

"Is Omar coming?"

"Why? You plannin' on playin' your man?" Juan asked.

"No!" I said quickly. "I was just wondering. He's fun to kick it with, that's all."

"Yeah, right. Play on, playa." He chuckled. "I'll see you up there, homie." I heard Keisha honking outside.

"Do you like my new braids?" she asked when I got in the car.

"Yeah it's cute." I admired her long extensions, which were done in an elaborate pattern. "Tonight is your night, Keisha—I want you to get some numbers. I'm tired of you being single."

"Find me a good man, Amber. It's not like I'm unwilling, but dang, I want some quality up in here!" We laughed together and she turned up the music and started singing as we drove to the club.

Keisha and I had a blast dancing all night, despite the fact we couldn't find any cuties. As we walked out to the parking lot we found our friends waiting for us there.

"Why didn't y'all come in?" I asked Juan and Lil D. Omar was in the car with Ray-Ray. My smile froze when I saw Ray-Ray glaring at me.

"We had our own party in the parking lot—you know we just come for the peep show," he said. The "peep show" was when people came to the club while it was closing, trying to get some action from all the drunks leaving.

The bouncers were already walking about, trying to clear folks out. "Move on, folks. Time to go home!" said one of the huge bouncers, looking our way. There had been a shooting a couple weeks before, so they had beefed up security.

"So what's the plan?" I asked. Juan jumped in a car that I had never seen before, probably stolen, and yelled out the window to us, "Just meet us at the 7-Eleven by Colorado Boulevard, we'll figure it out from there!"

There were three cars full of people at the convenience store, about ten or eleven of us, some Crips and some folks who had joined up with us after the club. I brought my own bottle of Night Train and passed it to my homies as we sat listening to Heavy D on Keisha's stereo. I didn't think there was a plan to do any dirt that night but then out of nowhere Ray-Ray said, "Let's do this store, cuzz."

"Word up," Juan said. "Come on, y'all, let's have some fun!" He rushed in and, without thinking, I followed him. Omar and Lil D came after us.

Keisha stayed in the car. "Amber, I don't like this—let's go!" she yelled after me.

"I'll be right back, Keisha, I promise," I said, with a pang of guilt. But as soon as I got in the store, the guilt was replaced with adrenaline. It was a madhouse. Everyone who was kickin' it outside saw a free-for-all, and joined in for a piece of the action. People started running in and grabbing all the shit they could get their hands on, then bolting out.

The older-looking clerk knew he couldn't do anything, so he just stood behind the counter. His hands were up in the air so that nobody would try to hurt him. Nobody had a gun on him, but I'm sure he thought people were packin'.

Keisha yelled to me, "Amber, I'm leaving! Are you coming with me or not?" She was getting frantic, so I grabbed whatever was in front of me and ran to the car.

"Don't ever do that to me again!" Keisha said as she drove out of the parking lot in a panic.

"I'm sorry, Keisha, I just got caught up," I said, going though the stuff on my lap. Razors, candy bars, and some nasty beef jerky. "It's 'cause I'm a little drunk. You know I didn't plan that—it just happened."

"But you didn't *have* to do it, not with me around. You're not being a very good friend to me, Amber. What if the cops came and took down my license plate? How would I explain that to my mom?"

I remained silent and Keisha turned up the music.

Keisha had a curfew, so she dropped me off at my house. "Keisha, I am sorry I put you in that position," I said when I got out of the car.

She sighed. "Fine, Amber. I'll talk to you later," she said, then drove off.

Everyone was asleep at my house, so I grabbed my mom's keys and took the car, heading toward T-Dog's, where I knew everyone was hangin' out.

"You wanna go outside on the porch?" Omar asked me as we were chillin' in the basement. I saw Juan eyeing me from across the room. I didn't want him to notice anything because he would probably give me shit.

Omar and I knew it didn't make sense for us to be together. I could never bring him home to my mom's house because of the way he dressed. He looked like a gangbanger and my mom watched the news, especially since there had been a shootout between the Bloods and Crips at our high school a couple weeks back. Lord only knew what she would do if she found out my friends were involved in that.

"Okay, yeah," I said. I was excited but also nervous. Everyone knew this was a Crip house, and sitting on the porch made us prime targets for a drive-by. But I would risk that to be alone with Omar. When I was with him, Jamal and all of our drama melted away from my mind, as if it was in another lifetime. Sometimes I felt guilty, wondering what was wrong with me. I had a perfectly good guy and I was messing it all up just like I did with Joe. But then I would remember Felisha's words, the rumors about Jamal playin' me, and my growing feelings for Omar and just go with it.

He handed me a forty. "So Jamal let you out, huh?" Omar asked. I hated when he brought him up.

"Yeah, he's busy tonight, he has a game or something." I took a swig. It hit me hard because I had already been drinking so much.

"I'm glad he's a busy dude," he said.

I knew it was hard for Omar to give me compliments, so in some strange way when he talked about Jamal he was showing me he cared. But I wished he would do it right instead of just making me feel guilty. I felt tears sitting in the corner of my eyes. Damn, I shouldn't have drunk so much Night Train. I was too buzzed.

Omar finally broke the silence. "Look at the beautiful moon." He motioned up into the clear sky. I looked up and felt my head spin a little bit from the booze.

"I see the moon reflected in your eyes," he said. I looked at Omar, who had turned his attention from the moon to me. He looked so good, his deep brown eyes, strong arms, and those juicy lips. I smiled at him.

"When are you gonna be just my girl?" he asked, taking my hand in his. "I don't like to share." He leaned over and kissed me. He wrapped his arms around me, squeezing me to him and sliding his hands into my jeans, grabbing my ass.

"Yo, what's going on up in here?"

Omar jumped back from me when some of the fellas showed up suddenly on the porch.

"What up, cuzz," he said, giving pounds to them. He stood in front of me. It seemed like he was trying to block them from seeing me, which was stupid because they knew I was there.

"Omar, let's bounce from this joint, man. There ain't no girls here, and I want to get some tonight, homie!" That was T-Dog's little cousin Trigga.

"Word up," the Crip next to him said, as he took a swig of his beer.

Without looking at me, Omar said, "Yeah, let's roll and see what's good in the hood." He walked back in the house. "Lemme get some drinks to bring with us. I'll be up in a minute."

The others drifted down to the front of the house, waiting for Omar. Nobody had said a word to me. Anger and embarrassment were fighting each other in my body and I couldn't tell which would win out. How could he disrespect me like that? My teeth clenched together. Fuck this shit, man. I'm leaving. As I got up I realized that Omar had unbuttoned my jeans, so I had to put down my drink and hurry up and fix myself before anyone noticed.

Just as I walked inside, I bumped into Omar, who was leaving to go find some girls. He put his arms around me to give me a hug but I shook him off. "Get away," I said.

"Don't trip, baby girl. You know you in my heart." He grabbed my face and turned it to his. "I hope you come by soon 'cause I drew you somethin'." He kissed my lips and was out the door. My tears came back and fell to my cheeks.

I went downstairs and said my good-byes. Juan was making out with some girl in the corner, so I didn't say anything to him, just grabbed another forty for my ride home. On my way out, two people asked me for rides.

"Nah, cuzz, I got plans tonight," I replied, not caring about making anyone happy tonight. I got in my mom's car and immediately turned up the radio as loud as I could taking the forty to the head.

I knew exactly where I was going.

Sitting in front of Jamal's house, I could barely remember how I got there. I looked at my watch and saw that it was late, but I didn't care. I walked up to the house, not sure if I should ring the doorbell or knock—I didn't want to wake anyone up. I was standing at the door for a good ten minutes, trying to make a decision, when Jamal's mom pulled up in her car. She had probably just gotten off the late shift at the restaurant where she worked. I quickly threw my beer into their bushes, hoping she didn't notice. She was surprised to see me.

"Hello there, young lady. What are you doing out here so late?" she asked, as she gathered her bags from the car.

I tried to act like I wasn't smashed. "Hi, Mrs. Davis, I'm sorry to be visiting at this time, I just wanted to see how Jamal's game went tonight." I tried to speak as evenly as possible.

"Oh, you didn't go see him play?" she asked.

"Um, no, not tonight, because my mom wanted me to help clean the house, so I couldn't make it. But I felt bad, so here I am." I smiled and tilted my head, praying she wouldn't ask me any more questions.

"Okay, honey, let me open this door and let you in."

Mrs. Davis was always so sweet to me, making me food when I was there, treating me like a daughter. She always told me that she liked me being with her son, because she felt the other girls he brought home were "rogues" who didn't care about anything but catching a man by having a baby. After she let me in, I hurried down the hall to the back of the house, which was where Jamal's room was.

He was asleep. I peeled off my clothes, slipped under the covers, and pressed my naked body against his. He woke up surprised, and happy. As we got our groove on, I thought, Fuck you, Omar, and basked in the feeling of being adored.

The next weekend came and I spent Friday night at Jamal's house. We talked to his brother Deshawn for a minute and then headed to his room. Jamal put on his famous slow-jam tapes and lit some incense while I sat on the edge of his bed, which took up the whole room. I glanced at the wall, where he had hung up all of his favorite album covers, like Eric B., Salt-N-Pepa, and LL Cool J. I chatted a little bit about nothing, butterflies of anticipation in my stomach. The bold girl from the other night was replaced with a meeker one, unsure of herself.

Although Jamal wasn't my first, he definitely was the one to teach me about sex. He was gentle and always treated me so good when we were together. I felt safe in his arms. When he learned I was shy about my body and still new to sex, he confidently guided me and taught me how to give and receive pleasure. By showing me how much he appreciated all I had to offer, he enabled me to feel better about myself. In our most intimate moments, he took the time to look into my eyes, to let me feel his adoration. At times, he would trace his fingers over my naked body, telling me how lucky he felt to be with someone so beautiful. I loved being with him, but I also felt guilty.

My mom knew I was dating Jamal and was okay with that, but she didn't know what we were doing. We never talked about sex, except for her reminding me I couldn't have it until I was married.

I pushed that out of my mind.

Jamal and I made love several times that night; he wanted me to stay over, but I had to get home. Even though he had a car, he decided to walk me, so we could spend more time together. He only lived ten minutes away from me. We were holding hands, walking and talking, when a cop car cruised by, slowed down, and pulled to a stop beside us. There were two white cops in the car.

"You got some ID?" the driver said to Jamal.

"I don't have my wallet on me 'cause I live right up the block," he said.

"Well, how about that, no ID. You know we could take you down to the station for that, right?" The cop had a nasty smirk on his face. I could tell that Jamal was getting upset, but he was controlling it.

"Officer, he's walking with me to make sure I get home safe," I said, trying to defuse the situation.

"Well, lemme tell you what, young lady. Why don't you just let us take you home? That way this gentleman doesn't have to be out on the street with no ID and you can get to where you're going safely."

The cop said it as a question, but it sure didn't feel like I had much of a choice. I looked at Jamal; he was pissed. But we both knew that it was better if I went with them. If we fought this, it would just mean more drama. I didn't even kiss him good-bye, I just got in the back of the cop car. Jamal turned and started back to his house.

The car ride was quick, but there was enough time for the cops to ask me questions like, "Do your parents know who you're hanging out with?" My anger raged, but the fear that they might talk to my mom kept me in check. The beautiful evening was draining out of me.

Here I was in the back of a cop car, getting lectured even though I hadn't done anything wrong. The cop pulled up to the front of my house. I prayed my mom wouldn't look out at that moment, because then I would be busted for lying about where I was. I knew I couldn't tell her what happened, even though I needed someone to make sense of it all.

Adults were always talking about "don't see color," and "treat everybody with respect," but when it came right down to it, they didn't live by those rules.

All it took was seeing a black guy with a white girl to bring out the worst in them.

Dear Diary

Song that I need in my life right now: Bobby McFerrin, "Don't Worry, Be Happy!"

Quote: "Prejudice is a burden which confuses the past, threatens the future, and renders the present inaccessible."

—Maya Angelou

Fifteen

Amber, we need to hang out!" I could hear the joy in Carmen's voice. "Mateo and I are having a party. I'll come pick you up."

Although we had talked on the phone a lot, I hadn't kicked it with Carmen for a while. It had taken some time for her to get over Kyle, but now she was in heaven. At seventeen, she was in love, so she moved out of her parents' house to live with her man. A lot had changed with Carmen—she and her parents had been arguing all the time, so when her boyfriend told her to move in with him, she agreed. To help pay the rent, she got a job as a waitress at a funky restaurant downtown where they could care less if she was old enough or not.

I liked Mateo and his crazy skateboarder friends. They were white boys living on the fringe, mostly punk rock, Red Hot Chili Pepper types. They dug rap music that had an aggressive edge to it. They liked anything hard core. All that really mattered was that Carmen was finally happy again.

"Pick me up? In what?" I asked, and she started laughing.

"Le Hooptie, at your service," she replied. She explained she had just bought a beat-up used car and lovingly named it Le Hooptie, because of its crappy condition.

Two hours later Carmen picked me up and we drove over to the apartment she shared with Mateo. "Carmen, tell me about your job. I need to start working too! I need some new outfits, but my mom wants me to shop at *Target*; those clothes are so ugly I'd be so embarrassed!"

"I can hook you up!" Carmen said, speeding down Sixth Avenue toward Capitol Hill. "I'm in good with the manager now. He likes me, a lot. A little too much, if you know what I mean!"

"For real? That sucks, Carmen."

"Yeah, I can't stand it when he tries to touch me—he always tries to cop a feel. But I need the job—my mom is still upset over me leaving to live with Mateo. She cut me off, so I gotta get that rent money, you know?"

Although our lives had changed so much and now we were running in different circles, we did make sure those circles collided once in a while.

I left Carmen and Mateo's after a beer and took Le Hooptie to the hood to see if Omar wanted to come to the party. I couldn't call, his family didn't have a phone. I wanted to widen the circles of both groups, maybe then people could see our cliques in high school were artificial. We all had some commonalities. We just needed to take the time to get to know one another.

I had forgiven him for the night he dissed me in front of his friends. When we saw each other after that, he explained how hard it was for him that I had a boyfriend. I knew it was complicated, so I didn't hold it against him.

I knocked on his door, hoping he was home. His mom answered.

"Hey, Amber, how are you doing today?" she said. She was a pretty lady, tall and slender, with a cute little mole on her left check. I could tell that Omar got his bright smile from her.

"Hey, Ms. Jones. I'm fine, how are you?" I asked as I walked in the house. The living room was very small, with just a couch and a small table with a TV on top of it. The light blue walls were bare, except for one picture in a pretty frame, a black-and-white of Omar when he was a baby.

"Omar," she called, "you have a visitor." She turned to me. "He'll be out in a minute, honey. Now excuse me while I fold up the laundry. Make yourself comfortable."

I sat down on the couch to wait for Omar. He came out of his room wearing blue dickies and a white T-shirt, as usual.

"What brings you to my hood today?" he said, flashing his beautiful smile.

"That would be you." I smiled back. "Come to a party with me."

"Word? Hold up, lemme check my schedule." He paused for a minute, putting his finger on his chin and looking up at the ceiling. "Okay, I checked my schedule and I'm free," he said as he walked over and kissed me on my cheek.

He got his stuff and we got in the car. "What's this?" he said, looking at the screwdriver in the ignition. I told him the story of Le Hooptie. It had been stolen a couple of times, so the ignition was all messed up, no keys necessary. The community car for all to use. We walked around with a screwdriver in our backpacks. The last person using it let Carmen know its location, so she could keep tabs on it.

"I want to get a car someday," he said, looking out the window. "But you know what I really want to do." He paused for a minute. "I really want to go to college for writing or poetry, you know. I think I could be really good at that."

"Well, before you get to college, you gotta start going to high school, Omar." I was worried because he was in and out of juvie all the time, missing tons of school. At this rate he wouldn't pass his classes at all.

"Don't you think I know that?" he snapped at me. "Damn," he said under his breath, "can you give a brother a break?"

I didn't want us to argue today. We rarely got to be alone because we usually were with the rest of the crew.

I put my hand on his leg. "Baby, c'mon, don't be mad. It's just that I worry about you sometimes."

"You know, Amber, I want it to be different, I really do, but I'm trapped. I'm just tryin' to stay alive long enough to figure it all out," he said.

I pulled up to Mateo's place and parked. We sat in silence.

"I guess we should go in," I said, not moving.

Omar turned to me. "Amber, I know that shit isn't perfect, and I know I've fucked up and not treated you right all the time—but I want you to know that I'm glad I met you, and I really like kickin' it with you."

For Omar, this was as romantic as it was going to get, which was fine with me. I could care less that he wasn't smooth and didn't have bullshit lines. I already had one of those in my life, and look where that was getting me. Jamal and I had been arguing lately over the same shit—his playa status. I loved Omar for who he was, and for what he hoped to become.

"Let's go party with the white dudes," Omar said, and we both laughed and walked up to the house, which had loud punk music blaring from the open windows.

The party was a blast; beer, weed, people shouting for the Broncos during the game, and just as I suspected all the guys got along great. We hung out there for a while and then Omar asked me to come home with him to chill. We got to his place around midnight, and went to his room to watch TV and cuddle. Both of us buzzed, we happily fell asleep in each other's arms. We woke up to Omar's mother yelling at us.

"What do you think you're doing, Omar? You are not allowed to have girls spend the night!"

I had never seen her angry like this.

"Ma, come on, we fell asleep. Why you trippin' so hard?"

"Amber, you gotta go. Omar, we'll talk later." She stormed out of his room and into the kitchen.

"Omar, why is your mom trippin' on the little things? It's like she's mad at you for us just being here, not the fact that you're out in the streets doin' dirt. What kinda sense is that?"

"Yo, Amber, you're talkin' about my moms. Chill with that."

"I'm not disrespecting her, I just—"

Omar put his hand over my mouth. "Sorry, baby, but you gotta go."

I pushed his hand away. "Whatever." I got up and started putting myself together. "I'll see you around." Omar walked me through the tiny living room and opened the front door.

"Yeah, whatever," he said, and closed the door fast and hard behind me.

I hated when things ended like that. But I had to worry about getting Le Hooptie back to Carmen's, and then see if she would drive me home. I needed to get there before my mom woke up.

Dear Diary

Songs I Love no matter what: Madonna, "Crazy for YOU!" (Jamal and Omar)

Phil Collins, "One More Night" (I wish that night with Omar didn't go down like that!)

Best Tag: the side of the Colfax bus! Juan was with me and he was so proud!

So much has happened. I still go out with Jamal, but things have been rocky for a while. Jamal's actions just bring out the jealous bitch in me! I just don't trust him anymore. Right now I'm confused. Omar and me have a strange relationship. We started hanging out a lot and one thing led to another and we've messed around three times now. It's unfair, though. The only time we hook up is when we're fucked up and during those times it seems like we're so close. We talk about deep personal things. We become almost like best friends/lovers. Then I'll come by the next day and it's as if nothing happened. He's sometimes cool, sometimes very distant and Crip-like. I guess that's reasonable 'cause he is a Crip. Gangs right now are on the rise, which makes it more danger-ous for my friends. Drive-by shootings are common. Omar even sells crack now just like everybody else. Being a Crip is taking over his whole life. He got locked up over the weekend for robbing some store with Ray-Ray. I know that he's not gonna live long. I just don't know what to do.

Over the weekend Felisha braided my hair in cornrows. She told me all about Omar going to jail because she was with them when the cops came. My heart hurt a little, especially because of the way we left each other, but I couldn't let Felisha on to that. I didn't want her knowing my business.

Anyway, I didn't have time to shoot the shit because I had to be at work. True to her word, Carmen had gotten me a job as a hostess at C'est Café downtown on the 16th Street mall. It was a happening spot for yuppies and businesspeople, and it felt like a whole other world, appreciative of diversity, so dif-ferent from the little cliques at Five Points High. The other workers were laid-back, and the tips were great. An additional plus was that one of the workers sold Ecstasy, so I had a new hook-up.

Juan promised to pick me up so I wouldn't be late. Felisha was on her last braid when I heard a honk outside.

"That's Juan, I gotta go, Felisha," I said.

"Okay, okay, lemme just put this rubber band in right quick." She pulled my head to the side to finish. "I told you it would look nice on ya," she said. "Damn, I'm good."

"Thanks, girl, I'll check you later." I went out to the car.

Juan was looking fly with his dark sunglasses and new ride. He had gotten a new tat on his arm, a half sleeve that his home-boy did for him.

"What up, homie? Dang, likin' them braids, girl. Now Jamal and Omar will really be fighting over you." He grinned. As hard as I tried, Juan knew me too well, and had peeped my game. Plus he was tight with Omar, so we couldn't keep our clandestine relationship a secret from him.

"Shut up, Juan. You should be classified as a clown as many girls as you jugglin'." I smirked.

"I gotta keep 'em happy, Amber. That's my job. Now where is this job of yours?"

Juan drove me downtown and dropped me off. "Stay up, homie," he winked at me, and I smiled back as I got out of the car.

"Love ya, Juan. Be careful." I shut the door and watched him drive away. I always felt warm and safe with him.

That day I was scheduled to work with Wendy, an experienced hostess. She was older than me and all the men loved to flirt with her because she had a nice body, bleached blond hair, piled-on makeup, and wore supershort skirts.

"Why did you do that to your hair?" she asked with a frown as soon as she saw me.

"I just wanted a change," I said.

"That's how black people wear their hair. Why do you want to look like them?" she asked. I was surprised, not sure what to say back to her. Luckily some customers came in, and when she shifted her attention to them, I walked away. The rest of my shift was chaotic, so I didn't think much about it.

Later on, right before it was time for me to clock out, Jamal came to pick me up from work at the café. He was waiting for me near the entrance of the restaurant. Wendy and I could see him from the hostess stand.

"Who is that guy?" she asked me when she saw us look at each other.

"That's my boyfriend." A slow smile emerged on my face. Jamal was looking really good leaning against the wall, in a new stonewashed denim outfit. With his hazel eyes and nice build, I was proud to call him my man.

"What?" she asked. "*That* is your boyfriend?" She put the menus down on the hostess stand and gave me her complete attention.

"Um, yeah." What the hell was she making such a big deal out of?

"I cannot believe you are dating a black guy," she said, with one hand on her hip.

"What are you talking about?" I asked, looking at her.

"Don't you know that people will think you're a slut? Dating blacks will really cause you to go downhill." I was speechless. I mean, come on, we weren't in white suburbia here—this was downtown.

"I'm really surprised at you, Amber."

It wasn't like Wendy was my best friend or anything, but I respected her; she had really looked out for me, training me and helping me learn the ropes. At the same time, I felt very protective of my boyfriend. How dared she talk about him when she didn't even know him?

"Whatever, Wendy," I replied. "How about you mind your business?" Not the most articulate response, but the only one I could muster at the time. I walked to the staff room, clocked out, gathered my tips, and left. The whole evening I was with Jamal, I was mad at myself. Why didn't I have what it took to really stand up to this woman, to tell her that she was being a prejudiced bitch?

I never told Jamal what happened. But I hated it when he came to pick me up and Wendy would smile in his face, like a snake. We were never cool after that. In fact, she got her schedule changed so we didn't work together anymore. I was relieved.

C'est Café gave me other challenges, especially with my hair. The braids were a magnet for comments from the mostly white clientele. How long did that take? Did it hurt? *How ethnic!* God, it was driving me so crazy, I could barely contain myself. Of course I had to smile and make small talk so I could get that tip, but in my head all I was thinking was, How long did it take for you to get so stupid? Does it hurt to be such an asshole?

When I got home from work I had to deal with questions from my family, my cousins, and random white people on the street. Two weeks later I took the braids out. I just didn't want to be a walking explanation of braided hair. I felt sorry for all my black friends who had to deal with white people asking them about their hair all the time.

What *was* wrong with my people? I asked myself that question all the time.

Sixteen

Dear Diary
I miss Omar. I heard he gets out soon,
That's all for now.

"Come eat some breakfast so we're not late," my mom yelled to us. It was still early in the morning and we were volunteering at the soup kitchen today. I was so tired from my late night with Juan. We got really high, and then we were inspired to walk what felt like twenty miles talking and tagging. My legs were sore and I didn't want to get up for anything.

After breakfast, my mom, TJ, and I got in the car. Driving downtown took fifteen minutes and we didn't have much to say in the car. We came up to the entrance of the church and saw a long line snaking down most of the block. I averted my eyes as I walked past the adults to get inside. I was never sure what to do. Smile and say hi, like everything was grand? Make eye contact with people and acknowledge them but don't smile and seem uppity? Let them see pity in my eyes? Instead, I just put my head down slightly and walked closely behind my mom.

My job consisted of standing behind the counter dishing out huge vats of chicken noodle soup and bread. We could always tell when the church received some extra donations, because then we'd have more of a variety, like some vegetables or some meat.

The kitchen was open from nine to twelve, and we served as many as we could. The worst part came when the food ran out. Then we had to tell hungry people that we had nothing left and see the pain in their faces. It was especially heartbreaking when little children came. It seemed like such an unfair childhood for them.

Once my shift was over, I chatted with a little kid who looked like he was five or six years old. He had stringy brown hair that hung on his thin, pale face. He seemed shy. He wouldn't really look at me and had his mouth full of food most of the time. I ended up just sitting with him for a while. When he finished, he pulled a plastic shopping bag from the floor, put it on the table, and pulled out some books.

"Can you read something to me? I got these from the library down the street from the shelter," he said.

"Sure, which one do you want to start with?"

"I like the looks of this one." He pointed to a Dr. Seuss book, *Horton Hears a Who*. Above the noise of a hundred people eating, and occasionally a scuffle from someone who was drunk and had to be "escorted" out, I read book after book to him. The young boy grew beyond his initial shyness, and would laugh out loud at the funny parts and ask questions when there were strange words involved.

After about thirty minutes, his mom came over and told him it was time to go. She was a really nice woman; after she fed herself and her son she always helped with the cleaning up.

"My way of giving back to those who give," she always said. When she first came to the soup kitchen, the bruises her husband put on her face were still fresh. We watched as they went from black to blue to yellow and finally faded away.

"Will you come back and read to me again? I can get more books from the library."

"Yeah, definitely," I told him and smiled. I waved good-bye as they left. I was still thinking about the kid when out of nowhere I heard my name. I looked up. Standing in front of me was Rodney.

"What's up, cuzz?" he said to me, and put out his fist to give me a pound. I looked to see if my mom was around, but luckily she was busy washing dishes with her back to me.

"Hey, Rodney, what are you doin' here?" I said, giving him a pound.

"The same thing you're doin', gettin' me some food!" he said, looking up at the clock, and then over at the line. "My moms drags me over here, 'specially at the end of the month when shit is tight."

"I hear you," I replied. I was all nerves. I realized that Rodney thought that I was here to get free food, just like him. I really didn't want him to meet my mom, who would shake his hand and ask him all kinds of questions. He had a blue rag hanging out of his back pocket and now everyone, including my mom, knew that having a bandana in your back pocket was a gang-related thing.

"You heard 'bout Omar? Five-o got 'im, cuzz. But he'll be out soon, bein' a minor and all."

"Yeah, I heard something about that," I replied.

He looked over at the line. "How's the food today?" Rodney asked.

"It's aight, man, you know." I replied, thinking of how I could get out of here without him realizing I was here to help, not to eat. Then the worst thing that could have happened did—the head volunteer came over and thanked me for volunteering at the soup kitchen again.

"You volunteer here?" he asked, looking at me quizzically as the guy walked away.

"Yeah, my mom makes me come," I said weakly, wondering what he was thinking. "She's into the church thing, you know?"

"No, I don't know—my family ain't like that," he said, looking uncomfortable. "You know, I gotta bounce. I ain't got time for that line and I'm sure the food is nasty, anyway. Stay up, *cuzz.*" He walked out, leaving his mother in line.

My stomach hurt. Now Rodney knew how different I really was from the rest of the Crips. I knew that from how he said "cuzz." He knew that I lied about coming here to get food, instead of serving it. I remembered Juan telling me that Rodney was one of those guys who sided with Ray-Ray and didn't want me in the Crips.

"Amber." I glanced up and saw my mom waiting for me by the exit. TJ was already outside.

As we were walking, my mom said, "I saw you sitting and reading with that little boy." She reached for my hand. "That's what this is all about, helping people in need. Life is about giving, Amber. I'm proud of you."

If you only knew all that I was hiding from you, I thought.

We went back to the same soup kitchen a dozen or so more times that year. Luckily, I never saw Rodney there again. He and I never even acknowledged what had happened. I guess he was as embarrassed as I was.

I never saw the little boy I'd read to that day again either. I tried to tell myself that good things had happened to him and his mother, and that maybe they didn't need to come back to the soup kitchen. Somehow I doubted that was what had happened, though, and my heart got just a little heavier each time I didn't see him.

"Keisha, you wanna play hoops with me and Jamal?" Jamal got along with my girlfriends, and since Keisha played ball, sometimes we'd hook up on the weekends to hit the courts. Plus, Jamal and I were always trying to introduce her to some guys—she was still single.

"I wish, Amber. But I have so much to do at home and my mom wants to go shopping at some outlets, so I'm out for today."

"Okay, girl. Well, I'll see you at school, then."

Jamal picked me up in his fly ride to play basketball. I was spending more time with him because Omar still wasn't out yet. We went over to the Rec Center in Aurora. But before that I made him drive by the throw–up Juan and I had done that night we walked forever. I was hoping that Jamal would appreciate it; I'd added a dedication to Jamal on the bottom of the piece.

"That's cute, Amber," was all he said. I crossed my arms, my good mood soured. I thought back to how special I felt when Juan dedicated his piece to me. To Jamal writing graffiti was just a waste of time. Basketball was where it was at. I could tell that it didn't mean that much to him. We were really different in that way. I was silent the car ride up to the spot, just thinking about our relationship.

Jamal knew everyone, everywhere—the Rec Center was like his own little fan club. His older brother used to play up there all the time. We had fun ballin' together because we made a good team. In many ways he was a coach to me, because he was always pushing me to do better. He would drill me, teach me new moves, and put me in situations where the competition was steep. He would make me join pickup games, and challenge whoever was winning that day; the top ballers.

That was how I got to be so good so fast. I was playing against guys who were really tough. They didn't care that I was a girl. On the contrary, the fact that I had enough nerve to get in a pickup game caused some animosity—not to mention that I was the only white person who showed up there.

The first time Jamal took me to the Rec Center, I was unsure of myself on the court. A guy on the opposite team pushed me hard while we were both going after the ball.

"Move, bitch!" he hissed.

The rest of the game I played terribly, and my confidence plummeted to an all-time low. When we lost, the guy who called me a bitch said to Jamal, "Get out of here with that shit and come back when you're ready to play, nigga."

Jamal was heated, and they almost fought, but a staff member came in and stopped it.

Jamal lectured me the whole ride home. "Them cats smell fear and act on it, Amber." He even turned down the music. "If somebody disses you—I don't care who they are, or how big they are, you need to give it right back. Show them they can't fuck with you. If you stand up for yourself, these dudes may not *like* you, but they'll damn sure *respect* you."

I took Jamal's words to heart, and the next time we played I gave back what was being dished out to me. And Jamal was right—after I pushed back, cussed back, and stood my ground, the guy's words went from "bitch" to "shorty." I even got compliments when my game was tight.

Several weeks later we played three pickup games, and won them all. We left sweaty and exhausted.

"Amber," Jamal said, "always keep your hand on his back when you d up—but don't get a hand check called on you—be aware of that. But you did good, baby. Let's go get some grub."

We drove off, bass bumpin', bodies feeling good from the exercise. My heart was smiling.

Dear Diary

Lyrics I love: "My pants are saggin', braided hair, suckers stare but I don't care!" —Ice-T

Wham! "Careless Whispers" is sweet!

Favorite Footwear: I finally got new British Knights—everyone's jealous. I crossed out the B, like Juan told me to.

I know I've had my doubts, but I love Jamal more than I've ever loved anybody!! This is special love—we feel mutual about it—it's not one-sided. I still like Omar, and if things were different, who knows? He's always getting picked up by the cops. But for now Jamal makes me so happy. I love spending time with him. Carmen got on the pill also. Carmen and Mateo seem happy, with their crazy selves. The pill is working out great! Me and Jamal make love and it's just wonderful. Sometimes I'm scared, especially when the rumors of Jamal cheating on me keep coming up—but mostly I'm pretty damn happy. What else—basketball is going good and I'm learning a lot. I'm all right on defense, and have been making all my shots. Me and Keisha got MVP's of last game! School's getting boring. My taggin' skills are getting better and better—Juan is proud!

Carmen picked me up to go shopping for lingerie. She bought a skimpy red satin nightie and I got a black lace set. She dropped me off at my man's house so I could surprise him.

"Thanks, Carmen. I'll call you later."

"Have fun, be naughty!" she said and drove away.

I was excited to show off my new outfit. I rang the doorbell. He wasn't there, but someone else was: that bitch Leslie. She was waiting for him in the living room; Jamal's father had let her in. At *my* man's house. I couldn't believe it—after I specifically told him not to let her near him. I *knew* she was after him. When he got home five minutes later, I cursed him out, broke up with him, and left him there with Leslie.

How could he do this to me, just when things were so perfect? I knew how I could get back at him.

Omar got out of juvie in time to go to my school dance. I knew it would get back to Jamal, and I couldn't wait to cause him pain.

We met at Carmen and Mateo's, because my mom still didn't know about Omar. I told her that I was going stag to the dance. We ordered Chinese takeout and enjoyed some wine, pretending we were grown as we shared laughs, romantic looks, and sexy smiles.

"You look good in that dress, baby girl," Omar whispered. I was wearing a new white dress with black polka dots and black satin gloves I had boosted. I was just happy he came. At first he said no, saying how hard it was for him to go anywhere without his homies; he'd have no backup if something went down. But after I told him how important it was to me, he finally agreed. I had counted down the days until the event.

"Thanks, baby. I dressed up for you," I said, leaning over to kiss him.

Mateo and Omar were busy bullshitting about football and guy stuff. In the right setting, Omar could get along with anybody. The sad thing was that many people wouldn't ever get to know Omar because he was a Crip. But he was so much more; a gifted poet, who would write scenes of tranquillity in one piece, and then the party flyer entitled "This is for the homies," including a dude throwing a big-ass Crip sign on the front. So in a certain way, he was like me. He was living a double life too.

I started feeling tipsy and got flirty with Omar, embarrassing him. I started grabbing his butt, and he ran off into the kitchen. I followed him and finally caught up and gave him a smack.

"Omar, what's up with your pants? They feel so thick."

"Well," Omar started, "you never know what's gonna go down, I got to be prepared for anything."

"Huh?" I stuck my hands down his pants despite his protest. "You got sweats on! Underneath your dressy slacks!" I started laughing hysterically. "What the—?"

"You know how you girls take off your earrings and grease up your face when you're 'bout to fight? Well, I ain't gonna fight in my slacks—I'm takin' them shits off so I can throw down!"

We had a blast at the dance, even though Omar was playing low profile and barely danced at all. The night ended in the school's parking lot, where we finished off a bottle of Southern Comfort. Luckily, it was one of the few times we didn't have any drama, so Omar didn't have to get Superman on me and tear off his pants.

Seventeen

Things went from bad to worse at my house. It seemed like our family didn't even like each other anymore.

Dinnertime was the same every night, a constant tension none of us could get a grasp on, but it had a profound effect on all of us. There was a total disconnect I just tried to ignore because I had no answers to our problems. What I did know is that my mom tried. She got off work early to come to my basketball games and she never missed one. Many times the only white person in the stands, she cheered me on loud and proud. She showed us love in all the ways she could.

"So how was your day, TJ?" my mom asked while we ate mac and cheese and green beans. A dull throb started in my head. It was only Monday and I still had the whole week of this to look forward to.

"Fine," he replied, disinterested.

"Is that it? Fine? Tell me something that you learned at least."

"Why? Who cares anyway? It's just school," TJ shot back.

Mom shut down and barely ate her food.

The big news was that TJ had decided to take a year off after high school. My parents were livid. College was a family traditon, and not something that you questioned. As far as I knew, he was still partying hard, but I hadn't seen him doing any coke lately. So I prayed he was just smoking weed and drinking. It still hurt that we were enemies instead of friends, but I had become numb to it, unable to break through the unspoken barriers between us. How did it get so bad? He was considering moving out to get away from us, I guess. I wondered if things would get better for us when he was gone.

Dear Diary

I'm listening to Howard Jones's "Don't Always Look at the Rain." Juan went to Florida last week to live with an uncle for a while to try and do better, and I'm missing him. I really love Juan. I learned so many things from him—I met people I would have never come in contact with, I did things I wouldn't even imagine doing. He taught me who to trust and who not to trust, when to get out so things aren't over my head, and about the ways of the street: gangs, fighting, stealing, drugs, guns, graffiti. He was my friend and mentor, and he always watched my back. Now that he's gone, there's an empty spot inside my chest. I guess I finally realize how much I love him.

Ever since the dance, Omar and I had developed a deeper relationship. He knew I'd left Jamal, so he was not between us anymore. Once Jamal found out about the dance, he called me and cussed me out. He called me all kind of names—bitch, ho, slut. I didn't care. I knew that he was doing dirt on me before I had done anything wrong.

It was Saturday, and after a shift at the soup kitchen my mom had given me the car for the rest of the day. I was driving down MLK Boulevard with Omar, Lil D, and T-Dog. Omar was mandated to work after being released and we were dropping him off.

The sun felt warm on my face, the tunes were jammin', and I was with my homies. Moments like this made me happy, until I looked up in the rearview mirror to see the red and blue flashing lights. My first thought was to move out of the way so they could pass me, but as I slowed down I realized that it was me the cops were pulling over. Damn, how fast was I going? I wasn't sure, but I knew I was going with the flow of traffic, which made it all the more surprising.

"Does anybody have anything on them?" I asked everyone in the car.

"You know I'm clean," Omar said.

"I got nothin', we're good back here," Lil D responded.

"Shit," T-Dog muttered. I was nervous as the cops approached each side of the car. I turned off Kool Moe Dee; smiled sweetly, putting on my innocent look, and waited to see what the deal was.

"License and registration, ma'am. Whose car is this?" the cop asked, removing his sunglasses.

"It's my mom's car. I'm taking my friends to work."

The chubby officer near me took a long look in the back, scanning the faces of the passengers. "Does she know you have her car?"

"Yes, she gave me permission to use it."

He took my license and registration. "Wait here." He and his partner walked back to their car.

We sat quiet, unsure of what would happen. After what seemed like forever, the skinny cop came back and leaned his head into my window. "I need you to come with me. Fellas, sit tight."

That White Girl 133

My heart was pounding. Was I being arrested? Would he call my mom? What would happen to my mom's car? How would Omar get to work? All these thoughts were running through my head when he brought me to the cop car. "Get in the back," he told me. The seats were an ugly blue with slashes in them, and the inside cushion was coming out. It stunk like sweat and body odor. The cops' radio kept beeping, a woman's crackling voice droning out descriptions of "suspects" and their possible whereabouts.

"How does it feel to be in the back of a cop car?" he asked, not too nicely. I knew the drill by now, so I stayed quiet.

"This is where you're gonna end up if you keep hanging with those guys." He paused for impact. "Did you know that you have members of the Crips in your car, little lady?"

I feigned surprise, to make things easier for all of us. Just endure it, I thought. The two good white cops felt the need to lecture the white girl on what company to keep. I still remained silent, recognizing their need for complete authority.

"Why are you with them? Are they pressuring you to take them somewhere? Are you in some kind of danger?"

"No. I know them from school." Neutral tone, not defensive.

"Take this as a lesson, young lady. Those boys are just gonna use you and then throw you away." The skinny cop spoke the whole time, the chubby one seemed bored. "It's in your best interest not to be with those characters. They're nothing but bad news."

I could tell that the lecture was almost over because the chubby cop started getting restless. I kept calm, counting down the seconds, and was almost out of the situation when the chubby one just had to make a comment.

"Get this white trash out of here, I'm hungry," he said to his partner, as if he could care less whether I heard him or not.

My anger burst out of me, almost as a reflex. "I'm not white trash!" I said, crossing my arms across my chest, shooting an evil glare.

"What did you say, girl?" The chubby one swung around and looked at me with such hatred, I felt fear creeping through my body.

His partner turned to him. "Calm down, Tony, c'mon now." Then he turned to me and said, "This is a warning. We're not gonna give you a ticket this time, but remember what we told you. Now get out of the car."

A ticket for what? He didn't even tell me if I was speeding or anything, but I knew better than to ask. Things could have been a whole lot worse. The chubby one stared me down as I jumped out. I barely had time to shut the door before the car screeched off, leaving me standing there bewildered. What did I represent that was so wrong?

As I walked back to the car I felt sick inside. I wasn't sure what to tell the guys. I didn't want to make them mad because then they might do something stupid.

"What happened?" Omar asked.

"Nothing—they were just giving me a hard time for going too fast. But it's cool—no tickets—I just had to listen to a lecture, that's all."

"Damn pigs, always fuckin' wit' people!" was the response from the backseat. I dropped Omar off at work, and continued up MLK with the fellas. It seemed like my luck was running out. My mood soured as I headed to the house.

Dear Diary
What a boring summer. I only went out bombing a couple times, 'cause Juan is still in Florida. Zap and Chaos took me out and we had a blast, but it was harder to get out of the house; my mom clamped down on me. Plus, Omar

got picked up for violating his probation. I felt so bad for him because it was just a stupid curfew law, but these cops, the gang unit, have it out for him. In his letter he said he'd be out by September. All I did was work and try to stay out of my brother's way. I can't believe I am saying this, but I can't wait until school starts!

P.S. I wish I didn't, but I miss Jamal.

Eighteen

$\mathfrak{I}$ was the girl with the getaway car, my mom's old-ass Toyota.

"Hey, baby," Omar said as he opened the door and kissed me on the cheek. "Come on in." Luckily, Omar had gotten out of juvie just before school started. He vowed to stay out of jail and go to school.

I walked in and sat on the couch in the living room. His mom wasn't home. We hung out there for a while before Omar said he wanted to hit up a store to get some food.

"Omar, you sure?" I looked at him. He glared back at me. "We don't have any food in the house, and I'm starving." "Okay," I said weakly.

"Let's pick up Rodney," he said as we got in the car. After we picked him up we drove to a gas station, far from the hood so that nobody would recognize us. Gas stations had the most variety of goods, which made it the store of choice to rob. When I wasn't around, Juan and Omar did jobs on everything from art stores to dry cleaners. They liked a challenge. I found out about the dry cleaners when all of sudden all the Rollin' 30s were wearing button-down business shirts.

I waited in the alley behind the store with the motor on. Rodney and Omar went in, and after what seemed like forever they came sprinting out, yelling "Go, go, go!" and jumped in the car. I floored it as hard as I could, but in the rear mirror I saw the clerk running out after us. I sped around the corner and Omar was yelling like crazy. After a couple of blocks we had lost him, but our blood was still pumping. I dropped Omar and Rodney off because I had to get home before my mom started worrying about me.

"Aight, cuzz." Rodney gave me a pound and got out of the car.

"See you, baby girl," Omar said. "Stay up." Omar gave me a Snickers bar (he always remembered my favorite) and I bounced to the crib.

I pulled up in the driveway and made my way into the house. As I was sitting at the kitchen table, eating my Snickers, the doorbell rang. My mom answered the door; standing there were two cops, hats in their hands. My mom let them in and as they were talking, she started looking at me, motioning for me to come to the living room.

I walked into the living room acting surprised and aloof, but I was nervous as all hell.

"Amber, these officers have my license plate number that a store clerk gave them." Mom was looking at me, puzzled. "They say my car was involved in a robbery."

"I don't know what you're talking about," I lied.

"You sure about that, young lady?" one of the cops asked me.

"Yeah." I couldn't look at my mom. Fear raced throughout my body.

The short cop took the lead. "Okay, so I guess we'll tow the car and do a full investigation to find out what happened."

Panic set in. My mom was staring at me, a shocked look on her face.

"Amber, what is going on here?" she asked. Her look cut me deeply. I didn't know what to do. I stood quiet. "You had the car for the afternoon. I need some answers."

"Maybe a trip downtown will refresh your memory?" While the short one talked, the meaner looking one was glancing around our living room as if searching for evidence. I looked up from the floor and met the cop's eyes, scowling at him.

"I told you already, it must be a mistake. I was at a friend's house!" No clever excuse was coming to my mind, just a whirlwind of disbelief that this whole thing was happening.

"Well, here's what we're gonna do." The short cop started getting his handcuffs out as he was talking. "We're gonna take you down to the station and take you a pretty mug shot."

"Amber!" Mom looked at me with tears in her eyes. "Tell me what happened!" I could tell she wanted to both protect me from the cops and find out the truth.

"And," the officer continued, "because your mother is the owner of the car, we're gonna take her down too." His partner got his cuffs out and advanced toward my mom.

I was paralyzed. Me going down was one thing, but my mom? Since I got in the Crips, I always prided myself on the fact that I kept the drama away from her. Despite our problems, my love for her was purer than any love I had ever given or received. This could not be happening!

My eyes were drawn to the table and chair that the mean cop was standing by. My mind flashed to when I was really young. My mom would brush my long hair as I sat at the table eating carrots and celery. I was her little girl, the one who did the dishes when she was too tired, who wrote notes with hearts and smiles on Hello Kitty paper, who made up for all the pain caused by the divorce. And now look at us.

She was talking to the cop, who now had one of her wrists in his hand, pleading, "This must be a mistake!"

"Okay!" I said. But they kept on. Now both my arms were behind my back.

"I said okay!" I yelled. "Leave my mom alone!" I tried to shake the cop's hands off me. "Stop!" He wouldn't let me go. Panic and anger rose in my chest.

"Oh, you have something to say now?" The short one waved at his partner to wait. He still had my mom's other hand behind her.

"It was me. I did it." I couldn't look up. I could not afford to see my mom's face.

"Amber, you did this?" Her voice cracked and she started crying. "How could you? What were you thinking? You were not raised like this!"

Silence.

"Okay, we've wasted enough time already. Let's get down to business," the mean cop said as he released my mom and motioned for her to sit on the couch. It looked like he felt sorry for her. Maybe he was the parent of a teenager too.

"Tell us exactly what happened, from the beginning," the short cop said.

"I went over to my friend's house to say hello," I answered back, giving as little detail as possible.

"But you did a lot more than say hello." The shorter one smirked. As the conversation continued, I could feel my mom's anger like a heat wave.

"Go on, then—what happened?"

"They were hungry so we went to the store," I replied.

"Why did you pick that store? Did you plan this ahead of time?" Short one.

"No!" I was irritated. "We just ended up there!"

"Do not get an attitude, young lady," my mom said.

Her respect for authority was killing me right now. Please let this be over with, I thought. I went through the whole scene feeling humiliated and afraid for me, my mom, my friends.

"Who was with you, tell them now!" She actually went over and got out my yearbook and said, "Point them out to the police." The cops had their little notebooks out and were writing things down, looking at me intently. The tall one refused to sit down. He was making such a big deal out of this, acting like someone had gotten killed or something.

I sat there with the yearbook on my lap. Two cops on one side, betrayed mom on the other, my fate with the Crips in the middle.

I chose.

I hated myself as I slowly turned the pages of the yearbook and pointed my friends out to the cops.

After the cops left, my body and mind were exhausted. My mom barricaded herself in her room, but I could still hear her sobs. I'd let down everyone in my life and there would be consequences to pay. I was sure Juan would be humiliated when word got back to him. After all, he was the one who got me in. Omar really wouldn't want to be with me anymore. It was true what Ray-Ray always said about me—you can't trust a white girl.

I wanted to die.

I locked myself in my room and looked for something sharp. Sometime last year I had thrown out my razor, determined to stop cutting myself. Now the only thing that could bring me relief was physical pain. I couldn't find anything. Fuck! I hit the wall with my fist. Over and over again.

The following day, my dad picked up my mom and me and took us to the police station to meet with the assistant DA. During the drive down my dad put on some jazz, but the upbeat music clashed with the quiet tension between my parents and me.

As we walked through the parking lot my mom was stiff, her lips sealed shut, her grimace set in stone. My dad was trying to tell me how to behave, but I wasn't listening. I felt cold, numb. My right hand was throbbing from the day before.

The police station was busy, and people barely even noticed us. A white man in a dark blue suit came over and shook my dad's hand. "Right this way, sir," he said politely. We were ushered into a small office with a desk with a computer and a huge printer spewing out paper.

"Attempted robbery, aggravated robbery, armed robbery, assault, assault with a deadly weapon, possession of an illegal substance for distribution, disorderly conduct, vandalism," the assistant DA said. He grabbed one of the sheets coming out of the printer and showed me the computer listing of several of the Crips's complete criminal histories. "That's just three of the guy's rap sheets. Shall I go on?" he asked.

Silence.

"Do you see what type of people you are hanging around? Do you want to end up like them?" He just wouldn't let it go.

Two things were on my mind. The first was the crawling fear that I could be going to jail. I thought back to when Juan got beaten down by the cops and thrown into juvie. Where would they put me? Would they put me in a place like that, but with all girls? How long I would have to stay? Would I have to wear one of those ugly orange jumpsuits?

Second, I was thinking about the gang's motto: "Snitches get stitches." It was true. I'd seen it happen. What kind of stitches would I get?

"Come on, you're from a good home, this life isn't for you," the assistant DA said. I could tell this was just going to be sermon after sermon. I felt trapped, angry and hateful inside, while I had to sit and listen to how "bad" my closest friends were. They didn't understand—none of them. My parents were not digging my reaction. I was stone cold, not crying, not giving any more information, not apologetic.

"Do you understand that aiding and abetting will get you two to four years in jail? We could put you in jail, if that will help you stay away from these gang members," he continued. "Would you like that?"

"No," I said icily.

"I'm going to speak with your parents for a while in a separate room, so I can go over the charges you're up against. Stay put."

My parents gave each other worried glances and got up and walked with the assistant DA to a room across the hall. I had to sit and wait. In my head I was trying hard to maintain, holding out for it to be over. Finally it was. The worst thing that could happen, did.

I got off.

When we drove home from the police station that afternoon dread sat in my belly, a heavy rock inside of me, barely allowing my heart to beat. I wanted to run away, but I knew that was a fantasy. Where would I go?

My dad dropped us off. My mom went into her room and slammed the door shut. I felt the rock inside of me expanding, taking over all of my insides, pushing against my organs.

I went to the basement and sat on the old leather couch. TJ's suitcases were half packed. As soon as summer hit he was moving to Boulder. That he was itching to leave caused my emotions to spiral down. He was still doing drugs, slipping further away from our family. I needed to talk to someone, someone who wouldn't judge me, who would let me be. I called Carmen. She picked up after the third ring, and I could hear laughter on the other end.

"Carmen, I have to talk to you," I started, my voice wavering. "Everything has gone wrong and I don't know what to do."

"Shut up, I can't hear!" she yelled to whoever was making noise on the other side. "What happened, Amber?"

I explained the whole thing to her, keeping my voice low just in case my mom left her room.

"Amber, calm down. I know it feels bad right now, but you gotta look at it like this: At least you're not in jail! Juan will forgive you. It might take some time, but that's your homie, right? I know that Juan would do anything for you! Omar too. Plus, none of them can be that mad, 'cause they're the ones that got you into this mess in the first place!"

"But they didn't force me. I wanted to get down with them. And now I look like a stupid snitch! They're not gonna want me around anymore!"

"Maybe that's a good thing, Amber. I have never said nothing to you before, 'cause it's your life, but you really changed since you got down with the Crips. I mean, you and me used to steal little stuff here and there, but cars? Robbing stores? That's different. You should take this as a sign."

Carmen and I talked for a while until I heard footsteps coming down the stairs.

"What the hell is going on, Amber? I heard you got arrested!" TJ yelled, getting up in my face, smelling like weed and liquor. I hung up with Carmen.

"Yeah, so what? It's none of your business!"

"None of my business? I'll tell you when it's none of my business, when it doesn't affect Mom or me! She's sitting in her room crying over all this!"

"Like she hasn't shed any tears for you, TJ? Give me a break. Since when have you cared how Mom feels? You're too busy getting stoned all the time—you don't give a fuck about anybody but yourself!"

"Bullshit! Just because I like to party doesn't mean I'm selfish. *You're* the selfish one in this family. Mom's given us everything, sacrificed everything for us, and this is how you repay her? What's wrong with you, anyway? Why the fuck are you hanging out with gangbangers?"

"What are you talking about?" TJ was never around, so I wondered how he knew.

"You think I'm stupid? My friends are always coming up to me asking me what's wrong with my sister. It's fucking embarrassing," he said, glaring at me.

"You know what, TJ, I've been hearing about you since I was a freshman! 'He's a stoner, he's a druggie' . . . Remember when our house got broken into because of *your* drug-dealing friends? When we came home from school and people were waiting by the house to beat you up because you owed them something? Don't try to be all innocent here!"

"Fuck you, Amber. You fucked up, this time." TJ walked to his stereo. KISS took over the basement and our conversation was over.

"You didn't even go to college like you were supposed to!" I added. He turned up the music even louder, drowning me out. I got up from the couch and went upstairs. It was late. Mom never left her room. I shut off the light and tried to go to sleep, despite my brother's music and the lingering thoughts in my head.

That night I had a terrible nightmare. Cops were raiding my friends' places, dragging them to jail cells, sneering when they explained who snitched: "that white girl." In the dream Jamal appeared, shaking his head at me, saying, "Why?"

I woke up knowing my nightmare was reality. The police would really come down on my homies. I wondered if anyone would still be friends with me after what happened. I tried to imagine Juan in this situation, but I just knew it'd be different.

My parents forbade me from ever seeing my Crip friends. If I did, they would transfer me to a Catholic school to finish out high school.

Days later the stress continued to build. I avoided Keisha because I knew she'd be upset at me. There was no way I could go to Omar's house to tell him what happened. My mom wouldn't allow me to use the car, and now she wanted to know my every move. She wouldn't let me take any phone calls, and Omar's mom had no phone anyway. I needed to talk to him and Juan, but I couldn't bear the thought of it. What would I say? What would their reactions be? Juan was still in Florida and, as much as I yearned for his comfort, I was glad I wouldn't be able to see the disappointment in his eyes.

When I went back to school, it was all I was thinking about, but I didn't see Omar. Monday, Tuesday, and then Wednesday passed. By Thursday, with no Omar in sight, I relaxed a bit, pushing the fear to the back of my mind. At times I pretended that the whole thing hadn't happened. Friday morning I was standing at my locker, searching for my World History book so I could glance at the assigned reading before class.

"Hey."

I looked up. Omar was standing next to me wearing creased

dark blue dickies, a white T-shirt, and a blue Windbreaker. He had a pencil behind his ear, and that smile that put love in my heart.

"Hi," I said, my voice an octave higher than normal. I fumbled with my books and papers, my hands shaking. *Say it, just say it,* I thought.

"Omar, I hafta tell you something," I started.

"What's that, baby girl?" he asked.

I hesitated for a minute, and then broke down and told him everything.

Omar's smile was gone, and he looked at me long and hard before he said anything. People passing us in the hallway said "What's up" but he paid them no mind. This is it, I thought. It's over, all of it.

"Damn pigs." He looked down and shook his head. "I can't believe they did that to your moms—that ain't even right. Don't trip, baby, there ain't shit you can do about it."

Omar took my hand. He was acting so nice to me. I looked away and focused on trying not to cry, I didn't want to make a scene. "What's going to happen to you?" I asked.

"They gonna add it to the list of citations we got. If I get picked up then I'll have to deal with it—but they ain't got time to come and find me for no ten-dollar robbery. All I took at that spot was lunch for the day and your candy bar. Rodney barely took anything. I told you, baby, it ain't nothing. Don't worry about it." He was holding my hands and looking at me the whole time.

There was one more thing I had to ask, but I wasn't sure I wanted to know the answer. I decided to take the risk.

"But are you mad I told them?" I dropped my head.

He ruffled my hair up. "I just have to teach you how to lie better. For real, though, don't say nothin' to nobody, you hear me? This is between you and me. I don't want to have to bust somebody's head in 'bout this." We were both thinking about Ray-Ray. If he got a hold of this it could be over for me.

"I gotta go, baby. Come to the house this weekend, if you can, so we can kick it, aight?"

"'Bye, Omar." I gave him a kiss on the cheek. "Thanks for havin' my back."

"I always got you, girl. You're my heart, you know that?" He looked at me intently before turning away.

I stood a moment, stunned at Omar's allegiance to me over the Crips, who, after all, were his family.

When I went to class, the teacher's voice lulled me into a daydream. I started asking myself questions like: How much was I ready to sacrifice for the Crips? Would I go to jail to protect them? Was my loyalty to my family or to them? I pictured my mom's face, and how upset she'd been since I got caught. We hadn't been getting along for a while now, but that didn't mean I wanted to hurt her.

Nineteen

"Keisha, I'm 'bout to come get you. I finally got the car," I told her on the phone. My mom didn't know I was going to a concert, or that I was going with people I was forbidden to see. We'd maintained a tenuous relationship the last couple of months.

"Okay, I'll be ready," she said. We'd been waiting to see our favorite artists, N.W.A. and Slick Rick, at the concert hall. After an all-out yelling match with my brother for use of the car, I won. I rolled through Forestville to Keisha's house, bumpin' Keith Sweat's "Make It Last Forever" on my mom's factory car stereo, the bass rattling from the cheap speakers. Embarrassing, but hey, at least I got the car.

"Who are we picking up?" Keisha asked.

"We gotta get Omar, Lil D, Juan, and them," I replied. Trying to keep Keisha and the Crips separate became too hard, so once in a while she would roll with me, as long as I promised not to do anything illegal.

149

Juan had finally come back from Florida—I didn't know what went on down there and he refused to talk about it. I never told him what happened, and, luckily, neither Omar nor Rodney got picked up for it, at least not yet. I was just happy he was back. I switched the slow jam to some party music.

"Who's 'and them' this time?" she shot back, laughing. It was always Russian roulette with the Rollin' 30s; we never knew who we'd have up in there.

"'I'm the dopest female that you heard this far,'" Keisha was singing MC Lyte's new cut, snapping her fingers and doing the snake in the car. We arrived at Omar's and waited in the car for the guys to come out. Omar winked at me when he got in the car, but didn't kiss me in front of the homies. Five blocks later the car filled with blunt smoke, and laughter. It had been a while since we'd gone to a show.

The concert was packed. People were definitely dressed to impress; the guys wearing designer jeans, silk shirts and big gold chains. Ladies rocked stonewashed jean sets with tight, low-cut shirts, their hair and nails done to perfection. I chilled with Keisha while the guys tried to get girls' numbers. I peeped Omar trying to kick game to a cute, short girl. Keisha noticed and pulled me away.

"Come on, Amber, let's go to our seats, the show is about to start." We left the guys and went to our seats, only twenty rows away from the stage. Slick Rick was masterful as he took the stage, patch over one eye and tons of gold chains, taking us on a ride with his storytelling craze. The energy was so high, the audience singing our favorite lyrics in unison, with Slick Rick egging us on. He knew how to move the crowd. When N.W.A. took the stage, the vibe went to another level. Shouts of gang sets could be heard from different sections of our area. N.W.A. brought out the hidden gangsta in all of us.

The fellas didn't even sit with us until the show was halfway over, they were too busy chillin'. It went so fast, before you knew it, security guards were shepherding us out, with people checking each other out, trying to get digits from the cuties, and looking for the afterparty. We filed out and made our way out to the car. I could tell Omar was fucked up, because, unlike before, now he was hanging on to me and flirting.

Passing through the parking lot, homies were yelling, "Caa-rip, Caa-rip," really loud, and everyone started staring at us. I was nervous because there were so many folks out, and you just never know who was among the masses. All of a sudden we heard sirens and people started running. We raced to the car, not sure if they were after us or somebody else. As I got in, I realized we had picked up some extra people who must have been at the concert. They opened my mom's hatchback and literally started piling in, yelling, "Get the fuck outta here!" I started driving slowly while the last of the crew was trying to get in.

"You can't fit man, let go," Omar yelled. The guy cursed and got his leg out of the car and started running in another direction. I wanted to get out of the ensuing chaos, but we could only snake our way out of the packed parking lot. Thankfully, nothing came of it.

After I dropped everyone off at Omar's and took Keisha home, I was finally alone. I realized how drained and exhausted I felt. Could I keep this up?

The next morning I got up early to put gas in the car, and get it vacuumed and washed, which was the trade-off for me using it. That was when I found it in the backseat on the floor. A gun. Damn, whose gat was this? I was tired of worrying about gats and gangs and cops. How could they have left it? What if my mom had seen it? I was so mad right then at all my homies; at

Omar, at Juan, all of them. But I was also mad at myself. Why did I keep getting myself into these kinds of situations? What was it gonna take for me to get out of them?

Jamal and I had gotten back together, vowing to make it work this time. I don't know how he sweet-talked me into it, but there was just something about him I couldn't resist. Omar and I still saw each other, but it was always the same. We just had a "thing."

LL Cool J's slow jam, "I Need Love," played in the background while Jamal made love to me. It was like old times—in each other's arms, safe and secure.

"I love you, girl," he whispered in my ears. I hugged him tight.

That was when we heard the yelling.

"Where the fuck is that bitch! I know you're fuckin' in there! Come the fuck out!"

Both of us jumped out of bed and started fumbling to put on our clothes as someone started pounding on the bedroom door.

"What the fuck, Jamal?" I asked, my heart beating wildly. He ignored me and opened the door. Leslie was standing in the hallway looking pathetic, crying, black eyeliner running down her face.

"I thought you said you were done with her, motherfucker! Was you just fuckin' her right now?" she demanded.

"Yo, Leslie, chill the fuck out! What the fuck you doin' here anyway? I told you to wait until I called you."

"So *do* you still love her?" Leslie's attention was all on Jamal at this point, staring him down.

"I just told her I do." Jamal had thrown on pants, but had no shirt. His chest was heaving.

"All you do is lie, motherfucker." Then she turned to me. "And you, you're such a stupid bitch! Jamal's been cheatin' on you since the beginning and you just keep coming back."

"Fuck you, bitch! Get the fuck outta my face!" My rage made it hard to see straight, and things seemed to be happening so fast. I brushed past Jamal and into the hallway, toward Leslie, ready to fight.

"Amber, don't touch her!" Jamal's voice was alarming. I looked at him in disbelief. He was defending *her* over *me*? After all we'd been through? He didn't say anything to her about steppin' to me. At that point Leslie didn't even matter to me anymore. I grabbed his baseball bat that was on the floor.

"Don't fuck with Leslie, huh? You sorry motherfucker. Fuck you, Jamal!" And with that I started for his head. Jamal started to back away and Leslie was yelling something at me when I heard Jamal's brother's voice. He came behind me as I started swinging for Jamal's head.

"Put it down, put it down!" Deshawn yelled. He grabbed my arms and Jamal snatched the bat from me and walked to Leslie's side.

"Chill the hell out, y'all." Deshawn was sweaty and upset.

"Why don't you tell her to leave?" I asked Jamal.

"Nah, I don't think so," he said, and she smiled at me smugly.

"Then why the hell did you fight so hard to get me back?" I choked back my tears, and ran into Jamal's bedroom and slammed the door. I was unable to control my anger. My head was buzzing. In the other room, I heard Leslie and Jamal laughing, and I knew they were laughing at me, at how long they had tricked me. I felt sick to my stomach. How could he do this to me? How could he humiliate me like this? Just fifteen minutes ago he was inside of me. I was so stupid to go back with him. I was crying silently, wondering what the fuck to do.

I must have been there at least an hour before I heard a knock on the door. It was Mrs. Davis. She sat on the side of the bed and put her hand on mine.

"Deshawn told me what happened," she said. "They're gone now. Honey, don't you worry about Mr. Jamal, you're just too good for him. He doesn't even realize how good he has it, with you as his girlfriend. I knew he was up to no good when that other girl started coming around. Let me drive you home. Don't cry over Jamal, honey." But I couldn't help it. We had been together for so long, been through so much. My head was hurting from crying. Jamal's mom gave me a ride to my house.

"You're gonna be all right, Amber. You're a strong girl. I'm sorry my boy hurt you." I gave her a kiss on the cheek, and she pulled me in close for a big bear hug as she wrapped her arms around me and squeezed tight.

"You're gonna be all right," she whispered again, and then sighed. I sighed too, desperately longing for just a little of the confidence she felt in me.

Dear Diary
Song of the week, "Fuck the PO-lice" by N.W.A.

What's up, cuzz? The latest? Jamal dogged my world for Leslie. It hurt. All this time I've been feeling better. I got a kitchen knife and opened up an old scar. 'Cause of Jamal.

The newest: LL Cool J, Too Short, and De La Soul to-morrow nite. Sweet is right—we got 14th row! I met a guy named AJ ——? I got really drunk and had a one-night stand with him. How sorry, I don't even know his last name. The fucker probably won't call me anyway—nobody else does. I still love Omar, but I am tired of his games.

Too many unsolved mysteries, too many unanswered questions. As guys come and go I'm left with crossed-out phone numbers and torn-up pictures. I don't understand. They claim me in my dreams at night and control my waking hours, as I sit here waiting for someone's call. All I want is someone to love me—no matter what the cost. Love Me! Love me, love me, lovemelovemeloveme . . . me love me?

It was Friday. Today, instead of Jamal picking me up, it would be Juan and Rodney, who had just gotten the sweetest ride. As soon as the bell rang, I bounced, heading to the side entrance of the school. Once outside, I slid on my sunglasses and looked around. I heard a honk, turned, and saw Juan waving me over. As soon as I opened the car door smoke swirled out. I sat in the back. Rodney handed me a joint, and started driving.

"Yo, pass that joint, homie," Juan said.

I took the joint from my lips and passed it up front as the smoke curled out of my mouth. I immediately felt the hit. I sat back and started thinking. After my breakup with Jamal, I lost complete trust in guys, and myself. I was dating all the time, looking for that spark, looking for that love. I still hung out with Omar, but it was hard because he was in and out of jail, and I couldn't bring him to the house or even acknowledge our relationship to my family. Both Carmen and Keisha started expressing concern about the choices I was making in guys, but I felt completely unable to stop myself.

We had gone back to a routine at my house. TJ had finally left for Boulder, promising to try to enroll in college when he could. I was gliding through my senior year, just maintaining. I felt old.

"This is some good shit, Juan," I said. The weed added to weariness from being out late with Juan bombing the night before. He just nodded, and started throwing up Crips signs to the music. I could tell he was in a zone. His fingers moved in an intricate dance of symbols, creating a language only the Crips knew. Juan got respect even from the O.G.s in the Rollin' 60s on his ability to throw signs faster than any other crew member, and on top of that he had the illest Crip walk. Watching his fingers move from the backseat I could read what was on his mind. I remembered when signs were foreign to me, and Juan would spend hours explaining to me what it all meant. A whole world opened up as I learned how to communicate silently, and although I never came close to Juan's skills, at least now I was able to hold my own. That seemed so long ago, now.

Juan interrupted my thoughts. "Before I forget, Omar wants you to come to the party tonight." My stomach tingled upon hearing that Omar was asking for me. When I had gotten back with Jamal, I stopped going by Omar's place. And then after the breakup I was just so depressed, I didn't want to see anybody. He had tried to call me from a pay phone a couple of times, but I was rarely home, so he just left short messages, asking me to drop by. I realized now how much I missed him.

Lounging in the backseat, I gazed out of the window at the usual scene in the hood by my school. It seemed like it was nothing but gangsters clad in blue and black, selling their dope on the corners. The tweakers were always easy to spot, skinny and dirty, jerking in every direction searching for something to ease their pain. Cruising by the next block, I saw three little kids playing in the front yard, throwing up gang signs at each other. Already the actions of the youngsters mirrored those of the older kids. Instead of learning their ABCs and how to count, they were learning Crip signs, not even knowing what they meant. They only knew that it made the older kids laugh and got them some attention. I tried to destroy the depressing images of baby gangsters in my mind.

I was feeling the high. My heartbeat took on the same rhythm as the bass in Too Short's "Life is / too short." Only one person could sit in the backseat because Rodney had set up two speakers that went from the seat to the ceiling, and today I was the lucky one squeezed in between them. The bass alone was enough to melt any negative thoughts in my head, but add the joint and we were in business.

As we cruised past the projects, I glanced at my watch. "Rodney, can you drive me by my house so I can change right quick?" I knew it was time to go home, where the silent tension of unhappiness drained me.

All I was looking forward to was the party in the hood that night—anything to get out of my house. At home, clothes strewn across the floor of my room, I picked my way to the bottom of the pile. I threw on my gear and was out the door in minutes. Luckily my mom wasn't home from work yet, so I didn't have any explaining to do. As I got closer to the party I could hear the house bumpin', drawing me into its magic. My lips curled into a smile.

After giving respect to the parents of the house, I started to party with my homies. Omar slid up next to me, supplying me with endless drinks. The house special that night was Crazy Train, which was Night Train mixed with Olde English malt liquor. It was a Rollin' 30s favorite.

"Juan, this is your song, baby," I said. We rhymed together, "Hindsight, Hindsight, Vapors, that's right."

I danced all night, with hip-hop mix tapes blasting out my favorite tunes—surrounded by Lil D, Omar, and Juan. My last thought was that nothing else mattered but this moment.

Then I passed out.

Twenty

The heat was on. A string of robberies and assaults the crew had committed was all over the news. Everyone was talking about it. Juan picked me up from school in a stolen car. I heard his favorite song, "Barbara's Bedroom," from a block away, the bass pumpin'.

"Yo, Corazón, what up?" he asked as I jumped in his new ride.

"I'm cold chillin' in the place to be." I was happy to be out of school for the day.

He passed me his piece book. "Check this out." His new design looked morbid, with dark colors and ugly creatures fighting each other, blood everywhere. It wasn't Juan's style. I closed the book and kept it on my lap, looking at Juan. He didn't look so happy.

"What's wrong, baby?" I made a funny face and tried to get him to smile. His lips twitched in a half-assed grin, and then he got serious again.

"Take whatever you want, girl, from me to you." As I was rummaging through the glove compartment to find a souvenir he drove me to a house near Aurora, where most of the Rollin' 30s were kickin' it. When Juan robbed a place he took anything and everything he could get his hands on, from clothing and money to a picture on the wall that caught his eye. I didn't find anything but junk, so I left empty-handed.

We got out of the car and walked inside the house. There was no furniture or anything—it was bare. I didn't know who owned the house and didn't ask. Everyone was telling war stories, reading the paper and laughing about how they hadn't been caught yet by the police. A couple of them had been documenting all of their crimes by keeping copies of the articles written about them. T-Dog told them they were stupid for having that stuff lying around.

"Y'all's egos are gonna get you locked up," he warned, shaking his head. But no one paid him any mind. At some point Juan grabbed me and pulled me outside to sit on the porch. It was there he told me what happened.

"Corazón, they went over the top this time. I can't get down with what they did." He was shaking his head. "It just ain't right." I had never seen such sadness in his eyes before.

"What happened, Juan? What'd they do? Was Omar there? Lil D?" Mad nervous, I waited for his response.

"They killed a homeless man for no reason." He was silent for a while. "And no, Omar wasn't part of it; neither was Lil D. Word on the street says it was Ray-Ray and some other Parkside hoods."

I was so relieved to hear that neither Omar nor Lil D had anything to do with it.

"They beat him with a baseball bat 'cause he cursed at them," Juan continued. "It's so sick what they did and I don't want no part in it. Killin' somebody for fun? I ain't down. I admit I'm a crazy motherfucker, you know, I'll rob a store in a minute, but he was helpless—how could anybody do that? I'm through with all of it." For the first time since I've known him, Juan broke down. It was hard seeing him like that, and a little scary, too. With an absence of his usual confident and defiant look, he suddenly looked really young, and vulnerable. A shiver ran through my body.

We sat for a while. He took my hand, looked me dead in my eyes, and told me to get out before it was too late.

"You know why we have to watch out? 'Cause it's all about 'guilt by association.' Five-o is gettin' real serious about gangs now. They even have a gang unit that they started just 'cause of *us*!" A combination of fear and pride mixed in his voice when he said that. I thought, Yeah, it does feel good to have some power, even if it is bad. I understood Juan's conflicting feelings.

The guys interrupted us as they came outside. "Yo, cuzz, we rollin' to the mall."

We stopped talking and strolled to the same car Juan had picked me up in earlier. We all piled in. I stayed close to Juan in the back.

Rodney got in the driver's seat and tried to start the car, but realized that there wasn't any gas. As everyone piled out I decided to take the bus home. It was a school night and I was broke, upset about the homeless man, and still pondering what Juan had told me. I needed some time to think. I gave Juan a pound good-bye.

"Call me, homie," he said. With the rest of the crew around he acted like nothing had changed.

I couldn't stop thinking about the dead man. I tried to cover the tears coming down my face while I was on the bus. *What was I doing hanging out with people who would do this?* I just couldn't understand it. It made me sick to my stomach. My heart hurt.

It turns out I got lucky.

That night everyone who stayed in the house got busted. To make matters worse, the cops found the bloody baseball bat, which had been hidden in the stolen car that Juan and I had been riding in all afternoon. There were so many things running through my mind: Juan had just promised to give this all up. Omar already had a record. I could have been at that house when the police arrived and arrested everyone. Juan and I could have been pulled over in the stolen car, and the bat could have been found then. What would my mom have said?

It was all over the news that night—they must have shown the house a thousand times. I found out that Juan got arrested when there was a phone call from the police. Juan had been talking about me during his interrogation, so the cops wanted to interview me as some sort of character witness. The police spoke to my mom. She was shaken to the core. The truth about the life I had been leading seemed unbearable for her.

My worlds had collided and burst into flames. Omar and my best friend Juan were in jail; my home life was shattered; and I had done the one thing I promised myself I wouldn't do— destroyed the little peace of mind my mother had left. More than anything else, that was what broke my heart.

Luckily, Juan and Omar weren't charged with the murder since they hadn't been involved in that. But they did get busted for all of the robberies they had been doing for the last year. T-Dog had been right; it was the articles some Crips kept bragging about that helped break the case. When the cops raided the house they used the newspaper clippings for proof of who was involved. They also found Juan's "trophies" when they searched his belongings and used that for evidence as well. So Juan and Omar both got hit with fifteen counts of aggravated assault, from all the fighting they had been involved in, among other charges.

Maybe I'd be better off dead.

Dear Amber,

Yo babe, what's up? Not much my way. I'm just chillin' in the place not to be. Right now I'm at Lookout Mountain because the committed unit was full, and since Juan and I were the last two people to get committed we won an all-expense-paid trip to "Club" Walnut, where you spend 23 luscious hours a day in your room! Isn't that great!! But wait, that's not all, it has the fragrant smell of piss and the blankets are made of 100% wool so you can stay up all night scratching your ass off. My mirror is a piece of metal that looks like a cat thought it was a mouse and scratched it up; my walls are decorated with blood and slime; and last but not least is the floor—it's so filthy I eat with my eyes closed to avoid getting sick. Juan is crazy. When he came upstairs and saw me he was laughing and I was still crying, then he started jumping up and down saying, "Smile, Omar we just got 4 LONNNNG years," but on the way back to the Hall, I was smiling and he was crying. Well darling I must close this letter with a simple "I love you" and "write back."

Omar

Juan and Omar wrote me a letter a week religiously, sometimes two if it was bad, like if someone got a beat down or got thrown in the hole. I wrote back just as fast. I visited them both when I could. I had to come up with elaborate lies to get the car and take the two-hour trip to the jail. But it was worth it. I never forgot the time Omar stood by me after the gas station incident. I needed to be there for him.

With Juan and Omar locked up, I stepped back from the crew a bit. I would stop by Omar's house to maintain some contact with his mother, but tried to stay away from the drama, which was very difficult for me. The Crips had become such an integral part of my life, of my identity. The RTS crew was also feeling the loss of its leader, and although Diablo, Zap, and Chaos would call me occasionally to go bombin', it felt so empty without Juan. I lost my desire to tag. Instead I mourned my mentor and friend, because being locked up was a lot like being dead.

Sometimes I still thought about Jamal, but I wouldn't admit that to anybody, not even Keisha and Carmen. Just as I found out I'd graduate high school, I heard that he got accepted to a college in Arizona. He got some scholarship for sports. I missed the times we would play hoops, but I didn't miss the drama. The last time I hurt myself was because of him.

Although in the back of my mind I knew that ultimately I must move on, I was still invested in the relationships that had been built. Another part of me understood the inequity in the fact that I had a choice whether I moved on or not, whereas my homies didn't. It made me feel guilty.

Denver was over for me. Too many ghosts, too many people and places that tempted a relapse into a dangerous lifestyle. My heart wept for Juan and Omar, for the murdered homeless man, for my mother—and for myself. One thing I was sure of, I needed to re-create my existence, search for a new way of being. I knew my future lay in other places, far away from the very friends I had once wanted so close to me. Now I just had to figure out how to get there.

Twenty-One

FRESHMAN YEAR, COLLEGE

Culture shock. The only way I could describe it. Looking out on the university campus in Los Angeles, California, I saw a sea of white people.

Earlier that day I had been trying to navigate the sprawling campus. Exhausted but excited, I went to grab a bite before heading back to the dorms. Occupied with finding healthy food, trying to keep the "freshman 15" off, I wasn't even thinking about where I'd find a seat in the crowded cafeteria.

I looked around with my tray of food to find a place to sit. Just like my high school, the place visually represented what was so wrong with the campus; each table was either white, black, Latino, or Asian. I walked around to the other side of the large cafeteria, hopeful for a different outlook. One table had some diversity to it, but upon further inspection it was all the athletes, mostly black guys with one or two white dudes. My happiness quickly dissolved into defeat. I wondered if this was just four more years of the same bullshit from whence I came.

"Dude, get another keg! Let's par-tea!" A blond guy wearing a striped rugby shirt tripped over my feet and fell flat on his face. I tried not to laugh. As I sat on a nasty beer-smelling couch, watching sloppy drunk college students acting stupid, I wondered how I landed here.

Only two months into the semester, I found myself in the same cycle I left in Denver, but this time with strangers, in a place unfamiliar to me. Living on campus, no place to hang out, no one I could count on, I longed for some security. I just wanted to feel normal. At times I wanted to grab my markers and go bombing, claiming victory over this new territory. But where would I go? With no car, no Juan, and nothing but freeways going down unfamiliar streets, it felt impossible.

It got so bad that a classmate down the hall, Belinda, talked me into pledging to be a little sister of a white fraternity. A sweet, chubby white girl from Arizona, her little sister obsession consumed her. That was all she talked about, thought about, and planned for. I reluctantly agreed to try. After all, the process seemed similar to joining a gang—tryouts, initiation, and if you're good enough, you're in.

The Beastie Boys blaring, the frat house trashed, and I just couldn't take the scene anymore. "Belinda, can we go yet? It's already one o'clock in the morning," I yelled over the pounding bass.

She looked at me with disappointment, even though not a single guy had approached her all night. "I thought you said you liked to party."

"Yeah, I do. Just not this party. Plus, all the alcohol is gone and the boys are getting restless." Toward the end of the night the guys who weren't hooked up with a girl started prowling. It was time to jet.

"Fine, Amber. But don't blame me if we don't get in. The guys like to see girls who have spirit. Remember what they said in little sister orientation?" She pushed up her glasses, and I said a silent prayer for her.

Frat parties occupied our every evening, and the scene was always the same: Older guys would get us drunk and try to sleep with as many freshman girls as they could before we passed out (some even after we passed out). And if you wanted to be a little sister, then you simply had to fuck somebody that was up in there and the position was yours. I managed to get through the entire pledging process without sleeping with anybody. That feat alone should have granted me a degree.

Three weeks into the grueling process Belinda was waiting for me in the hallway, sobbing, when I arrived in the dorm after my classes.

"It isn't fair! You didn't even care if you got in and you did! If it wasn't for me you wouldn't have even known what to do!" she said.

"What are you talking about?"

"You! You got in! They left a message on the machine for you, and your roommate rubbed it in my face." I walked in the room and Belinda followed right behind me. She kept pushing her red-rimmed glasses up from her nose, attempting to pace in my small dorm room only there was nowhere to go.

I had pretended to like the whole thing—the parties, the guys, and the idea of belonging to something. I did it for Belinda's sake, but I had reasons of my own, too: I needed something to fill the void left from RTS, from the 30s.

Belinda's sobs continued. I knew why she didn't make it—her size wasn't quite what they wanted. Too big. "You can't let them bother you," I said. "They're nothing. They don't care about you or me or any of those other chicks! Don't let this get you down. You know what, if you want I won't even accept—I'll tell them I'm not interested."

"Don't do that!" She turned very serious. "Maybe if they like you, then you can put in a good word for me, and then I'll still be able to be a little sister." I felt sickened. Here she was, totally dissed by these assholes, yet she was still trying to find any way to get in.

"Please, Amber, please. Just give it a try for me, 'kay?"

Promises flew out of my mouth as I told her I would give her the inside scoop.

The week flew by, and I got a call that Friday from Adam, my new "big brother." He wanted me to come to a function for little sisters. He seemed nice enough over the phone, although we stumbled through the conversation trying to find some commonality.

My total time as a Little Slut? One month. I thought I'd last a little longer than I did. Adam came to my dorm room a couple of times (that way I could introduce him to Belinda), and he invited me to some parties. Then he tried to kiss me while we were at a function. Upon my brush-off, he asked, "Is it 'cause you're with some nigga?"

"What did you say?"

"Well, I mean, you know, I've seen the pictures on your walls, so maybe you only like black guys."

"Why did you use that word? What the fuck is wrong with you?"

"No, no, you don't understand—I'm from New York, and everybody is okay with that word out there. The black people don't care—they even call each other that! It's all the rap songs. What's the big deal?"

"That doesn't grant you permission to use it! You're white!" I thought back to Juan and my lesson on the "N" word. "I don't even want to see your face right now."

"You are making such a big deal over this! I just asked you a question. What's your problem? You're so defensive! I'm the one that got you into the little sisters anyway!"

He was drunk, and I was buzzed. I knew this couldn't end well, so I said good-bye. I heard him saying all kinds of things under his breath as I walked away. I ignored it. I went to bed with my head spinning. I longed for people who knew me, who understood me. Maybe it was a mistake thinking I could start over here.

Adam called me the next day and apologized.

"Just don't say that word around me, all right?" was all I said. But that was just the beginning of the end. During a couple of other drunken frat parties I got into fights with some of the guys who were talking shit. Needless to say, I didn't last long as a proud little sister of Drunk White Boys fraternity.

Dear Diary
My New Life, College—
I hate FRATS! This week was bad, I cried twice and was feeling lonely, depressed, and out of control. I miss my friends. I've gained weight, which I am fighting by running three miles every other day. Racism is disgusting and on the rise. I don't know how to handle it—it goes both ways, black and white just don't integrate here. It really depresses me . . . I wish I was an ignorant dizzy blonde who didn't give a shit about important things, just dances and men. I'm trying to leave negativity and vio-

lence behind but I feel so disconnected. I ache for the
past. I tagged up Corazón a couple of places on campus,
but with nobody to care, I just felt emptier. Pictures of my
homeboys flashing guns, money, and drugs saturate my
dorm room walls, just to make sure people understood
where I'm coming from. But they don't.

I'm so broke that even with two part-time jobs I have
to sell weed to pay for books and food.

My first stop at the dorm was the mailbox. As soon as I saw the
envelope I knew it was from Juan because of the handwriting.
I ran straight up to my room to read it. Luckily my roommate
was never there, so I had the place to myself.

Hello Corazón,
What's up, homegirl? I wonder how you are. Are you
happy? I hope I haven't caused any damage to you emo-
tionally. If I have, please provide me with a chance to
make it up, okay? I realize I have caused great troubles
inside you, starting with getting you involved with the
Crips, but all I can say for myself is that I made some
wrong decisions that hurt my friends and me. I caused
turmoil in my family and yours, and this I cannot take
back, but Amber I have learned from this and I will ben-
efit from this. I shall grow as a person and so shall you.
Are you following a path to a goal, or are you just having
short-term fun? It's time to look to the future. I know all
this sounds weird, coming from me, but I want you to
know that my head is in the right place. You'll do okay. I
know you are going through some very hard times out
there in California, but remember that Plato once said
that if we took all the world's problems and asked each
person to take his/her own share equally, most everyone

would gladly take their own sorrows over someone else's.
I hope you can look around and appreciate what you
have and realize that the only way to a goal is through
positive forward movement.
Just remember, I love you and Keep the Faith, baby!

Juancito aka iRoniC

Even from jail, Juan made me think about my life more critically. After Juan and Omar got locked up, I knew I had to leave Denver. That became my focus. What I didn't think about was what I wanted to accomplish once I got out. My whole first semester had been about just getting by, and all I'd managed to do was get caught up in some petty social bullshit. Juan was right. I needed to stop complaining and figure my life out.

Twenty-Two

You people just need to stop making such a big deal out of everything!" My white classmate started getting flustered and red in the face as she tried to further explain her comment about slavery being over. The class got silent.

"You people?" one of the black students repeated. "That's what I'm talking about! You have to be more conscious of how you talk. I can't even go there right now, I'm so upset!" She shook her head. We all looked to the professor, who seemed at a loss for words.

"Just because slavery is over doesn't mean the effects of slavery are gone," I added, feeling the need to break the uncomfortable silence, and come to the aid of my black classmate. "In fact, have you ever heard of the Willie Lynch letter?" I had just learned about this in one of my Africana Studies classes, and was proud to show off my knowledge.

"Okay class, let's get back to more important things, we

have an exam coming up," the professor said, shuffling some papers on her desk.

The young woman threw her books in her backpack, tears streaming down her face. "Yeah, I guess four hundred years of oppression isn't very important!" She stormed out of the class.

There was a long pause. "Well." The professor cleared her throat. "Some people are just so *angry*. Please get out your study guides and follow along."

I had a hard time dealing with that kind of attitude, and as a result many white students in the dorms and my classes didn't understand me, or just plain didn't like me. Thankfully I did find some refuge. A cool white boy named Terry was in some of my classes, and we'd talk afterward about how fucked up our people were. Surprisingly, an old high school classmate, Sam, wound up in LA too. Sam and I bumped into each other on campus, and he invited me over to check out his apartment and hang for a while.

The following weekend, I rang the doorbell at Sam's spot. A beautiful man with milk chocolate skin and light eyes opened the door. He rocked a Malcolm X T-shirt, and a jean jacket covered with buttons spouting political messages.

"Hey, come on in." He opened the door wider for me to slip by. "I'm Drew, what's your name?"

"Amber." As our eyes locked, I tried to control the automatic blush.

"Welcome to our humble abode." He smiled at me. A Tribe Called Quest serenaded us in the background. I thought I was in heaven. "Sam, your Denver homie is here," he yelled.

Sam came out of his room and we all kicked it, drinking cheap wine and talking shit all night about hip-hop and college life. That night I learned Drew was an LA native and his eyes lit up when he brought up political things. Most of it was stuff I'd never heard of, but he explained it in a way that made it interesting, and his excitement was contagious. I was hoping Drew would ask for my number when I left, but no such luck.

It felt so good finally finding some peeps I could kick it with. I ended up hanging out with them all the time, and was really diggin' Drew. The more I got to know him, the more I respected him. He was going to school full time and working, all while dealing with some major family drama.

Slowly things evolved, and after a couple of weeks we started "talking," LA speak for dating. After that he came to my dorm regularly to chill.

Journal Entry
Drew is incredible! Roses, cards, and romance. This feels different to me, because unlike all those guys in Denver, Drew makes me a better person. He makes me think about things in a very different way, like I'm more conscious of why things are the way they are, and what is because of "the man," and how we need to defeat it. The best part is that I feel myself beginning to trust in love again. I am so happy right now! I don't want anything to mess this up!

Drew stopped by to visit me on Wednesday after his classes, for some quality time. It started getting late, so I put on my slippers and we strolled to the front of the dorm to say goodbye. I walked back to the elevator alone when two guys, reeking of liquor, got in.

"You must think you're real cool, huh?" one guy said, slurring his words as he swayed from the alcohol. I recognized the blond one from my dorm, but had never talked to him. "Huh?" he said, more insistently.

I looked over at him, frowning. "What are you talking about?" I asked.

"Yeah. You must think you're cool with your *homeboys*." His friend with the Birkenstocks on started to laugh. "What, you got to college and you wanted to experiment or something? You wanted to start being a slut or something?" His friend continued laughing.

I looked to see what floor we were on. Thankfully I only had two more to go.

"Do I know you?" I said.

"I know you, 'cause I see you all the time with black guys," he slurred.

"Yep," said the other one, leaning against the wall.

I start inching toward the door. I didn't think these guys would do anything to me, but there were two of them in a confined space, and they were pretty wasted. The elevator landed on my floor, and I stepped out. "Why don't you just mind your business?" I spat out as the doors closed behind me.

"What'd you say, bitch?" I could hear them still, even with the elevator rising. "Fuck you, you stupid whore!" I walked away quickly, trying to distance myself from the voices.

I got to my room and locked the door, chest heaving. I sat on my bed holding on to my pillow. Why did those guys feel entitled to comment on who I chose to be with? Alone in my room, I wondered if it was all worth it. But when I heard Drew's voice whispering sweet things on the phone, all the anger and questioning melted away—after only being together two short but intense months, I was already in love.

I floated back to Denver for Christmas, excited to see my family and friends, and to share the news of my boyfriend. I was also going home to see Omar. We set up a visit. It felt like so long since I had seen him. My stomach did flips just thinking about it.

My mom was waiting for me at the airport gate. We hugged and hugged. "Oh, I've missed you, Amber. I'm so glad you're here," she greeted me. We didn't stop talking all the way home. She told me about her job, gave me the latest updates on my cousins—which I *was* interested in—and let me know how her personal campaign against smoking was going.

"I haven't had a cigarette in three months!" she proudly reported. "So tell me, how is school going?"

"It's okay, Mom. I'm learning so much from my classes, and I have a couple of friends that I hang out with." Ever since I left for college, I'd made a commitment to mend our relationship. I didn't want to mention the negative things happening in my life. Instead, we chatted about my classes, midterms, and friends. She listened, happily.

My brother was still up in Boulder, so it was just Mom and me. When we got home she made lunch, and showed me articles that she'd cut out and saved for me. Some dealt with cultural diversity, others were about black authors who had new books out. She was beginning to if not understand me, then at least support me and be open to my changing ideas and views. And, like when I was a child, before our lives became so complicated and messy, she made me feel completely taken care of.

Evening came and I caught up with Carmen when she dropped by. She gave me a copy of her first official mix tape, and told me about her new life as a DJ, and how she was getting into the club scene.

When Keisha came over a couple days later, I had already received two letters from Drew. Each one had his favorite quotes all over it, little sketches and drawings on the envelopes. I showed her Drew's letters, sharing stories of our love.

That night Keisha and I stayed up eating snacks and talking until one in the morning. She told me all about her life: boys, school, work. She explained how hard it was because there were very few black people at her school, so she encountered ignorance by some and tokenism by others who just wanted her around so they could say they had a black friend.

"Keisha, are you gonna make it out there? It sounds dismal," I said, passing the last batch of popcorn.

"Girl, I'm just gonna do what I came out there to do—get my education and bounce. I'm not trippin' off of all these other people. I know it's not personal, and most of them just don't know any better. I'm gonna be fine."

I was proud of Keisha holding it down like that.

Dear Amber,

The weeks have been unbearable without you. I went to a club last night, and all my homeboys were trying to get me hooked up with this chick, but I couldn't get you out of my head—your gorgeous eyes, your long hair, your laughter, all the experiences we've shared. I'm not sure I can wait for you to get back. I want us to do so many things together! Travel the world, eat different food, lounge on the beach drinking (no, not Night Train, margaritas!). I told my family about you and they want to meet you. Amber, I love you and really need you in my life.

Peace,
Drew

Although Drew's letter filled me with happiness, I got some bad news the following day. Omar's mom called to tell me my trip to visit him had been cancelled; he'd been moved to a different prison just days earlier. It had taken months of letters and expensive collect calls to set the whole thing up because of the prison's lengthy process to get an approved visit. I wanted to get out of the house to take my mind off it. I called all my homies to find out what was going down.

"Keisha, let's hang out," I said.

"I can't tonight, I'm cooking dinner for my family."

"Okay," I said, "I'll let you off the hook. Call me tomorrow."

I called Carmen, but she wasn't home; probably out with Mateo. I was so happy they were still together. I decided to take a chance and do a "drive-by" to see if any of the old crew was around. I drove to T-Dog's. As I pulled up I saw him, Rodney, and Lil D on the front steps. I got out with a huge smile on my face and flutters in my stomach. Being close to them made me feel closer to Omar and Juan.

"What up, y'all?" I said. I didn't feel like I could say "cuzz" anymore. I mean, how could I sound like I was still bangin'? I was a fuckin' *college student!*

"Yo, Amber, what up, girl?" Both T-Dog and Rodney gave me the customary pound.

Lil D hadn't said anything to me yet. I waited, wondering what the hesitation was about. Finally, after some small talk, he looked at me. "Where you been, sis?" he said, with his arms crossed. "How comes I hear that you write to Juan and Omar, but I can't get a letter, huh?"

"Lil D, why are you acting like you're mad at me?" I said. "I been in Cali, man. Why do you think I'm here? This is my first time back, and y'all are the first people I've been to see beside my fam!" He still didn't move to give me any love.

"You wanna smoke this joint with us right quick?" asked Rodney, still rocking his now out-of-style Jheri curl, which was peeking from beneath his black Raiders cap. He motioned me into the house with a nod. "Don't worry 'bout him; he glad to see you, he just missed you, that's all."

Lil D walked in front of us and went into the house. T-Dog

put on some music and we proceeded to get lit up. He didn't have anything but forties and old Chinese takeout in his fridge, so we were sippin' and eatin' as the joint got passed around, just like old times. It felt good—familiar. Thirty minutes into our blunt session Lil D finally started talking to me like nothing happened. I understood it was hard for him when I left for college. We got in our own zone, talking about Lil D's life, his plans. I heard Rodney's voice calling my name.

"Yo, Amber," he said as he puffed on the blunt.

"What's up?" I asked, annoyed, because Lil D and I were still talking.

"You seen Omar's baby yet?" Rodney asked, and then let out a stream of smoke.

"What the fuck you talkin' about?" I asked. Rodney looked at Lil D and Lil D glared back at him. "Omar has a baby?" I was staring at Lil D. My head was fuzzy from the weed.

"Shit," Lil D said. "Rodney, why you always gotta bring shit up at the wrong time?"

"I'm sorry, man! How was I supposed to know Omar didn't say nothing to her. I thought they was tight like that!" Rodney said, flinging both hands up in the air.

My heart was pounding, eyes squinting. "T-Dog, why didn't you tell me? Who's the mother? I can't believe I'm hearin' this right now."

"Don't trip, baby girl. You know Omar got love for you. It's these other tricks out here, they be triflin', fo' real. He don't love her anyway. She just tryin' to get a baby by a Crip so she can be down, that's all," T-Dog said. "Omar fucked up."

"But how could he have not told me this? I go visit him every chance I get, we write each other like every week, and *this* is the first time I hear about this shit!"

"You need to just let it go, Amber. Ain't nothin' you can do about it now," Lil D said, puffing on the last of the joint. The doorbell rang, interrupting the conversation.

"Oh shit, I forgot we got some bidness to handle with Killa," Rodney said. "Come on, we gotta be out."

Upon hearing Killa's name, I got a flashback to that night in Kyle's car and him bleeding all over the place. I still felt strange around him.

Lil D put his arm around me, but I pushed him away. I went to the bathroom to wash my face, and forced the tears forming to stop. *What a fool I am,* I thought. After I calmed myself down I went back to the living room.

"Yo, Amber, can you take us somewhere?" Rodney asked.

I sighed, remembering all the times I was the getaway car, the taxi, the errand runner. I knew I was upset because of Omar's baby, and because I had a buzz too. But it also triggered resentment from before, when I felt used.

They were all looking at me for an answer.

"I can take you one place, and then I gotta roll," I said and walked out to the car.

"Yo, hold up, cuzz, lemme serve this customer right quick." Before I could protest Killa was hustling toward a tweaker who was slowly drifting up the block, his body wasting away. T-Dog and Rodney got in the car.

"I'm bouncin', y'all. I'll get up wit you later," said Lil D. He looked at me, waiting for me to say something to him. He looked so young, so vulnerable. There was no reason to take the news of Omar's betrayal out on him, so I smiled at him and waved good-bye. Relieved, he broke out in a smile, and then jetted.

I was trying to lift the fog from my head to focus on driving when I heard someone shouting. I looked around and saw Killa running toward us. The blunts and alcohol caused a delayed reaction, so it wasn't until he jumped in the front seat and screamed, "Get the fuck outta here—he got a gun!" that I even tried to start the car.

Killa bent his body down to use the dashboard as his cover. I saw the tweaker stumbling toward us, pointing a gun, yelling with all the strength his body could muster, "Give me my shit, motherfucker!"

I jammed the keys in the ignition, started the car up, and floored it as hard as I could.

"Go the other way! Go the other way! He's gonna get a shot at us if we drive past him!" Rodney yelled from the back. Shit, I don't want to get shot over some craziness! I shook my head. Come on, Amber, wake the fuck up!

I threw the car in reverse on the one-way street and sped backward toward the intersection. I was driving so fast in reverse and was so high that I started swerving like crazy, trying to control the car. I heard a shot fired.

"Oh shit, the crazy nigga is shootin'!" Killa said, and he started laughing.

"What the fuck you laughing about?" T-Dog yelled. "What the fuck is wrong with you?"

As I got near the intersection I started slowing down, because now I had to back into oncoming traffic.

"T-Dog, *help me,* I can't see!" I screamed.

Another shot. It rang out loud even though we were at the end of the block. All I was thinking now was that the cops were going to come. I was high. I was sure Killa got some dope on him. Fuck!

"Go now, no cars are comin'," T-Dog yelled, leaning forward from the backseat with his hand pushing on my shoulder, urging me on.

I backed into the intersection and shoved the car from reverse into drive. "Is he near us? Where's he at?" I asked.

"I can't see him but keep going just in case," T-Dog said.

Killa turned around to look behind him. "Homeboy is gone. He ain't nowhere to be seen," he said, throwing Crip signs in the air. "This is Crip, fool, don't try to fuck wit' me!" I looked over at Killa to see who he was talking to, and saw him looking out of the window and smiling. He was saying it to himself.

Relief poured over me. Killa was laughing again.

"Damn, that fool has some balls, man! I didn't think that tweaker was packin'," he said.

"Why'd that fool bust on us like that?" T-Dog asked angrily.

"'Cause I took his money and didn't give him no dope, that's why!" Killa said.

"Why the fuck you gank him like that, fool? Do that shit on your own time, not ours. We coulda got blasted right there over one rock, cuzz. That ain't cool." T-Dog was mad as hell. "Matter fact, get the fuck out the car. Amber, pull over and let this fool out."

"Word up, cuzz. I got a new baby at home, I am not tryin' to get smoked by a crackhead, cuzz," Rodney said.

"Come on, man. Why you trippin' so hard? Fuck!" Killa grumbled.

I pulled the car over, happy to get rid of him. He slammed the door shut and just started walking, not looking back.

"Amber, take me back to the crib. I had enough for one day," T-Dog said.

"Yo, cuzz, you should come to my crib. You can't go to yours right now, 'cause of that fool Killa. That tweaker could be waiting for you over there, " Rodney said.

"Fuck!" T-Dog said. "Amber, take me to Rodney's. Killa's a bitch nigga, man!"

The rest of the car ride was silent except for the radio churning out old rap songs the DJ claimed were new. I was glad that Lil D hadn't been rollin' with us. We were all with our own thoughts as we said good-bye. I didn't know when I would see them again.

Or if I even wanted to.

Twenty-Three

Drew occupied my thoughts the whole time I was in Denver. Just thinking about him made me smile. I couldn't wait to get back to see him. I wanted to tell him all the things that had happened to me in Denver with the Rollin' 30s. I felt he could give me some perspective, help me figure some things out. I knew he'd had to make similar choices about who he was kickin' it with, and had to let some friends go in order for him to try and succeed. The faint flutter of butterflies in my stomach betrayed my desire to not be so caught up in this dude. I was still burnt over learning about Omar's baby. Despite that, I couldn't help calling Drew my first day back. I got the answering machine at his apartment.

I left the second message on day two. Day three I started getting that nervous feeling in my stomach. My birthday was coming up and I wanted us to make some romantic plans together.

We met randomly when I saw him at a lunch spot on campus. I was thrilled to be running into him.

"What's up, stranger! You can't call nobody?" I asked, flirting with him.

"Hey, girl. Been busy, you know." He remained standing, so I asked him to sit down at the table. He seemed reluctant.

"How come you don't seem happy to see me? I thought you missed me over the break. At least, that's what it seemed like from your letters." I smiled again. He fiddled with the books in his hands, and didn't say anything. "What's wrong, Drew? Are you okay?"

"I have to tell you something." His face turned toward the floor. "I'm pledging a fraternity."

"Congratulations, I guess. Is that why you haven't been able to call me? Can we hang out this weekend?"

"You just don't get it, Amber. Let me spell it out for you. This is a black fraternity. I can't have a white girlfriend. It's in contradiction to our mission. You and I are over."

I tried to hold back my tears as I stared at him in disbelief.

"Think how that would look, me in a black fraternity, speaking out against racism in the school—standing for my community—with a white girl on my arm. I just can't do it."

"After all those letters you sent me over the break? After the flowers, telling me it was just you and me?"

"Amber, you gotta remember the struggle that I've been teaching you about. Black people are still working for basic rights in this country. If I have to pick my community over dating a white girl, well, my community comes first. Remember the Malcolm X book I gave you?"

"Thanks for the birthday present, Drew." I looked down at my food. My appetite was gone.

"Anyway, I gotta go. See you around."

Just like that he was gone. It was over so fast. I hardly had time to adjust to having my heart broken. The very thing that I loved about him, his love for his people, was the very reason we couldn't be together. As mad as I was, part of me did understand. But it hurt.

It was only a week later I saw him speak at a protest on campus. He said that for African-Americans, interracial relationships were a step in the wrong direction.

I was not prepared to hear those words. Standing in the back of the crowd, I kept hearing him. "Interracial dating is destroying the black community." I got a flashback to our most intimate times, sharing our secrets, loving each other. "Anyone in their right mind would stick to their own." I rushed away before he saw me, tears welling, heart tightening. It made me feel everything between us had been a total lie.

THREE DAYS LATER, GO SEE THE DOCTOR . . .
—KOOL MOE DEE

Belinda and some of the girls from my dorm dragged me to a club to get me out of my depression. I had resolved that I would never get what I wanted. Things just didn't work out with me and guys. In Denver, it was the playa and the gangbanger. Now it was the race/political issue. Would it ever change?

My friend Amara met us at the spot and forced me out on the dance floor to shake my ass. She was wild, crazy, and one of the sexiest girls alive. You could have asked anyone about Amara's beauty and they would have told you the same thing— irresistible. She was so fine, with jet-black hair that she wore straight and long, deep blue-gray eyes, and an Arabic tattoo on her lower back that always peeked above her low-cut jeans.

Amara represented a particular mind-set when it came to women and sex, which for me was empowering and revolutionary. She was a sex fiend: She'd pick up the cutest guy at the club, take him home, fuck him good, and then tell him to get out and "don't bother to leave your number—I'm not calling you." When she would recap the scene for the girls at the next party, we'd laugh hysterically and give her much respect. Now *this* was sexual liberation!

We were doing shots all night long, and ended up at a house party near campus. Drunk and depressed, a cute boy cheered me up, even though he was not my type. I had revenge sex. Or maybe I was inspired by Amara's ideals of sex equals freedom. But also I just wanting to get back—to get even. I thought about Drew the whole time.

After spending the night together, the guy gave me a ride home on his motorcycle. He was sweet, but we didn't have too much in common. He said he'd call me. And he did. But not with an invitation for our next date.

"Umm, Amber?"

"Yeah, who's this?"

"It's Mike, um, we met the other night, at a party, the motorcycle?"

"Hey, Mike, of course I remember you." We did sleep together, right? Idiot, I thought to myself.

"Well, um, I have to tell you something." A pause. "I went to the doctor, and, well, um, he told me that I got chlamydia." Pause. "So he told me I should tell all my partners, so um, you know, they can, you know, get checked out too."

I was shocked. Mike and I hadn't used a condom because I was on the pill, and he seemed really cool, and, I don't know—I was really drunk. My mind was racing. How stupid of me to sleep with this guy.

"Amber, I just wanted to make sure you knew so you didn't pass it on to other people."

"Pass it on to other people? What do you mean by that? Just

because I slept with you that night doesn't mean I do that on the regular."

"I don't want to argue with you. I was just trying to be nice by letting you know."

Things were going from bad to worse.

"Well, thanks for calling. Peace," I said bitterly and slammed the phone down.

The next day I went to the health clinic.

My name was called over the intercom, and I had to do the walk of shame down the long hallway to the doctor's office. I felt as if everyone knew what I was there for. I mean, really, what else could it be but a sexually transmitted disease, right? I hated this. No more men, I told myself.

I opened my mailbox and found two letters from Omar. Great, like I need more guy drama on my mind. On one envelope Omar had drawn a detailed picture of my face, with a teardrop coming out of the corner of my eye. Next to that he drew himself sitting in his cell, his head down in his arms. The letter opened with "Forgive me."

Ever since I found out about his baby I tried to distance myself mentally from him. It was easy to do if I put my mind to it. I put away all the photos, the drawings, and the love poems he sent me from prison. I knew that the chances of Omar and me being together were not too good. He had to get out of jail, get an education, get a job. Could we ever make it work?

All these questions whirled around my head. Before I found out about the baby I fantasized that we could beat the odds. We had grown with each other over the years, our roots were deep. But the bond we shared in Denver seemed like nothing compared to what transpired between us once he was locked up. There were aspects of our relationship that were denied when he was free, because of my family and his lifestyle. Strangely, now that he'd lost his freedom, our connection was able to thrive.

But now I wasn't so sure. I wondered if his baby's mama came to visit him. Jealousy seared through my body. She had more of Omar than me. Their child would connect them forever.

I read through the letter slowly. His poetic words touched me. Forgiveness washed over me slowly. I picked up his other letter, which he had written before he knew I had found out about the baby.

Amber,

Greetings and good wishes, loved one. It is my hope that your thoughts of life are accompanied by a smile. Every time I get a letter from you it really brightens my week. I feel intense, warm affection for you, and the more time goes on, the deeper my affection for you. You inspire me with hope, and I thank God for letting me meet you. I just pray that He allows me to hold on to you and eventually be with you.

As you may have noticed, my address has changed. I have been removed from the general population and placed in a maximum-security segregation unit because I "pose a serious threat to the security of the general population." I will not divulge the specifics of the incident leading to my removal until you write me back, but I will disclose that it is a consequence of my intelligence.

I found out the root of my name is Arabic, and it means "Flourishing, long-lived; Speaker; Disciple," and that's how I feel in here, I always gotta be the speaker for the inmates, 'cause there is definitely no justice up here, it's JUST US!

Still in Love, Omar aka THE DISCIPLE

As I finished the letter there was a knock at my door.

"What's up, Amber?" It was Yvette from down the hall. "What are you doing?"

"Just sitting up here bein' sad," I replied, and sighed.

"Come on, come to my room and I'll cheer you up," she said. Yvette was one of the few black girls in my dorm, and although she was really quiet and my exact opposite, once we met we hung out together all the time. She was from southeast San Diego, and was one of those super-smart kids who graduated early from high school.

"Since you're in my room, we listen to my music, 'kay?" she told me.

I plopped down on her bed. "Well, what are you gonna put on?"

"Bebe and CeCe Winans, the best in gospel music." She smiled at me, knowing I had never heard of them before.

"I am always down to learn, girl, let's hear it." I looked at the pictures of her family members and Whitney Houston she hung neatly on the walls. Something soothing and soulful began playing. I thought about Omar, and the fucked-up things they were doing to him in prison, what I was learning in my classes, and then the white boys from the elevator a while back. It was all bubbling around in my mind. "Yvette, can I ask you something?"

"Yeah."

"How do you deal with it? All the racism here?"

"I just don't let them bother me, I go about my business. There is so much more to life than worrying about some white kids being ignorant." She paused, looking down. "You know, Amber, I see the world through such different eyes." We both sat there, uncomfortably silent. "Come on, let's go ball. I need to get my mind off of some things, *tu entiendes*?" She smiled at me, lifting the mood.

"*Si, si,* I understand." I laughed. "Maybe it will get me out of my bad mood. I have a need for a victory in my life right now."

"If it's victory you need, you shouldn't play against me; try the elementary kids down the block, they're more your level," Yvette said, zipping up her gray GAP sweatshirt and grabbing the basketball. Our relationship consisted of Spanish classes, her tutoring me in math, and me trying to get her to drink, smoke, or otherwise corrupt her saintly ways.

We played ball for hours that day, and afterward went to eat before heading back to the dorms.

"Do you feel better now?" Yvette asked me at the corner taco shop.

"Yeah, Yvette, I do. Thanks for kickin' it with me today— things just seemed to be going from bad to worse." I drank some horchata to try and swallow the lump in my throat, as the negative thoughts popped back in my mind.

"I got your back, amiga, I got your back."

Twenty-Four

3 say we stop this meeting until the devil leaves."

Someone I didn't know spoke in a voice so cold and detached, it clashed violently with the warmth of the uncontrollable blush creeping up my cheeks. It was plainly evident he was talking about me, since I was the only white person at this meeting to discuss the Rodney King incident. With panic rising, I tried to assess the situation and decide what to do.

"Don't make her leave," said a young woman who looked vaguely familiar. Maybe she was in my Psychology of Blackness class? "If she wants to do the right thing, then good for her. That's more than what most white people on this campus are doing."

"We are wasting time. Let the cracker stay. Please, we need to focus," said an irritated voice from the other side of the room.

"What if she's an undercover?" This discussion was going on as if I wasn't even in the room. Until then I had only known what it was like on an intellectual level, after reading Ralph

Ellison's *Invisible Man* for one of my classes. I was rendered invisible, which is probably what most black and brown people felt all the time.

"I know this girl and she's cool, y'all are trippin'," said one of my study buddies. "You don't even know somebody and you're trying to cast them out. You doing her just how the white man has done us. Don't be like the oppressor!"

Even though it felt like an eternity, only fifteen minutes had gone by.

"Fine. Let's just proceed. We have some critical things to talk about. We have got to get organized!" The leader of the Black Student Union who convened the meeting spoke with conviction.

"Fuck y'all!" said the guy who called me a devil, and he walked out. I breathed a sigh of relief, not at the verdict that I could stay, just that the focus wasn't on me anymore. I stayed for most of the meeting and managed to make a couple of suggestions that seemed appropriate.

College life was becoming my own personal civil war, the campus a battlefield with daily casualties. Cultural misunderstandings, angry voices during class arguments, heartbreaks like I suffered from with Drew, and the lost possibility of human connection. My school was totally segregated. I came along and fucked that up. I would go to Black Student Union meetings, black fraternity dances—most places I wasn't wanted. But I kept going. I was still new to the West Coast; it was impossible for me to find clubs and parties that were about hip-hop and had any type of mixed crowd. So I hung out where I felt most comfortable. I would stand my ground, regardless of the consequences. I had to be true to what was in my heart.

"Walk with me to my office, young lady," Professor Brown said, grabbing his bulging, ancient-looking bag, papers sliding out everywhere. He pushed his glasses back up on his nose and motioned me to follow. I had asked if I could meet with him one day after class. Two weeks had passed since I was called a devil at the Rodney King meeting. The stress of the color line kept growing.

Before Drew had broken it off with me, he raved so much about Professor Brown I signed up for his class. I figured I could gain more knowledge *and* meet more black folks my age. In a school of 30,000, only 3 percent were people of color so I had to search far and wide to meet anyone who wasn't white.

In my Africana Studies classes, my eyes were opened. I felt awareness seeping through my mind, allowing me to see the world from a new perspective. I learned the ugly truths about how racism was part of the very foundation of our institutions. The lessons helped me understand a lot of what was going on in Denver, LA, and with Drew.

We walked briskly across the campus grounds, as Prof. Brown expounded upon an earlier lesson of internalized racism and its effects on people of color. A familiar feeling of pride came over me as we passed people on campus, reminding me of what it was like when I was first kickin' it with the Crips. Strange. Such different circumstances, yet the same reaction. I filed it away so I could focus on what Professor Brown was sharing with me.

We got to his little office which was crowded with books and papers. He shut the door, lowered his chin, and looked over his glasses at me. "So what can I do for you, young lady?"

At that moment I knew he would understand what I really needed help with. I broke down and told him all about Drew and what happened between us. It wasn't what I had planned to talk about, but it came pouring out of me anyway. We spoke for hours. I felt my world open up, and with it came both pain and understanding.

"You see, young lady, this is all a consequence of living in a racist, unjust society. Black people have to fight every day for things white people take for granted—like dignity and respect. That takes a toll on us. Also, for black students, many of them are learning the history of their ancestors, their family, for the first time. Can you imagine the feeling of being lied to your whole life? By teachers, by the news, by adults who taught you that you came from slaves? That you should feel *lucky* for what you have now? Black rage is normal after enduring centuries of abuse."

My heart was breaking all over again, for all the fucked-up realities people of color had to deal with in this racist world; for my getting involved with the Crips when I didn't have to; for remembering what Darnell had told me about how kids were dying over colors.

I walked away asking myself the very question Prof. Brown left me with: "Are you part of the problem or part of the solution?"

I vowed to never be part of the problem again.

Journal Entry
I just got back from an Africana Studies class where we talked about internalized racism and self-determination. Sometimes in class I get so upset. I can't stand hearing what white people have done to people of color. It makes me hate myself sometimes. I have a lot more respect for Drew after learning so much in my classes and in my talks with Professor Brown. The unfortunate thing was that I could have supported the work and activism that he fought so hard for, but racism wouldn't allow it. Because unfortunately love doesn't conquer all, and until shit changes in this world, a righteous black man with a

white woman, no matter who she is, will be considered a sellout. And I can understand why. In fact, as crazy as it sounds, as hypocritical as it seems, even I get upset when I see a good black man with a white woman. What a trip, right? So although my heart is still throbbing, I'm beginning my healing process. But I become more and more enraged with the racism that keeps me from being me; that keeps me from loving who I want to love; that keeps all those white kids at my school so ignorant, just as I was. What will become of us?

I was just trying to get my party on, the night I fought with Gibran.

Amara invited me to a house party ten blocks down from the dorms, and I talked Yvette into going with me. With my baggy black jeans, a black sweatshirt under a fly vest, and my Raiders hat on backward, I was ready to go. Yvette picked me up from my dorm room, rockin' a new Nike sweat suit, and we headed to the party.

"Yvette, put on a little lipstick. Maybe you'll meet a hottie tonight!"

"Nah, that's all right. I'm not into that," she said.

"I know, I just gotta try sometimes, right?" I laughed. "Yo, let's stop at this store right quick so I can get a beer before we get there."

We stopped in my favorite liquor store near the campus. The guy there knew me and always hooked me up. I grabbed a forty and a bottle of Night Train.

"You gonna walk on the street with that?" Yvette looked at me as I smiled back at her. "You are so crazy, Amber."

"Yvette, I have a brown bag, okay? I'm not stupid!" I was downing my beer as we walked toward the spot. We heard the music a block away. When we got there, I knew it was my type of house party: a DJ playing the quintessential hip-hop jams, alcohol, and cuties. It was on.

Yvette and I danced all night, sometimes with each other, sometimes with friends, and sometimes with random people. My classmate Terry was there, and we grooved to a couple songs. Then Amara and her friend Sandra came over to join the fun. Amara put her mouth to my ear. "I got some really good ecstasy, you want in?"

"Oh, I wish, Amara. But I'm with Yvette, and you know she don't get down like that."

"Next time," she replied.

I broke out the bottle of Night Train and we started taking it to the head. As the night progressed one of our classmates, Gibran, was all up on Amara, trying to get his grind on. She was all smiles, because Gibran was definitely a cutie, dark chocolate with long dreads; respected on campus as one of the emerging young black leaders, like Drew.

I went outside to get some air. I was starting to feel a little dizzy from all the drinking. A bunch of people were hanging out in the backyard, and I saw Sandra kicking it by a car in the driveway.

"What's up, girl, you having fun?" I asked as I walked over.

"You know who I'm meeting out here for a rendezvous?" She pulled me in close to her. "Gibran!" she whispered in my ear.

"Gibran?" I looked at her. "Girl, didn't you see him in there all up on Amara? Be careful with that, I think he's trying to double dip!" She looked upset. "I just don't want you to get played, Sandra, that's all."

"No, thanks for telling me, Amber." She gave me a hug. "I can't believe that asshole, he knows that's my girl! Why would he try and play us like that?"

"You know how men are: straight-up scandalous! They'll do anything if they can get away with it," I said. "I'm going back in to find Yvette."

An hour later I had forgotten all about it. Yvette and I were standing right in front of the huge speaker, which was pumpin' out X-Clan. Sandra and Amara bounced, but not before putting another drink in my hand.

Gibran stepped up to me from out of nowhere and shoved me from the side. I lost my balance and stumbled to the floor, my drink spilling everywhere.

"What the fuck!" I said as I tried to get up.

Gibran pushed me back down, yelling, "You fucking cock-blocking cunt!"

By now Yvette had rushed to my side and was helping me get up. People around us stopped dancing. Terry asked me if I was okay and Yvette started pushing me through the crowd, away from Gibran and toward the front door.

"Fuck that, Yvette! Homeboy is really fuckin' wit' the wrong bitch!" I yelled.

"Amber, calm, down, you're drunk! Leave it alone!" Yvette ushered me outside. Tears of anger streamed down my face, and my sweatshirt reeked of alcohol. Gibran followed us out, a small crowd gathered behind him.

"Why the fuck you throwing salt in my game?" he yelled.

Yvette grabbed my arm and led me to the sidewalk. "We're getting out of here, Amber," she said.

"Yeah, run away, you cunt bitch! You just mad 'cause I ain't kicking game to your ugly ass! Run, bitch!" Gibran threw a bottle toward us and it shattered at my feet.

"Y'all need to chill out, 'fore the cops come," somebody from the party yelled.

"Fuck you, cocksucker!" I yelled up at Gibran, as he stood

at the top of the steps. "You fucking pussy! I'm gonna get you! You don't know who I'm down with, cuzz!"

Yvette was trying to push me up the block and I was struggling against her, trying to get back to Gibran, when I heard the sirens. A neighbor must have called the cops.

"Amber, come on! The cops are coming!" Yvette yelled. "We gotta get out of here, let's go!" She pulled me, and this time I went with her.

"Fuck the cops!" I said to Yvette, but I knew I didn't want to be sitting in the back of a squad car, so I hurried with her toward the dorms. I looked back as a car pulled up to the house, where about twenty people now stood. Yvette and I turned the corner and kept walking.

"Are you okay, Amber?" Yvette asked. I started crying hysterically. "What happened? Why did he do that to you?" She put her arm around me.

"Damn, man, I don't even know! All I did was tell the two girls he was trying to play to be careful!"

We got to our dorms and Yvette opened the door for me. I knew I must look really awful by the way people were staring at me.

"Come on, don't pay them any mind," Yvette said as she walked with me to the elevator. She came into my room with me. Luckily my roommate was away for the weekend. No sooner had we walked in than the phone rang.

"Fuck that, I don't want to talk to nobody!" I said, taking off my wet clothes.

"Yeah," Yvette said as she sat on my bed, "don't bother with that."

The answering machine came on and, after the beep, I heard Gibran's ugly voice. Yvette and I looked at each other, surprised.

"Hey! You fucking white bitch! You just don't know who

you are fucking with, do you?" He was laughing and I heard other laughter in the background too. "You ain't in Denver, you sorry ho. Lemme tell you something. From now on, anytime you are on campus, you better watch your back. I got every single black girl on campus waiting to whip your ass. Watch your back, stupid white girl. Your shit is gonna be jumped Cali style!"

> BLACK CAT IS BAD LUCK, BAD GUYS WEAR
> BLACK / MUSTA BEEN A WHITE GUY WHO
> STARTED ALL THAT.
> —MC SERCH, 3RD BASS

Twenty-Five

I had beef with black people who wanted me to stay out of their space, with white people who were straight-up racist, and with the few white kids who were into hip-hop, just like I was.

The white hip-hop kids were funny, because although we had a lot of commonalities, they had beef with me just the same.

"Yo, what's up, Denver, how about them cows?" Max laughed as I came through to eat with Yvette and some classmates. Max was a white dude from the Bay Area, a popular DJ in the nightclubs. Everyone agreed that despite his red hair and green eyes, Max played the serious hip-hop, dancehall, and roots that always made people dance. He went to my school and hung out in the same circles I did. We ran into each other quite often. Terry was sitting next to Max.

"Max, have you ever been to Denver? Then shut the fuck up." I wasn't in the mood to defend myself after dealing with Gibran the week before.

"Ohh, lemme be quiet. The cow-banger has spoken!" Max looked so smug. How I wished my homegirl hadn't mentioned anything about me being involved with the Crips. I don't know how we had gotten on the topic the week before at the club, probably we were just all drunk when it came up. But Max had not let it go since.

"Shut up, man." I started eating my stir-fried rice, telling myself to just ignore him.

"Why do you act like you're so bad? Like they have gang-bangers in *Denver*! Please. They don't have time to be in gangs, they still doing the running man out there."

"Dude, Max, shut up, man," Terry said with a disgusted look on his face. But he wasn't done. Max got up and started doing the running man dance, and everyone started laughing. Then I lost it. I was already stressed out from Gibran's threat, and now this? It was just too much.

"Motherfucker, if you don't shut the fuck up I'm gonna fuck you up! You don't even know what the fuck you talkin' about and you steady talkin' shit. SHUT THE FUCK UP!" I pushed my chair back as I stood up. People at the table were telling me to chill out, but their advice was like a soft buzzing in my ear that I could not really hear because the rage in my blood, pulsing through my body to my ears, was so loud.

"Whatever, *Amber*," he said sarcastically. "I gotta bounce anyway, see y'all later." And he walked away.

"Sit down, Amber, come on, don't worry about him. He's just an asshole," Yvette said to me.

"No. Fuck him. He think just because I ain't from LA that I don't know what's up. I wish he could tell that to the Crips I know. They would *show* him how real they are! He's fucking corny anyway!" I sat back down and tried to relax, but the anger just would not go away. Max made me the enemy because I was a threat to him. I was pushing at the "cool white kid" quota, which meant that Max wasn't the only one who could get down in the world of hip-hop. I was his competition.

"Amber, what's up with you? Two fights in two weeks—Gibran at the house party, and now Max? Why do you let them get to you?" Terry walked with me to my next class, after we finished lunch.

"Why are you putting this on me? It's not like I go out of my way looking for assholes to fight with."

"All I'm saying is it seems like you attract drama. Maybe you should peep out why that is happening. Some people are addicted to drama."

"Thanks for the profound insight, Terry," I said sarcastically.

I was thankful we were approaching the classroom so that the conversation could end. *Is* it me? I wondered. Terry was raising issues that struck my core. Even if it was true, who was he to be pointing it out? He didn't know me like that.

I spent the rest of the day zoning out in class, my mind analyzing all the things that were wrong with my life. Terry's comment forced me evaluate who I was rollin' with and how I was reppin'.

I didn't have an answer, I just knew I didn't want to live like this anymore.

I came home that night to a message on my answering machine: "Come home for spring break, Amber. I miss you!" Hearing my mom's voice, I almost started to cry. "How about if I pay for your plane ticket? It'd be so nice to have you here."

When things got really bad for me in LA, I relied heavily on my friends at home. Keisha was in college in Maryland, but came home for the holidays. Carmen got more and more into hip-hop, and was getting good as a DJ, even getting local gigs. Letters from both of them, Omar, and Juan kept me going.

My mom became a huge support to me. We began speaking religiously every Sunday night. I always looked forward to our talks together. Even though I wasn't able to share everything with her, our relationship began to blossom in a way that somehow couldn't take root in Denver. I think part of it was my struggle for independence as well as my quest to find out who I was beneath the family role that had been projected upon me. Whatever it was, Mom helped me keep sane during my college years in ways she couldn't even imagine. For the first time since I was a little girl, I was able to reciprocate. She helped me manage my stress during midterms and I helped her quit smoking. Though I had left Denver, I didn't lose my connection to it. How could I? It was my foundation.

"Mom, I'm coming home."

"Amber, what are you going to do tonight; you wanna hang out?" Keisha called me for some quality time before I bounced back to LA. The week had flown by.

"I'm going to the hood to try and find Lil D. I want to see how he's doing," I replied. "I'll call you tomorrow so we can do lunch or something."

"Okay, girl, have fun—and Amber, please be safe."

"Keisha, you're starting to sound like my mom! What's up with you?"

"I don't know, Amber, you just never know. Things have changed around here, and you don't have Omar or Juan around to protect you."

It was true. With Omar and Juan still locked up, I was on my own. But I still wanted to feel connected with my homies, and that desire was bigger than my concern.

"Thanks for lookin' out, Keisha. I'll be cool, promise," I said.

I needed to go feel that vibe, see my old friends again. The last episode with the Crips flashed through my mind, giving me second thoughts. Then I thought about Max, making fun of me, claiming I wasn't part of any gang. Was he right? Had I lost my street cred by going off to college? I blocked those questions out of my mind.

Even at this age I was still making up stories to protect my mom. With my brother out of the house, I didn't have any competition like I did in high school, so getting wheels was no problem. I quickly changed into some cute jeans and a black baby tee with "California" in white olde English lettering on it, and threw on a little eyeliner and lip gloss. I grabbed some beers from the fridge and was out the door.

I drove down the familiar streets near Five Points High, sipping on a Coors while looking out for cop cars, and giggling like crazy hearing all the old-school music on the radio. I looked forward to seeing Lil D. I got updates about him from Omar's letters, but we hadn't kicked it since last Christmas.

I cruised past the house where he lived the last time I was in town. I saw two guys dressed in blue hanging out on the porch. They looked like Crips by the colors they rocked, although I didn't recognize either of them. I parked the car halfway up the block, made sure my makeup looked right (I knew that how I looked would get back to Omar), and approached the house. The guys were watching me with scowls on their faces.

"What up," I said, standing at the bottom of the front steps.

"You claimin'?" The guy asking me had a scar from his ear to the corner of his mouth.

"Not no more. Just looking for a homie."

"C'mon in, maybe he's inside," the other one said, and opened the door. He seemed a little nicer than scarface.

I walked up the steps and through the front door. The first thing I noticed was a child lying asleep on the couch. He had nothing on but diapers and looked way too old to be wearing them. I glanced over to the next room: Four dudes were sitting at a table, dividing up rocks and baggin' them. I didn't recognize them either. My stomach started turning.

"So who you lookin' for?" The nicer one sat on the edge of the couch, waiting.

"I'm looking for Lil D," I said.

"Oh, you want Lil D, huh?" Scarface looked over to the cats sitting at the table, who turned their attention to me, getting all up in the conversation.

"Yeah, you know where he's at? He use to live here."

The nice one got up from the couch and started walking slowly toward me. Scarface started laughing and said to his homie, "Yo, you handle this, cuzz."

I started backing away, not sure what was going down.

"Yeah, I can show you where Lil D is, if he comes back here again. I'ma be serving his head on a silver platter, bitch!"

I made a run for it and got my body through the front door but my arm got caught when the dude slammed it shut. Engulfed in pain, I was half in and half out. Crying, I pushed the door as hard as I could and managed to get my arm out. The door barely missed snapping my fingers.

Holding my arm, I ran down the block to the car. Three of them ran out of the house onto the front lawn.

"We're gonna get you, stank bitch! You gonna get deaded with the rest of those fools!"

I fumbled to get the keys out of my pockets and looked up to see a couple of neighbors looking out of the windows and then closing their curtains. I knew I couldn't count on anyone right now, not with all those guys after me.

I gunned the engine and backed up, hitting the parked car behind me. I looked in the rearview mirror, and to my horror saw the three dudes getting into an old Impala. One of them was carrying a heavy pipe.

I hit the corner and ran the stop sign, cursing to myself. Where the fuck should I go? I can't drive to anyone's house with them following me. Fuck!

I tried to ditch them by turning corner after corner. I was headed back toward the other side of town, hoping that they wouldn't want to go too far from their pad. Then I got the idea of heading to Forestville Park, where Juan and I used to hang. There would be a lot of people there, and I could probably ditch them.

As I was driving, it seemed like every car looked like theirs. I was crying and sweating, and my arm was throbbing. His words bounced around in my brain: "We're gonna get you, stank bitch!" What the hell was I thinking? I wasn't no Crip anymore. I didn't know the scene anymore. I had to face that. I couldn't have both worlds.

After driving around randomly for close to half an hour, I knew I had finally lost them. I looked at myself in the mirror. My eyes were red and puffy. I drove home slowly, hoping that my mom was already asleep, so she wouldn't see me. I parked the car in the garage, just in case. Since I didn't know who I was dealin' with, I couldn't be sure if they knew anything about me.

Mom had left me a note on the kitchen counter saying she had gone to bed. At the bottom she had written, "I love you, so glad you're home!" Next to that she'd drawn a smiley face.

My arm throbbing, I went into my old room, lay down on my bed, and cried.

When I got back to LA, a letter from Omar was waiting for me. I had decided not to mention my recent confrontation in

Denver because I didn't want to be the cause of any more violence. I had to wear long sleeves for a while, even in the warm weather. My bruised and sore arm had become a constant reminder of my two worlds, and the pain caused by their collision.

Lately Omar's and my love letters had intensified, and even though I was dating people, he remained close to my heart. My pulse raced whenever I received his beautiful works of art. The envelopes themselves were pieces of artwork, so detailed and vivid—and then violated by a huge black stamp reading "UNCENSORED INMATE MAIL" over the intricate drawings, as if to prove that no amount of beauty could ever come out of a prison.

Dearest Amber,

Hello again. In general all is well for me, but there have been several unfortunate individuals who can't say the same. The most recent incident occurred last night. Some dude got stabbed to death in the shower, and about two weeks before that, this young fellow who lived above me was strangled for reasons unknown. It's really a trip being back here at Limon. About a month ago I changed jobs, and I am now an assistant teacher in a poetry class. The job is difficult at times because there are several Mexicans whom I have the honor of teaching English to, but it's rewarding because I've learned a lot of Spanish as a result. It also pleases the humanitarian in me to know that I am educating folks.

There are countless deeds that burden the core of my soul, all of them self-inflicted. The only remedy that I can offer you for my asinine behavior is a promise to do better. The love that I want from you is my motivation.

I want to carry you across the threshold of happiness, into the land of forever. Once there we can stroll through meadows of sensuous memories and make love in gardens of endless compassion as we savor the gentle smell of rose-covered love. I want to walk with you in love, through eternity.

Straight up! Omar the Disciple

It took about three weeks for the bruises on my arms to fade. By that time, I had pushed the incident in Denver to the back of my mind. Although I had Omar in my life, I yearned for some affection. But after my first college heartbreak and the drama of my one-night stand, I slid into my next relationship much more carefully.

Terry and I had been hanging out more. I always dug his sexy goatee, and the big tattoo with the word "Hip-Hop" in olde English lettering spiraling around a microphone displayed prominently on his forearm. We had several Africana Studies classes together, and he loved hip-hop as much, if not more, than me. He had taken me to my first black frat dances on campus.

The most important thing we had in common, though, was that he was white.

I didn't normally go for blond hair and blue eyes, but there was something about him. Terry was from Atlanta. He had gone to a predominantly black school and found that culturally speaking, he related more to black people than white people. We vibed together on so many things—and it just felt so good to be with someone who understood my struggle. We stuck by each other through the difficult decisions we had to make, especially things that dealt with race.

Terry and I were on campus, sitting on the grass after class.

"I gotta talk to you about something, Amber. I made up my mind and I'm gonna do it. I mean, what do I have to lose? It's important to me!" We had been dating for a couple weeks before he made his decision to pledge a black fraternity. Of course I was worried for him. I thought back to Drew and his fraternity's perspective on race.

"It's just hard because I know how they feel," I told him. "They're all about self-determination. About strengthening the black community. If people in the fraternity can't even be with white people, why do you think they would want you up in the mix? There are very few places where they get to carve out their space and make it their own."

"You know what, Amber, you may be right. But the thing is I just don't fit in with any other group. I am just more comfortable 'round black people. And I want to show that. Being in this frat will explain who I am to everyone, before I even open my mouth."

"It's not like I don't understand, Terry. I just don't know if this is the best way to prove you're down."

"I don't have to *prove* anything," he shot back.

"You know I didn't mean it like that. I know how hard it is, when you have to explain to all the white people why you're different, and prove to all the black folks you're not fake. Come on, Terry, you know that's the story of my life too."

We were silent for a minute, watching all the students walk by.

"All I want is to feel part of something. Something that feels real to me. I'm tired of being out of place everywhere I go. I'm just tired." He took my hand. "I know it won't be easy for me or you. But I feel like I gotta do this. I gotta find my place in this world."

"Listen, I'll support you, even though I don't know if it's the right move. I mean, what about our hip-hop crew? Can't you find peace in that?" By now our multiracial community of hip-hop heads was growing, slowly.

"That's cool, and it makes me happy, for sure. But I need a little bit more right now. I need some brotherhood."

For weeks he went through the whole pledging process: wearing the same clothes every day, walking in a line through campus, doing a trial step show. We rarely spoke because of the rigorous pledging routine. Late at night he would call to check in. There was a big Greek step show happening in LA at the end of the month, and he would find out the decision right before the event.

When it came down to it, they decided against him. They told him that it would go against tradition, and that maintaining a place for African-American men in this crazy racist world was their top priority. It could not be compromised for him.

He was crushed.

It took him weeks to get over it, partly because he felt they hadn't been straight with him. Why had they made him go through all that if they'd never planned to let him in in the first place? The betrayal cut him. He stayed in his dorm room, only coming out to go to classes. But he got through it, and as the semester came to an end he slowly became social again. He and I would go to events together, raise hell together, and keep it moving.

Though I was thrilled it was summer, it meant my weed income came to a halt with my market gone from campus. I needed a place to stay, because they shut down my dorm until September. If I had to work, I wanted to at least enjoy it, so I got a job at a clothing store near Venice Beach. But saving for rent could take weeks, so I started couch surfing, my first stop: Terry's.

The first week I stayed we had a blast with each other. I felt grown up, staying with my boyfriend. We cooked dinner for each other in the evenings and he'd drop me off at work in the mornings.

The second week he shared his biggest secret with me.

I came home after work and there he was, looking depressed, drinking a forty.

"My whole life is a lie," he said flatly.

"What's wrong Terry? What are you talking about?" I dropped my things off by the door and went over and put my arms around him. That's when I saw he had his high school yearbook out.

"I made it all up. My school. Where I'm from. Everything. It's all a lie." He broke down as he told me how he had painstakingly created the Terry that I knew, or thought I knew.

"I'm from Marietta, it's a white suburb in ATL."

"I thought you said you grew up in a black neighborhood?" I pulled my arms away, confused.

"Yeah, that's what I said." His eyes looked dead. He stared out into nothingness.

"I don't understand," I started.

"I made it up! All of it!" he yelled. "I drove through East Point in ATL and picked out my address. I made sure it was a real rough block, and hung around enough to hear some people's names and what crews ran what—nobody could tell me something about that block that I didn't already know." He stopped and took another swig of his drink. "Then I went to the school in that neighborhood and got hold of a yearbook and studied it just in case people asked me questions, so that I could throw out names of students and teachers."

I was in shock as I began to comprehend how far he'd gone. After the shock came the sadness. Why did he feel that he wasn't enough? Why did people like us have such a hard time finding our place? This world made it so hard just to be honest about who you were. But making all that shit up? Nah. I vowed to myself that I would never fake jakes about who I was or where I came from. It just wasn't worth it to me.

Throughout my life people told me I "talked black" or "acted black." In Denver, most black people said it like a compliment. One of my black friends, April, gave me a picture of her, and wrote on the back, "To the blackest white girl I know—stay cool!" She liked me for me and I prided myself on staying true to who I was. I had to stand my ground, even when it was uncomfortable, even in the face of Max making fun of Denver.

Terry and I talked for a while that evening. It was during this conversation that something shifted in our relationship. I knew we could never go back to the way we were.

A month later, we broke up. We had been arguing a lot, and finally we both decided it wasn't working. We had never been whole after that night. I think he regretted telling me. I think I regretted hearing it.

I had to move on.

BLACK MEDALLIONS NO GOLD . . .
—DE LA SOUL / JUNGLE BROTHERS /
Q-TIP / QUEEN LATIFAH / MONIE LOVE

Twenty-Six

COLLEGE, SOPHOMORE YEAR

Yo, rock that Africa medallion," one of my new roommates, Sasha said. "It matches the sweatshirt." We were going to see De La Soul and Jamalski in downtown LA and were tearing through our closets to find the right outfits. "Lemme do your hair, 'cause you suck at that!" Sasha was a white girl who had grown up in the hood.

"Stop moving," she said as she cracked her gum. She was putting some braids in my hair and was hurting my head. "You are so tender-headed, Amber. Girl, you gonna look good to-night!" I was hoping to meet a cutie. I hadn't dated anyone since Terry and I broke up.

"Hey, is Yvette coming?" Sasha asked, getting out the hair spray, drowning me in a mist of ultra hold.

"Damn, girl, you're gonna suffocate me with that shit." I coughed. "Nah, she don't feel like goin' to the club tonight, but

217

she said she'll come through tomorrow. Amara might come, though." By now Yvette, Amara, and Sasha had become good friends. Yvette was always over at our crib, and Amara was our clubbin' friend.

The phone rang and I answered with our customary greeting. "What up, black?"

"What up, Amber? It's C-Loc. Look, I can only get two of you on the list for the concert." C-Loc was a club promoter we were cool with because we were regulars at the hottest hip-hop spots in the city. Sophomore year was quickly becoming all about clubs, parties, and trying to get to class without having alcohol seeping out of my pores.

"Cool—we can work with that," I said. "See you tonight, C."

"Aight then. Peace."

There was a huge line to get into the club, but we were on the guest list, so we slid up to the door and got right in. First stop, the bar: We were already dancing as we ordered two shots each of tequila, which we took to the head, and followed that with a Corona. "La di da di . . ."

"Hell yeah, they playin' Slick Rick, Amber, come on let's dance—" Sasha made her way through the crowd to the dance floor, singing, "La di da di, we like to party." We danced for hours. It was as if the DJ was spinning just for me and Sasha—song after song—from Jeru to Cypress Hill to the Jungle Brothers, we were in heaven. At least before we got kicked out. We ended up getting into a drunken fight after some bitch pushed Sasha. The bouncers threw us out of the club, but not before Sasha caught one of the girls in the face.

"I hope you used a condom." The voice of Vicky, my other roommate, cut through my dream-like state. Was she talking to me? I flipped over in my bed and opened my bloodshot eyes. There she was, hands on hips, all ready to condemn me for having unsafe sex. I thought back to last night, the club, the alcohol, the fight, getting kicked out—nope, there was no sex in that equation.

"What are you talking about? I didn't even sleep with any-body!" I rolled back over, and heard her breathe a sigh of relief.

"Thank God," she said, then left for work. I was glad she was gone.

Vicky was from southern California. She was tall and white with light brown eyes and dark brown hair. She grew up in a white upper-class neighborhood in La Jolla. When she started living with us she became curious about black culture, and how Sasha and I were able to negotiate different worlds.

Sasha was a native of LA, and the first time I met her she was sitting on a couch smoking a cigarette, bright red lipstick, nails done, and a real cute outfit on, everything matching per-fectly. We talked for awhile before she promptly lifted one of her butt cheeks and farted, with a "S'cuse me" before con-tinuing on with her point. She had never dated a white boy before—ever—and really didn't think much of it. She was hilarious. A college dropout, all she did was work her little cashier job and party, but somehow she ended up hangin' with us college girls.

Then there was me—Denver born; straddling two commu-nities, one black and one white; not having a lot of money, but eating out at fancy restaurants with Pops; tagger and ex-Crip, but going to college. In a sense I was in the middle, having experienced a lot of both worlds that my roommates inhabited. So there we were, the three white musketeers, riding through life trying to make sense of it all.

The following weekend we all went out to hip-hop night at the Palladium. I met Q.T. Nice body, cute face, and clean-shaven, with creamy brown skin. He wore his clothes well, but mostly

I loved the way he moved. We ended up on the dance floor all night, and I gave him my number before leaving.

"He's mad gay, Amber." Sasha was laughing hysterically.

"Did you see the way he danced?"

"Oh, you got jokes, huh? Did you get any numbers, Ms. Thing? I didn't think so!"

"He's just what we call avant-garde," Amara said, shaking her hips to the beat. "Girl, go get you some. And I want to hear all the juicy details." She laughed.

Q.T. and I started talking. He'd call me late at night after his shift as a bartender. He was different, but I was open to getting to know him. In the back of my mind, the whole bisexual thing kept coming up because of little things here and there, but when I asked him about it, he was adamant about being straight. "People are trying to bring me down—that shit ain't true!" he said.

We'd been seeing each other for about three weeks when I brought him to my apartment one afternoon. As we were kissing, he picked me up and took me to the bedroom that I shared with Vicky. Nobody was around. Everyone kept crazy schedules, so most days the apartment was empty.

He put me down on my bed, kissing me on my mouth, my neck, all over. His hands felt the curves of my body, softly lingering in all the right places. I began to touch his strong arms and then I tore off his shirt. I let my nails gently scratch his back.

"Baby," he said, "you are so fine, girl. Take off your shirt." I pulled it over my head. He looked at me and licked his lips. He slowly took off my bra and began caressing my breasts, licking my nipples, swirling his tongue around the right one until it got hard, and then moving to the left, giving it equal attention. I started getting wet with excitement. He reached down and started to pull my pants down.

I decided I was going to go for it. "Go get a condom, over in the drawer," I whispered seductively.

He looked at me and pulled my panties off. I lay naked on the bed. He stood up, and took his pants and boxers off, and then got on top of me, fingering and kissing me feverishly.

I returned the kisses, but when he started to go further, I pulled away.

"Baby, get a condom—it's right over there," I said, pressing my hand on his chest.

"I don't use those things," he said, his knees separating my thighs. Then he started trying to fuck me.

"Q.T., I'm serious. You have to put on a rubber." There was no way I was having unprotected sex. I had learned my lesson.

He started flippin' out.

"Why, Amber? Are you fucking somebody else?" He started putting his dick inside of me.

"Stop it! I'm not playing. If you don't put on a rubber, we ain't doin' this!"

He wasn't stopping. In fact, he seemed to be getting more turned on. His body was pressing hard into mine, and I was having trouble breathing. He was trying to push his way inside me.

"Give me your cunt, you fuckin' slut! You're a fucking white whore anyway!" His voice became strange—a hoarse whisper—and all of a sudden he sounded crazy.

"I only fuck white whores—and I knew you were one of them when I met you at that club," he kept whispering in my ear. "White girls who go to black clubs like fucking black men like me, right, Amber? Right, you fucking slut! Come on, let me squeeze those titties of yours. You know you like it." He was doing his best to force himself inside me.

"Get the fuck off of me! Get off!" I started crying and yelling at the same time. I was wiggling my way up, trying to get his dick out of me.

"You know you want this. You like playin' hard to get, huh? Come here, girl, I'll show you hard." His hands were all over me, pulling, pushing, shoving.

I managed to get my arms out from underneath Q.T. and started scooting myself off the mattress completely. He lost his grip on me, and I pushed backward until I was able to get up. I ran in the bathroom and locked the door. He banged on it for a while, before finally giving up.

"You made the wrong move, Amber. You don't even know the power I have, you fucking little bitch." I heard him walk out of the apartment and slam the door. I sank to the floor and started sobbing. I wondered when Sasha and Vicky were coming home. The thought of being alone in the apartment was terrifying to me.

Eventually I got up and took a shower, scrubbing myself as hard as possible. I started thinking of that story of the guy with AIDS who knowingly transmitted it to as many women as possible. I should have listened to my friends when they told me Q.T. was no good. After the shower I went into my room, put on my sweats, and got into my bed. I was rocking back and forth and crying. I found myself thinking of Omar. *Where are you? You should be here to protect me.*

My next stop was the campus clinic.

Again.

Journal Entry
I feel dirty. I keep taking showers and baths, but it won't wash away—soap and water won't wash it away. I close my eyes to it. But I feel it, hear it, deep down. Don't understand it. Can't touch it.

A week later, as I was waiting for my test results, someone was waiting for me.

I started shaking as soon as I saw Q.T. standing by my apartment door. "Now I know why you wanted me to wear a rubber. You've been a bad girl, haven't you?"

"What do you want, Q.T.?" I was pretending to be tougher than I felt, afraid of what he might do.

"I knew something was up with you. My friend got me in the campus clinic file room, and I saw that you had been burned before. Hmm, I wonder who would be interested in that type of information? Or should I keep your dirty little secret?"

"Fuck you, Q.T., you're fucking crazy. Just stay the fuck outta my life!" I started walking away. I heard him laughing but didn't turn around to see if he was following me. I just kept moving. I headed to the main walkway of the campus, looking for a place where people would be, in case he followed me.

I didn't feel safe until I saw some other people. I felt so violated, both physically and psychologically. Who was it that gave him access to my file? What could he do with all the personal information it had on me? Everything felt fucked up.

For the first time I looked back, but he wasn't there. I didn't want to go all the way on campus, so I turned back toward our place, but took the long way home. I walked and walked and walked, crying the whole time.

My roommates were livid when they found out. Sasha called Yvette, who lived ten minutes from us, and she came right over.

"That motherfucker! What is wrong with you, Amber? He was so fucking weird to begin with—" Vicky began.

"We can't think about that now," Yvette interrupted. "Amber, are you gonna call the police or what?"

"Hell no! I don't want anything to do with this guy. And I'm not going to give him any more reasons to bother me. He has already caused enough drama in my life. I just want to forget the whole thing!" I said. "Plus, you know how racist shit is, I don't want to give the police something else to justify their racism."

Sasha had her arm around me, trying to comfort me.

"That's crazy, Amber, this has nothing to do with race! This is about attempted rape!" Vicky said.

"Everything is about race, Vicky," I said. "And it looks bad. Black man tries to rape white girl. What if it gets out or something?" I shook my head. I refused to let my personal situation make things worse. It was my fault I got myself in this mess in the first place. If I told, not only would I face ridicule and be called a slut, but I might be thought of as a traitor by the students of color. I knew it would look bad.

"Well, you should at least do something about your file. Do you want me to call the clinic and talk to a supervisor for you?" Vicky was ready to try and fix something, anything.

"It's so humiliating. I don't know what to do." I was tired from crying so much. I just wanted to sleep and pretend it never happened. But the nervousness in my stomach wouldn't let me relax.

"You should call and report it," Vicky said again. I waited to hear Sasha's input, but she didn't say anything.

"It's your decision, Amber," Yvette said, giving Vicky a look. Yvette could tell that Vicky was pressuring me. "We're just here to support you."

"No," I said. "I just want this whole thing to be over."

Vicky went into our bedroom and shut the door, clearly disappointed in my decision.

"It's cool, girl, I got your back. Do what you feel is right," Sasha said, wiping my tears.

Yvette and Sasha stayed up with me all night. They made an emergency ice cream and junk food run, rented stupid movies for us to watch, and tickled me until I couldn't stop laughing.

We all woke up in the morning with sore backs from falling asleep on the couch. But I didn't care. I woke up to my friends.

I called the lab the following morning. Sasha sat next to me for moral support.

"The results are negative," the cheerful lab tech said.

I hung up the phone, I closed my eyes, and said thank you over and over and over again.

Twenty-Seven

Amber, Amber, guess who called?" Sasha practically tackled me when I walked in from class. A couple of weeks had passed since the Q.T. incident, and I had begun building my life back up and reclaiming my happiness.

"Was it your husband, Q-Tip? 'Cause I don't know who else could get you jumpin' up and down like that!" Sasha was in love with Q-Tip of A Tribe Called Quest. I put my backpack down on the couch and walked into our kitchen to get some grub.

"More like *your* husband!" Sasha said with a sly smile on her face, following me.

"Who called me?" I looked in the fridge, and pulled out cheese to make a quesadilla. I wished I had Carmen's home-made guac to go with it.

"Omar! And I talked to him! He seems so nice, Amber, just like you always said."

"*Omar!?*" I put the cheese down and turned around to face

Sasha. "I can't believe he called over here! What did he say?" Omar rarely called because it was so expensive for me. The phone company had a crazy monopoly on prison calls, making money off the families of the prisoners. I didn't find this out until the first month I was in college and my phone bill was five hundred dollars. It was one of the reasons I had to start making cash on the side. After that, I told him we had to write each other.

"Not much. He just said that he really needed to talk to you, but it was a surprise. So romantic," Sasha said, grinning.

"Did he give you a number?"

"No, he said he'd try and call you tonight. Maybe you can have some phone sex." Sasha laughed. "Just put on some music so I can't hear you."

I waited all night for his call, but it never came.

"Yo, Corazón, you wanna go bombin'? I'm a free criminal!" a familiar raspy voice asked me when I picked up the phone two days later.

"Juan! You're out? I thought you got four years! How'd you get my number?"

"Damn, girl, slow down! What's up wit' the questions—you ain't happy I'm out?"

"Shut the fuck up, man, you know I'm fucking happy!" I yelled. "Juan, come visit me! We'd have so much fun out here together."

"I wish I could, but I'm on parole. I can't leave the state for a while or they can lock me back up. But when you coming out here?"

"I'm coming my next break, I just gotta make some money first," I said.

Juan and I talked for over an hour, catching up on things. He told me that he was done with the Crips. But he did link up with some of our old RTS crew and was painting again. Toward the end of the call I asked a question about Omar, and Juan got serious on me.

"Hey, Amber, I got some bad news," he said, and my heart dropped. I started pacing in the living room.

"What happened, Juan, did he get hurt?"

"No, *he* didn't get hurt."

"Juan, just tell me, c'mon, man."

"Here's what happened." Juan proceeded to tell me Omar had also gotten out on good behavior, and the whole crew welcomed them home. His first night out, there was a jam happening at one of Denver's hottest clubs, so they all went up there to celebrate. Juan decided to visit one of his favorite chicks to catch up on some lovin'.

"They was all at this jam, just having fun, when Bloods rolled deep up in there," Juan continued. "The Crips were outnumbered, so Omar had to step in. They say it was a bloodbath, but I can tell you right now, Omar was framed."

"Framed for what, Juan?" I asked, my head already shaking back and forth as I tried to imagine Omar, his first night out of jail. What had he done?

"A Blood got stabbed. He died. They said Omar did it."

I started crying. "No, not Omar, he swore he was done with all this." I could taste my salty tears as they streamed out. My body felt weak. "So what's happening now?" I asked. My voice was trembling, but I needed to know what came next. "What'd he get?"

"The prosecuter's going for the max."

"What?" I wailed, and started shaking uncontrollably.

"Listen to me, listen to me, Amber. He's gonna try and fight this. He was framed. He was there, but he didn't do it. I know he didn't." Juan kept talking, but I couldn't hear his words anymore—they blended together and became background noise to my cries. We hung up, and I shut my bedroom door and cried myself to sleep.

Amber, my sanity's salvation:
Greetings and good wishes. By the time you receive this letter I will be sentenced to 16 years in a maximum security facility. My greatest concern is that you'll meet someone before I'm released who will captivate you so completely that our relationship will be sacrificed. A lot of people ask me how I've been able to retain the love of my life, you, after all these years of tortuous incarceration. In my soul, I can blame my strength on hope. My sanity resides in my fantasies and my dreams. Without them, I would have fallen to pieces long ago. Your words, your voice, and your image have been a pillar of support to my hope for many years, Amber. So do not doubt the intensity and depth of my endearment for you. In one of your letters you said you weren't sure if we would still be compatible when I got out. I am confident we will, because I will shift the direction of my thoughts, if required, to see you glow.
                    Forever Your Friend, Omar the Disciple

I sat with the letter for a long time. Before, whenever I met a guy, I told him about Omar, explaining I had a man but he was locked up. That way there would be no misunderstandings, nobody caught off guard when my knight came for me. My dream was shattered the day I received Juan's call. Four years was now sixteen. I went into my room and pulled out my box where I kept all my letters from him. I placed the new letter inside carefully.

I wasn't sure if my heart could take this anymore.

The day after the letter, I called Keisha and Carmen to tell them what happened. They both felt bad, but also urged me to try and move on.

"Amber, I know that you love Omar with all your heart, but what kind of life are you going to be able to live with him?" Keisha said. "What about your mom? You finally have a great relationship with her. How do you think she would feel if she found out the love of your life was Omar?"

I took the phone from my ear for a minute.

"Amber? Are you there?"

"Yes, I'm here," I said. "The thing is, Keisha, we are so close, closer than I've been with anyone before. It's hard to hear you say give that up."

"I know it's not easy, but you have to think with your head, not your heart. Can you really wait sixteen years for this guy? I mean, come on, Amber, you'll practically be an old lady by the time he's out."

"I know."

"And think about it—he's been in jail since he was a teen-ager. He will have spent over half his formative years in an in-stitution. That can't end well."

"Okay, Keisha, I got it. But you know what, that is not what I need to hear right now. It's just too hard."

Keisha sighed. "I'm sorry, Amber, I know you're upset. Why don't we talk about this later, sweetie?"

"Yeah, okay," I said. After we hung up I decided to try and focus more on my life and my goals. And right now the top priority was money.

Sasha had gotten a really good weed connection from one of her old homies. She was working at a drugstore struggling to pay her bills. My part-time job barely covered my food. So we decided to sell weed. Our hustle helped ease our financial stress.

"I don't ever want to go back to the way I grew up." Sasha and I were getting tighter and tighter. We would spend time listening to hip-hop and talking about our issues of growing up different from everyone else; what it meant being white and hanging out in black communities. She told me how rough things had been in the past, especially with money. There were many times when she didn't have anything to eat.

I never had it that bad, but I definitely didn't want to bother my mom with my money issues. She was already covering my tuition and she definitely wasn't making big bucks. My dad— well, things weren't so great between us. I would hear reports from TJ that he had a new girlfriend, and that he had bought her a car or given her some expensive gift. Yet here I was scraping together money just for food and rent. We rarely talked, although I did see him when I went to Denver.

Sasha and I were in the middle of bagging up the first pound when Vicky came home from school. She looked mad hyped.

"Amber, can I wear your overalls for this party I'm going to tonight? A lot of famous people are gonna be there." Vicky and I shared a room, shared clothes, shared everything. For a long time I felt good about our friendship, but lately things were changing.

I was a little hesitant, which usually isn't the case for me. But these were my signature overalls, one-of-a-kind, airbrushed overalls that Juan had made for me. Coveted by many, owned by me. Anybody who knew me knew about my overalls. So she wasn't asking to borrow just anything.

"I guess . . . *if they're clean.*" I knew I was being passive-aggressive, but I was still trying to figure out my feelings. Sasha looked up at me, hearing my tone. Vicky didn't even notice because she was so excited about the party. Which was another thing. This was no ordinary party. It was a private record release party for the then-unknown, but loved by us, Del the Funky Homosapien. Our friend was throwing it, and he liked Vicky, so she got hooked up.

Vicky didn't know *anything* about hip-hop, except for what she picked up from Sasha and me. Most girls we knew liked the music but weren't fiends about it, like us. They couldn't understand the realness of it; how it was so much more than *just* music to us. It was the one force that managed to get beyond skin color; that allowed peace where before there was drama; that spoke to something in all of us that was universal. Meanwhile, we, the true hip-hop junkies, were left out in the cold while she got to roll with *Del*! That just wasn't right!

"And what if I wore your black leather Raiders hat to bring it all together?" Oh Lord, not the hat too? She was biting my whole look! She floated out of our place, a cute girl with my fly-ass outfit on, going to the album release party of the hottest new hip-hop artist. That should be me, I thought.

It was partly jealousy that overtook me that night. Also pride and ego. Before that infamous date, Vicky was like a pupil of mine—much like I was to Juan—at least in the areas of hip-hop and black culture. Don't get me wrong. We definitely had an equal relationship in other areas, and she helped me through a lot as a friend. But she looked to me to help her negotiate the color lines. I did. Now I regretted it.

I was starting to feel suffocated, sucked dry. My mannerisms were becoming hers, my style was being duplicated. In fact, I felt like my whole existence was being coopted.

The problem was I had a hard time talking about it. That was my fault. Things had been building up for quite some time and because I couldn't articulate it, Vicky had no idea what I was feeling and how her actions started to grate on my nerves.

"Nah, black, I can't get with that!" I heard Vicky laughing

on the phone. Just hearing her say that pissed me off. I went straight into our room and didn't even say hi.

It was a slow descent into the demise of our friendship. No dramatic scenes. No yelling in each other's faces, or cussing each other out. Rather, sensing the negative vibes, she spent less and less time at our place. Consequently, Sasha and I spent more and more time together. When the lease came up for renewal, Sasha and I decided to move out and get our own apartment.

Twenty-Eight

COLLEGE, JUNIOR YEAR

After I got over the initial shock of Omar's sentence, I tried to put him out of my mind for a while. It never lasted long, because as soon as I got comfortable not thinking about him, another letter would arrive. As soon as I saw it, my heart would flutter.

My dearest confidante,
There are not many people I can talk about my true feel-ings with, so I'm afraid I must burden you with them. As they led me off the bus, I was acutely aware of the cold-ness of my new surroundings that I would call home for the next sixteen years. As I was shuffled in with the other inmates, all of us feeling like animals, I began con-templating how I would maintain my sanity and stay alive. At that same moment, a fly perched itself proudly

235

on my shoulder. With my hands and feet shackled with steel handcuffs, I remained powerless, unable to do the simplest of all tasks, brushing off a fly. At that moment, I felt the little fly had conquered me, had conquered my manhood. And that, my friend, is the clearest way I can describe what it feels like to have your freedom taken from you.

Pray for me.

Your devoted soldier and disciple, Omar

The letter, having been read several times, landed in the bottom of my box. It crushed me that I had absolutely nothing to offer Omar but my love. How could he survive on just that?

Sasha and I got our new place together in Echo Park. It was a fly little spot, with a little backyard and patio. Now sailing through college, I found my salvation in our friendship, my work, and hip-hop. I finally found a multiracial crew of heads that came together because of our love of the culture and our faith in one another as human beings. Our crew got bigger and bigger. I felt like I truly belonged.

My campus was still riddled with issues about race. I had to take a stand or risk being like any other white kid, or worse, a total hypocrite. The more I learned about hip-hop, the more I discovered it was as much about justice as it was about music. Understanding people of color started the culture, and it helped to elevate consciousness, I began to see that if I wanted to be part of the culture, especially as a white person, I had to give back.

That gave me the strength to declare my major in Africana Studies, which was controversial on campus and somewhat confusing to my family at home. When the news hit my brother, he let me have it over the phone.

"Amber, do you know that black people are probably laughing at you right now? Do you think they *want* a white girl with that major?" he asked me. Boulder wasn't what he thought it would be, so he'd come back to Denver and was working at a restaurant while taking classes at a community college. Whenever I called home, my mom made us talk to each other.

"I haven't had any problems with that, really," I lied. Although Gibran, the guy I'd gotten in a fight with back when I was a freshman, never made good on his threat, he was still around and talking shit about me.

"Why don't you study up on *our* culture, Amber? The Irish were considered black when they first arrived here. Did you know that? Do you even care about where *you* come from?" I could hear my mom telling him to pass the phone. "Really, Amber. Don't you feel a little ridiculous? All you have to do is look in the mirror to see that you're just another *white girl*." I heard my mom's voice in the background again.

"Here's Mom," TJ said.

"I'm sorry, dear. I didn't know he would say all those things to you," she started.

"It's not your fault, Mom." I was numb to it by now. "You know, it is really hard to believe that TJ and I came from the same household. Are you sure that he is my biological brother?"

My mom started laughing. "Oh, Amber, I don't know why things are so hard sometimes. But I want you to know that I am proud of you."

"Thank you, Mom, that means a lot to me."

"You know, when I was growing up things were quite different. I disagreed with many things that I saw and heard, but I was taught not to question it. What makes me sad is that I obeyed."

"I know it was different back then."

"I am so thankful that you are doing all of the things that I just thought about." I was quiet, and she continued, whispering now, "I am so proud of you, honey."

I knew my mom might not understand everything I was doing, but she could feel I was doing something right.

Declaring my major forced me to put out what was in my heart. As a white person, I was always free to decide when, where, or if I wanted to deal with racism. If I was at a restaurant and just wanted to eat, I could make the decision to let a racist comment by the waitress go by. Every day I had the *option* to stand up for what was right or not. But as college students know, the number-one question you get asked by *everybody* is, "What's your major?" With the declaration of an Africana Studies major, I was forcing myself to take a public stand. I couldn't change the color of my skin, but I could open up a dialogue with people, where we could explore new possibilities and spark change.

"He won't ever be able to father a child." That was the first thing in Robbie's file. He was fifteen years old, homeless, and a heroin addict. "Client is not to wear socks, long-sleeve shirts, or anything covering his neck or head." Feeding off my desire to give back, I started volunteering at a homeless shelter for kids. I loved it there, but it evoked painful feelings. We never had enough to feed everybody, and seeing families and children out on the streets tore at my heart. It brought back memories of my time spent at the soup kitchen in Denver.

I learned Robbie had exhausted all the veins in his arms, so he went to his legs, ankles, feet, neck, face, and then, in desperation, his penis. He shot up his dick so much, the doctor said the damage was irreversible. It was hard to believe, but I read his own father got him hooked on heroin at the age of twelve, and the street became his home. His mother had died when he was a baby.

I couldn't wait to get home that day. I didn't know how Sasha would take it, but I had to tell her.

"I just can't do it anymore," I announced as soon as I walked in our apartment. I knew I had to quit selling weed. Not that weed and heroin were even close to being the same, but I felt like such a hypocrite. Here I was helping young people stop using, seeing how drugs fucked up their lives, and then I went home to sell weed. What would happen if I got caught and the kids I worked with found out? All my justifications for dealing disappeared. I just couldn't do it anymore.

"Slow down, Amber. Put your bag down and sit on the couch. I ain't going nowhere." I plopped on the couch and Sasha handed me some coffee. "So what is it that you can't do anymore?" she asked.

I told her everything that happened at work. I remembered Juan saying to me, "I'm never going back." Now I really understood it was my time to pull myself out of this character I had created.

"Are you done?" Sasha said. I nodded. "I don't know who you are trying to convince over here. If you wanna stop, then stop. I'm not gonna get in your way. It's more trouble than it's worth, anyhow." I was surprised it was so easy. I didn't know what I was expecting, but it was definitely not this.

"We just need to figure out how to make some extra cash," she said. "Legally." We both started laughing. "Well, we can't let what we have go to waste. Let's roll up a joint and celebrate the end of our drug-dealin' days!"

"Word up," I said. "Roll that shit up and I'll put on some music. Whatcha wanna hear?"

"You know what I want to hear. A Tribe Called Quest! You know I love me some Tribe!"

"Yo, it's Trade Show time, baby! I'm coming out to see you!"
Carmen left a message on my machine detailing her trip out
to Cali.

The following week I picked her up at the airport. When we
saw each other, we started screaming and hugging. I put her
stuff in the car and started checking her out.

"Damn, Carmen, you look hot!" I said, eyeing her new look.
Carmen had always been attractive, but now she had an extra
layer of style about her, with her long black hair, small frame,
and dope wardrobe.

"Amber, don't call me that no more."

I looked at her. "So what is it that I'm supposed to call
you?" We jumped in the car as a cop approached with his ticket
pad out.

"DJ Empress! Things done changed since you bounced. I'm
down with the DJ scene in Denver, and I've been out bombin'
too, takin' up your legacy, Miss Corazón!"

"That's so fresh, girl! Isn't it crazy how we are a world apart,
but somehow our lives always seem to be in the same place?"

"Word up, baby girl. Now let's go wreck shop."

Sasha had already gotten the party started when we arrived.
She had called Yvette, Amara, and some of our homegirls to
come over, and they were already drinking. We spent the next
hour gettin' cute. It took a whole bottle of Southern Comfort
and several collisions in our bathroom tryin' to get at the mirror before our clique of hip-hop divas were ready to drive to
San Diego for the weekend. The whole thing was just funny
to Yvette, who still didn't drink. She used us for her personal
entertainment.

We were attending the legendary 432F Trade Show at a hotel in downtown San Diego. The hip-hop clothing market had
been exploding on the scene, and clothing companies came to

sell their new products at the Trade Show. That was what *they* came to do. We came to meet fine-ass men, get some free gear, and party!

"Let's stop and get another bottle before we hit this spot," I said. "I'm feelin' the Night Train callin' me!" I was already buzzin' from the Southern Comfort.

"Cool, there's a liquor store right up the street from where we are going," Sasha said. We got a couple of bottles and stashed them in our bags. The rest was hours of nonstop partying. Each room was a different company with crazy gear, hip-hop beats, and, of course, men.

I got introduced to mad famous graff artists, O.G.s who Juan had me studying back in Denver. It was like a dream come true for me. We kicked it in the Tribal Gear booth for hours. Tribal had a bangin' clothing line, plus the owners, Bobby and Carl, were real cool. As we talked, I started telling them about the shelter I worked at.

"You know what would make those kids' day?" I said, taking a sip of the Night Train and passing it on. "If I could have you guys come to the shelter and you could tell 'em your story, how you make money and everything off of your true love, hip-hop! And maybe you could bring them some gear—these beautiful young people got nothin' but hand-me-down rags."

"Lemme tell you somethin', we came from the hood," said Carl. "We will never forget where we came from. You want us to come talk to those kids? We're there, no playin'. This company was built on love. We don't use sweatshops. Them people are *our* people. We do this for the hood."

Bobby handed me his business card. "You call us directly. We'll set a date, bring a shitload of clothes, and chill with the kids at your shelter."

The warmth seeping through my body was not from the alcohol. I had found my salvation, and its name was hip-hop.

From that day forth, I began getting my hustle on in another way—my goal was redistribution of wealth, from hip-hop clothing companies to the homeless kids who could never afford them. It felt natural to combine my hip-hop life with my work.

In many ways, seeing these kids took me back to my teenage years—the struggle to find myself—to wade through the difficult decisions to find the right path. It felt good to finally be in a place where I was really beginning to understand myself.

Journal Entry
"I got so much trouble on my mind . . ." —Public Enemy

The future? You mean the next minute, hour, day? What's around the corner, a cop, a killa, a hooka, a john. Manchild, womanchild, living a life on the streets, getting love from a fuck and seeking comfort in a needle. Doing anything to numb the pain, so thankful for that bottle of Night Train, it swoops away the dreary day. The night seems less cold, the concrete not as hard.

These are the children of the night.

They try to blend in during the day but they are everywhere if you open your eyes. Their pain is too real—it forces people away. Suffering the abuse started back in the womb—born already an alcoholic, a crack baby, weaned on molestation, a fist to the face, a curse with no love. Brought into the world to be destroyed; left to the junkies and the users, preparing them for runnin' and hoin', and then nothing at all. They keep surviving, striving to live, searching for one last chance to be loved.

The rage implanted in these kids' hearts and minds— where is the release? Some things bring validity to the street kids' lifestyles. Hip-hop music has a certain power to it—a strength that at times is what gets people through the day. In a world of disillusionment, of invisibility, of feeling beyond worthless, it can be the thing that postpones the decision to give up. All this is talked about in hip-hop—the hard times, the pain, the streets, the game. Livin' like a hustler, doin' whatever it takes to stay up. In this music the words are the Bible, the verses the lessons, the bass the heart and the bond.

In a society where capitalistic greed permeates our most powerful institutions and people, street kids are looked at in terms of dollar signs, using the quickest solutions at the lowest costs. Presenting these problems is easy; determining the solution takes unity, power, and strength. Each one teach one—for all who have succeeded to some extent in this society, it is our responsibility to assist others in reaching their dreams, or maybe just ending their nightmares. We have the heart, but we are losing the beat, which will be the demise of the whole body.

Forward Ever, Backward Never!

I feel better now.

Twenty-Nine

SENIOR YEAR

Upon making it to my senior year, I decided to celebrate. On a whim I took a trip to New York by myself and stayed with the only person I knew out there, DJ Breeze from Cali. Breeze worked nights, but he gave me the 411 on the scene, so one night I went out on my own.

I was rocking my purple Tribal baggy jeans with my new historically black college sweatshirt. I liked to travel light, so I only carried my ID, money, and lip gloss, and was ready to take on New York. While walking to a spot Breeze told me about, I passed a club that was playing hip-hop. I stopped to listen and peep the scene. The music was right, for sure, and it definitely looked packed. As I was debating with myself about whether I should go in or not, a young Latino cutie approached me.

"Peace, sis. Are you joining us tonight?" he asked.

"I'm not sure, I was just walking by," I said, my body slightly swaying to the music. "Should I?"

"No doubt, sis. This is the place to be tonight, but only if you are looking," he said.

I guess this is how they kick game out here in New York, I thought. Well, since I'm here, I'll play it their way. "Lookin' for what?"

"Truth."

"What?"

"Truth. This is not your ordinary hip-hop party. This party is about a revolution of the mind, body, spirit, and the hottest beats. It's about embracing hip-hop culture as a tool to unify and restore balance in the world—to bring back truth, justice, and, therefore, freedom."

He stopped, waiting for me to say or do something. I, however, was immobile for the moment, because of the increased activity in my head.

"So?" he said, after waiting for me to reply. "I want you to know right off the top, we are universal, despite what people may think. We welcome all, including our white brothers and sisters." He paused, seeing the look of surprise on my face. I was still trying to digest the first part of what he said, and now this? He was so up-front about everything. People in Cali just didn't talk like that.

He interrupted my thoughts. "Sis, why don't you come in. We can continue to build, to talk about the state of hip-hop culture, and the world? You can be my guest." He held out his hand to me, "Welcome to the K'Arma Collective." I took it, and he escorted me into the club, and into a community whose principles and ideology spoke to everything that I stood for and believed in.

K'Arma, I learned that night, stood for "knowledge as our

weapon." The "K" stood for knowledge, and *arma* meant weapon in Spanish.

As soon as I came back to LA, I applied to become a member of K'Arma. I talked to all my friends, encouraging them to join too, so we could begin to *do* something. Two months later, I was in. Upon my acceptance, I decided to reclaim my graffiti name, which had been my first entrance into hip-hop culture. Before you knew it we were thirty deep. At the first meeting I introduced myself as Corazón.

Journal Entry
Song I'm listening to: "She keeps on passin' me by." I love the Pharcyde!
Why I love hip-hop!

Hip-hop, the culture, the way of life, the realities, and the attitudes, has always been an outward vehicle for inner expressions. Hip-hop music and culture was created out of the feelings of social stratification and economic injustice. Those same issues of yesterday are confronting us today. Hip-hop culture is misunderstood in a society that allows people outside of hip-hop culture to define who we are and what we represent. As people outside of our culture attempt to expound upon our principles, the general public is misled into believing us to be a negative element in society. Rap music is under the umbrella of hip-hop, but rap is not synonymous with hip-hop. Hip-hop is about searching for truth—anywhere you can find it! K'Arma has helped me take all these feelings I've had about hip-hop and right and wrong, and turn it into organized action. My cypher is complete.

> IT WAS ALL A DREAM / I USED TO READ
> WORD UP! MAGAZINE
> —NOTORIOUS B.I.G.

Thirty

The leaders of K'Arma, the Originals, called a meeting to discuss how the West Coast unit was progressing. The person running it, Scientific, announced he was setting up a Central Committee, CC for short, for the LA K'Armas. For some crazy reason he appointed me to be in it.

I was almost done with school, working at the shelter, kickin' it with Yvette, and living with Sasha. I was proud of Sasha, who had turned her life around. Now attended community college, and got a job with me working with kids, in which she flourished. She also was involved in a serious relationship. Living together since my sophomore year, our relationship had evolved from friendship into sisterhood.

Just as I was getting more involved with K'Arma, Empress called me from Denver. The first thing she told me was that her and Mateo split up.

"It was over a long time ago, and we both knew it. We just didn't know how to say good-bye," she said. "Anyway, since all that happened, I've been thinking a lot, Amber. I just don't want to stay in Denver anymore. I'm tired of it out here. On the DJ tip, I've conquered the scene already. I need a challenge: new music, new beats, new peeps. I want to be part of the movement, and I need a strong tribe to run with to make this world better, you know?"

"I hear you, girl. I told you Cali's the spot."

"It's calling my name, Amber. I want more out of life and the signs are everywhere. You remember my friend, Ajaya? You met when you were out here last."

"Yeah, she was a real cool chick. And deep too. She was on that spiritual tip."

"Yeah, that's her." Empress laughed. "I think me and her are gonna move out there. We are both saving our money now. We'll probably be out there in a month or so."

"It is so gonna be on when you get out here! I'm so glad we'll get to chill like back in the days. You remember when your man crashed the car when we were all on acid?" I started giggling.

"That shit was insane! We were like a block from my house, right?"

"Yeah!" I said. "And he just had to have the perfect song on the radio, so he was trying to put a tape in—"

"And he swerved and hit a damn parked car! What an idiot." Empress paused. "Damn, girl, I can't believe we didn't die. Think about all those times we were fucked up and driving, poppin' E, and acid, and going all over town. We were so *crazy* back then."

"Crazy, Rowdy, Insane Pimps," I said. Empress knew all about what the Crips name stood for in Denver.

"Word up! Now us pimpettes will be runnin' shit in Cali!" Empress's other line beeped. "I gotta take this, Amber, it's business, but I'll get up with you later."

"Love you, girl," I said.

"You too, Amber. Peace out!"

Now it was perfect. My Denver homies joining my LA folks. I started looking for an apartment for them right away. I could hardly wait for them to come. Everything was working out perfectly.

Empress and Ajaya came out one month later. I got them an apartment down the block from us, and we spent our time going back and forth, cooking, getting fucked up, and going to clubs. I tried to study from time to time, but it was becoming less and less important to me. I didn't have the energy and time anymore for all the petty bullshit happening on campus. We were building a hip-hop revolution. Empress and Ajaya got down with K'Arma immediately.

One night Ajaya and I were kickin' it after she made me some fry bread, her specialty.

"You know what's crazy, girl?" I said as she handed me some tea. "I can't believe we never knew each other in Denver. All that time being so close and never meeting each other."

"You know what, we're meeting now because it's time for us to meet, you know what I'm sayin'? People come into each other's lives at the right time, for the right reasons. It's up to us to figure out why, you know, like what we're supposed to be learning from each other."

Ajaya and I had a lot in common. We were from middle-class families, we got involved in the gangsta lifestyle, and we both got out. The only difference was that she kicked it with the Bloods. Chicana and African-American, with beautiful long hair and sexy body piercings, she inspired many a guy trying to get close to her. We continued babbling about life, looking back at our hometown of Denver.

"Sometimes my grief is so great, I just have to smoke a blunt to keep it all in perspective," Ajaya started.

"What do you mean?" I asked.

"There's so much pain in the hood, on so many levels. People are trying to survive, to pay their bills on time, to feed their kids—it's just so hard. And on top of that is the violence." Ajaya started choking up. She wiped away a tear.

"Do you want to talk about it? Sometimes that helps. It can be like a release," I offered.

"I saw stuff go down all the time, I mean, that's just the way it was. But one day—" She shook her head. "It hurts to think back on it." I put my hand on her arm. "I was at my house when I heard the gunshots and screaming. I ran around the corner, and there she was, my homegirl, on the ground. All I could see was blood." She stopped, sipping her tea. "Three people got shot: my homegirl, her husband, and her aunt, and none of them had nothing to do with gangbangin'." Her neighborhood was Blood territory. They had all been sitting together in front of the house when a car full of Crips did a drive-by, shooting every one of them.

"But that wasn't even the worst part." Her face went from anguish to a cold stare looking somewhere off in the distance, as if invoking the image in her head. "The ambulance came while I was there, trying to help everybody. Her husband had been shot in the chest, but he was still alive. The paramedics, who were all white, grabbed him by his feet, and literally dragged him all the way from the porch into the ambulance, his head thumping against the concrete." I started to visualize the scene, my anger rising. "Then they came back for my girlfriend and was like, 'You're too fat for us to pick you up—you need to walk,' and just left her there. I scrambled to try and help her up into the ambulance, even though her leg had been shot. Those racist motherfuckers. The evil in their eyes—I saw it that day. How could you treat another human being so bad? They were the victims!"

Tears were coming down my face, mixing with Ajaya's rage. The story brought so many emotions to the surface. Memories of what I was involved in, and all the trouble I caused in my selfish need for what, power? For fame? To say I was "down"?

It wasn't until the end of the night that we found out that Ajaya knew the Blood Omar was accused of murdering. In a moment of truth we looked into each other's eyes, realizing the reason we were just meeting now. If we had met in Denver, instead of being the best of friends, we would have been the worst of enemies.

"I got the ill connect, girl!" Amara was smiling from ear to ear. "It's gonna cost, though, because it's good Ecstasy," she continued.

It was the whole clique minus Yvette, who wanted nothing to do with this. We planned on doing E for a while, and this weekend it was finally happening. Amara and I were both graduating this month, so we were celebrating.

"Cool, we can make it happen, right y'all?" I was sure that we could scrape the money together.

That night everyone came over to our apartment. We dropped the E, turned up the music, and chilled. After a while, the drug started kicking in and we were all feeling good. At one point Amara, Ajaya, and I all went to the bathroom together. Amara pulled down her pants to pee and she had on a super-sexy G-string. Ajaya and I both were staring at her fine ass.

"Damn, girl, you are so fly!" Ajaya said.

"O-kay!" I reiterated. I was laughing and feeling really good.

"You guys are beautiful too, come on, pull down your pants, lemme see your panties!" She giggled mischievously. In the face of this gorgeous girl there was no way I was going to do what she asked—I just wasn't worth it. My mind spiraled downward and all the negative thoughts of my body imploded inside. Everything came bubbling up as tears started spilling down my cheeks.

"What's wrong?" the girls chorused together.

"I'm fat and I hate my body!" I was trying to control my tears and my sobs, but suddenly both were unstoppable. Amara finished peeing and she and Ajaya were hugging me and stroking my hair.

"Girl, you are far from fat. You've got to stop that tape in your head that says these things!" Amara looked intently into my eyes and Ajaya held my hand. I leaned on their support, physically and emotionally.

"That's just society's view of women reiterated by the men in your life. You have to destroy the programming and replace it with love and respect for you and your body," Ajaya said. "It's a gift from the Creator. You are the only one who thinks you're fat. Turn that negativity around. If you love yourself, the universe will love you right back!"

I grew tired and hot and claustrophobic in our little bathroom. I sighed. "Okay, you guys, I'm gonna try and let go of this negativity inside of me. I'm sorry I broke down like that."

"You never have to apologize, Amber. You know that we love you and just want you to see the Amber that we see, the queen that you are!" Ajaya smiled and gave me another hug.

"Let's go join the party, y'all." Amara opened the door and Bob Marley's melodies welcomed us back into the high that was happening in the living room. I so valued the relationships I had with my girlfriends. They were my voice of reason when the irrational self took over. We walked out with our arms wrapped around one another, euphoria claiming our souls.

College life was coming to an end. Mom and TJ were flying out for my graduation ceremony, which produced a mix of excitement and nervousness in me. I got tense when the separate components of my life came together. I felt like I had to make everyone happy.

The weekend of graduation crept up on me, and before I knew it I was sitting in a stadium of students, family, and friends. Pride and happiness swelled inside me as I crossed that stage and received my diploma. I made it. Not just through college, but my life. Things were so right. I found my community of friends, my job was exactly where I needed to be; even K'Arma was so powerful to me. I felt complete. In the back of my mind, I knew it was time—I had to fully let go of the past.

That night we went to a fancy restaurant with all of my homies: Sasha, Yvette, Amara, Empress, and Ajaya. TJ was enjoying himself, flirting with my friends. Balloons and flowers were everywhere. I couldn't help but notice the shine in my mom's eyes, and the smile dancing across her face as she sat next to me.

A peacefulness came over me. I was finally able to make her happy again.

Thirty-One

COLLEGE GRADUATE

Once I graduated, I turned all of my attention to working with the homeless kids and K'Arma. Yvette moved to San Diego to pursue her master's degree. I saw her about once a month, when me and the girls would visit her and party. Ajaya bounced to Miami to start a hip-hop fashion line. Empress was getting gigs on the regular at parties and shows. Sasha was busy with work and her relationship with a guy named Terrance.

Omar's letters continued. I cherished him and them. Our love ran deep, but I tried not to have any expectations of what would or could happen with us. Juan was doing really well in Denver. He had a job and resisted going back to a life of crime and gangbangin'.

K'Arma was better than ever. Our focus was using hip-hop culture to educate young people and give them an alternative to gangs. We created an application process and took over a local coffeeshop, with forty deep out in the parking lot, waiting for their turn to be interviewed. The rules: Leave your forties and blunts outside.

Skillz had already been a member for a while, so for him it was just a formality.

"What are some ways that you could teach someone who is racist to search for the truth?" Scientific asked.

"I'll just fuck that motherfucka up." We all started laughing. "Nah, I'm playin'. For real, though, I always put people on when I can, through my own way. But I don't allow for disrespect, not from anyone."

"I hear you, Skillz, but—" I looked at him.

"I know I know, Corazón, no violence, we about peace," he answered, smiling.

We moved through the interview quickly but thoroughly. By the time Shadow came through the door we were almost done. We already knew we had found a solid base for our youth chapter.

"If you believe a truth exists, and you are shown new knowledge that conflicts with your truth, will you discard your former belief and adopt the new one?" I waited for his reply.

"Truth is truth. I'll always go with that, as long as you have the evidence to back it up" was Shadow's response. We were satisfied; another mind ready to get down.

K'Arma had a hierarchy to it, with strict rules and regulations. Nobody questioned outright why Scientific had chosen me for the CC, but that was all the K'Arma members talked about. I understood that I had to show and prove before I'd really be accepted as a CC member.

We threw park jams and loft parties, held meetings, and raised money for youth centers. We were makin' some serious noise. Internally we had our own shit going on. By that time,

Empress had joined the CC, and there was mad talk about us being in leadership positions. There was beef all the way around: Besides me being white, neither of us were from LA, and we were both women. Had we paid our dues in hip-hop? Why did we get to be on the CC? Questions lingered in some of the chapter members' minds.

It was the type of situation that needed time, effort, and action for people to see where we were coming from; that it wasn't ego or us wanting power but our life calling. What we didn't need was something tipping us in the other direction—but that's exactly what we ended up getting.

We were at a critical meeting with the West Coast K'Arma leadership. Scientific told me and Empress to represent at this meeting; Originals from San Diego, LA, and the Bay Area would be there.

"K'Arma is my life," said Slim, an Original who outranked Scientific. "I don't mind taking yours, if you fuck with it." I looked around, surprised at the tone that Slim was opening with. I tried to catch Scientific's eye, but he wouldn't look at me. "There have been rules laid down since its inception, and they are not going to change every time a new member comes into what they think is power. I am here to show you where the power is, and where it will stay." Slim began slowly walking around the room. "All new CC members at this table, your status is revoked until further notice. The only person who can reinstate it is Prophet." Prophet was one of the highest-ranking Originals.

We were devastated. How could they do that to us? I don't know how I held back my tears. My rage blocked the rising possibility of anything coming out of my body. I looked around the table and nobody was saying anything. Being the new jack, there was no way I could contest. Slim and the others had been part of K'Arma for more than fifteen years. Then there was me. They saw me as just another white girl.

"This meeting is adjourned."

Once our status was taken away, Empress and I had some fast thinking to do. This could really hurt our chapter and the upward battle we were facing. But we had some things going for us. I refused to give up my voice this time, because I knew I had something to contribute. I could not allow this to threaten the community that had taken me so long to find.

While Empress and I were trying to renegotiate our status within K'Arma, things were going downhill at the house.

"I can't believe this bitch is trying to fuck with my man!" Sasha was pissed when I got home after a shift at the shelter. She and her boyfriend, Terrance, had gotten really serious, really fast. Even though she fell in love with him I never understood why. He was drama from the beginning.

"You won't believe the message I heard on his phone!" She often checked his messages, and had good reason. Terrance hadn't always been faithful.

"What happened?"

"While I was at work today I was bored, so I called him up and left a message. I wanted to hear how I sounded, you know, so I called back to listen to my message, and there was another message on there too. A giggling little bitch talkin' 'bout beep her later tonight if you're not busy type shit."

"Did you talk to Terrance yet?"

"I called him like five fuckin' times, but his punk ass ain't called me back yet. I'm gonna kill him!"

"Okay, calm down. We're gonna work this out, just chill out, let me get you some coffee."

"Fuck coffee, get me a damn forty!"

"You want me to run to the liquor store right quick?"

"No, no, I'm just so upset right now—just when shit is so good between us, why does he do this to me?"

"I don't know, Sasha, I don't know."

Sasha sat on the couch, tears streaming down her face. It wasn't the first time he had made her cry, and definitely wouldn't be the last. He didn't call her until late that night. I was in bed and heard her yelling at him for what seemed like hours. But the next morning, as I rushed off to work, she told me they had "worked it out." I could tell she didn't want to tell me the details.

"I hope you're happy," I said, and ran out the door.

I was trying not to be judgmental with Sasha about her relationships. Lord knew I had had my fair share of unhealthy men in my life, and I was still trying to change that about myself, but I was worried about her. She had come so far since we first met, taking classes and advancing in her career. I didn't want to see her with a man who was not only refusing to better himself, but also bringing her down in the process. Terrance became a barrier between us. I remained silently concerned, and sad.

TODAY I DIDN'T EVEN HAVE TO USE MY A.K. /
I GOT TO SAY IT WAS A GOOD DAY
—Ice Cube

Six months after the notorious meeting with Slim, we got some news from Prophet. Despite our stripped status, we had continued our events. Working in our community meant so much to us, especially witnessing our kids transforming from gang-bangers to K'Arma members.

We were making so much noise that the West Coast O.G.s were taking notice. We began getting regular visits from them, including Prophet. We treated them like royalty, and they loved it. Although they had been in the game for quite some time they weren't getting the recognition they deserved for taking hip-hop to where it was now: a worldwide cultural movement influencing everything from the music industry to the latest commercial trends.

"Peace, Corazón. Prophet is requesting your presence." K'Arma security escorted me to where he sat during one of our huge park jams, reppin' all the elements in hip-hop. Although I was summoned quietly, all eyes were on me. I was extremely proud and extremely nervous.

"Corazón," he started, not looking at me. "It has come to my attention that the work you and Sister Empress are doing here is of the utmost importance. You have proven yourselves as loyal members of this organization." I had never been so close to him, alone. There was one thing I knew instinctively, though, and that was to keep my mouth shut.

"I have decided, after careful consideration and discussion with other Originals in K'Arma, to reappoint you and Sister Empress. The ceremony will be tonight. The CC will be convened at seven PM sharp. Call this number for the location. That will be all." The whole time he never looked at me, but even his detached, businesslike manner couldn't dilute my joy at the fantastic news.

That night we gathered in a fancy restaurant in Hollywood, in a private room reserved for us. Prophet held the ceremony, and with all the CC members present, we regained our status, and our dignity.

Sasha poked her head in my room, "Amber, Amber."

"What, Sasha—it's late!" I said, squinting my eyes from the hallway light she'd turned on.

"It's Prophet," she said, and handed me the phone. "I wouldn't have woken you up, but he said it was urgent."

"Corazón," the low voice on the other end said.

"Yes?" Why was Prophet calling *me,* at one o'clock in the morning?

"I have given it much thought. I believe that you are the one." He paused and I remained silent. "I am requesting that you begin to study under me at once. There is much to learn, and critically important decisions to be made that could affect our entire organization. I need you fully briefed. Be prepared for my next call. Peace."

And that was it. I had been asked to study under one of the highest-ranking Originals, and I was ecstatic. It would be an honor to be his student. My lessons began immediately and we were on the phone daily; private meetings were held; plus I was getting archival video footage, books, and lecture notes about everything from the New World Order to historical documents of Malcolm X and the Black Panthers.

Sasha only called me at work for important stuff, because she knew the shelter was crazy hectic. So when I got her call that day, I was immediately worried.

"Hey Sasha, what's up?"

"Well, I wanted you to be the second person to know. I'm pregnant."

I plopped down in the chair, not sure what to say. "Um, wow. That's crazy. Are you sure?"

"Yeah, I just got the results."

"So what are you gonna do?"

"I want to have this baby."

"Well, I'll support you in whatever you decide. But I'm kinda disappointed." I had a flashback of Vicky. Being judged was no fun, but I had to tell Sasha how I felt. This would change everything. She was only twenty-one, and doing her thing in college.

"Well, let's talk later. I just wanted you to know."

I felt like shit. I should have been happy for her, and excited when she told me. I went back to work with a heavy heart.

We had ups and downs throughout Sasha's pregnancy. She was happy about it, but she and Terrance fought constantly, usually ending with her crying on the couch, depressed. That was hard to watch.

I was there by Sasha's side when baby Macala came to be. What a beautiful experience it was. Something shifted in me that day. I had never witnessed a child being born, and what shined through the most was the power and perseverance of women. Never had I looked at life in those terms. It was so simple yet so profound. I was so proud of Sasha and her new baby girl. I felt something in me opening up that had been closed off for a long time.

Thirty-Two

Omar had never sounded so bad, so I knew it was time to schedule a visit. It was my first time back to Denver since becoming involved in K'Arma, and I wanted to share what my life was like with my family and friends. Being a college grad made me feel more grown up. I felt it was time to come out of the closet with my family. So I began working on making my relationship with them, choosing to be more honest and open. I decided that regardless of whether they understood or agreed with everything or not, I would speak up about the issues that were most important to me.

"It's an organization that helps kids stay out of trouble using hip-hop," I began to explain when my dad asked about my life.

Up until that point, dinner with him and my brother was going smoothly. We were on our second bottle of wine, and had been laughing and talking, but when I started describing

265

K'Arma and hip-hop, things toned down a little. A look of confusion came over their faces.

"Amber, you're still a white girl! Or did you forget that out there in California?" TJ said.

"TJ, it doesn't have to do with the fact that I'm white. Hip-hop is universal! K'Arma is for all people!"

"I just don't understand you. What's so wrong with being white?" TJ blasted back.

"Just forget it, TJ. I don't want to talk about this anymore!" I could feel tears bubbling up in my eyes, and I did not want to cry. My arms crossed, I slouched down in my chair.

"Amber, you gotta lighten up," Dad said. "You're too serious. You're not going to get your way in life like that."

"People are dying every day, Dad, and you want me to tell a joke?" I got up and went to the bathroom. When I came back to the table, another topic was being discussed. I joined the conversation as if nothing had happened. That was how we usually dealt with difficult conversations. We just made them go away.

Later that night, I went over to Juan's new house to hang out. It was just the two of us.

"You want something to drink, Corazón?"

"You got some Night Train, dog?" We both started laughing. "Nah, for real, what you got for me?"

"We can go old school with some Ol' E, or we can be more adult like and drink a chilled bottle of white wine—you pick."

"I'm feeling like a grown-up tonight, let's do the white."

Juan poured us two glasses of wine and we sat on the couch in his spacious living room. I was impressed with his nice house. He had framed graffiti murals on the walls.

"So Juan, what's up with your life now? How'd you get this house, man?"

"Hold up; before we start philosophizing I got to put on

something from our past." He got up and soon enough N.W.A. bounced off the walls. "You remember that lady photographer that used to follow me around, taking pix of all my pieces?"

"Yep, I remember her, vaguely."

"We kinda became cool. I mean, she was all right, for an older white lady. So right after you bounced for college, a big article came out in the *Rocky Mountain News* about street art featuring three of my pieces. This business guy really liked my style, so he contacted the photographer, and she told him where to find me. He tracked me down after I got out and asked me if I would take him out painting with me."

"Word? That's crazy, Juancito. Yo, pour me some more wine, this story is getting good."

Juan nabbed the bottle from the coffee table and filled up my glass.

"Hell yeah! Of course I was surprised as all hell that this old white guy wanted to go bombin', but I said fuck it. So we went one night and I did a crazy burner, and he said, 'Juan, my boy, you have a job with me, if you want it.'"

"What did he do?"

"He was the CEO of a graphic design company. So he brought me in as, like, an assistant. Everyone in the company loved me—and they got to see my art. Six months later I got promoted, and now I do artwork for their website and stuff. See, I got my own business card and everything." Juan pulled a card out of his wallet and handed it to me.

"Damn, dude, that is so cool! I'm so proud of you!"

He looked at me with a half grin that quickly turned into a grimace. "I'm just lucky I made it out." I knew he was thinking of all the others that didn't.

"Let's not think about that right now," I said, gently massaging his neck. "I want to celebrate your victory."

"Victory?"

"Yes, Juan. Victory over the odds. You beat 'em. Let's drink to that."

We sat close to each other the rest of the night, reminiscing. Despite all the madness, drugs, violence, and crime, we were here now. There was an air of intimacy, possibility, and evolution.

Journal Entry

I just got back from visiting Juan. I am filled with so many feelings. Longing, desire, the past. I don't even know why. As I sat with Juan I realized something. Despite the fact that both he and I "survived" our gangbangin' experience, I know that it was way easier for me to get out than Juan, than all of the 30s. I think I always knew that, but didn't want to accept it—because I knew it had everything to do with me being white. I felt a sweeping wave of guilt remembering the times we all got busted and everyone but me went to jail. When the cops tried to "save" me, not beat me like they did to Juan. My whiteness protected me in so many ways. My decisions to be reckless in all areas of my life didn't get me so much as a time-out, whereas my friends got life sentences. My games were their lives. And like I learned from my mentor Professor Brown, the historical legacy of white people is that when shit gets hot we get out of the pan. Because we have that option—other people don't.

The day finally came to see Omar. I decided not to tell my mom, not out of a desire to deceive her, but to protect her feelings. We were so close now, if I brought this up, it would just bring back memories of a horrible period in our lives. I wanted to preserve her sense of peace.

I picked out my outfit the night before, knowing I had to

leave early Saturday morning. The prison had a very strict dress code, so I planned carefully. I had plenty of time to think about the upcoming visit. What would Omar be like? Would we still feel the love when we sat next to each other?

The four-hour drive flew by. After parking and checking my appearance in the mirror, I walked to the main entrance. I felt good about myself. I wore a white fitted skirt that was a little long for my taste, but it had to be to my knees because of the dress code. At least Omar would be able to catch a feel of my skin. I knew he would like that. I also wore a cute snug top that accented my chest without showing my cleavage, another rule. My hair was long, almost to my ass, and I let it loose.

As soon as I walked in, the guards scowled at me. They made their contempt of us visitors of "criminals" crystal clear. To them we were just as bad, just as savage. Why else would we be associated with the prisoners they so detested?

"I can tell you right now to just turn right around and go home," said the security guard by the metal detector. I turned around to see if someone was behind me, but I was the only one standing there.

"Excuse me?" I said.

"You heard me, turn around and go. You're not visiting anyone in that getup," he said to me, and then turned chuckling to the heavyset black female security guard who was standing next to him. "They think they can get fresh in here, Gracie, but not on my watch."

"Um-hum." She nodded at him.

"Excuse me, sir, but my skirt is to my knees, just as the person I spoke to about the visit explained to me." My heart was beating fast. I was trying to control my breathing and maintain my composure.

"Well, whoever you talked to was mistaken. No skirts allowed. Period. Now good day." I started to panic.

"But I just drove four hours to get here," I stammered. "You have to let me in. We set this visit up a month ago . . . he's waiting for me!"

"Excuse me?" He turned sharply and stared me down. "I don't *have* to do anything, miss! I'm in charge here, not you! Now, I do not want to repeat myself. Go home!"

I looked at the female guard for help, but she wouldn't even look at me. I turned and pushed the door open, stumbling into the parking lot, bumping right into a woman.

"I'm sorry," I said, wiping the tears from my eyes.

"No problem, young lady," she said. "Are you okay?"

"Yes, I mean, no, not really. They won't let me in to see my boyfriend. I drove four hours. I don't even live in Colorado, I'm just visiting," I blabbed.

"Slow down, honey. Just breathe for a moment." She put her arm around my shoulder. "I come here to see my son every week, and I know how the guards are—not too friendly," she said. I looked into her kind face. She was an older white woman, the beginning signs of wrinkles around her eyes. "Let me see if I can help. Come with me to my car."

We walked through the parking lot to an old beat-up car. She smiled apologetically. "All my spare money goes to my son's commissary," she explained, "and the collect calls, well, you must know how much they cost, being three dollars a minute and all. Let's see what I have in this old trunk." She started digging around a bunch of bags, pulling out clothes and smelling them.

"I collect clothes from family and friends and sell them at flea markets. The extra cash helps keep away the collectors." She smiled. "Here, try these, I think they might work." She handed me the ugliest pants I had ever seen. "I'm sorry, dear, you look so beautiful in that skirt, but if you want to see your friend, I suppose you don't have much of a choice. You can change in the car."

I knew I had to put my pride and ego aside so that I could see my man. I sat in the front seat and quickly slid my skirt off, then put the ugly pea green pants on. They were baggy on me, but they had to do. The woman bent down and started rolling up the legs so that I wouldn't trip.

"Thank you," I said with relief. "Thank you so much for helping. I don't know what I would have done."

"Sure, dear. Please, it's nothing. Now let's walk in together, because they know me here. I'll help smooth things over." I put my skirt in my bag and walked with her back to face the security guards.

When they saw us, they looked at each other and shook their heads. The guy looked at me with disgust the whole time I was being frisked and led through the metal detectors. Finally I was free to sit in the waiting room until I was called to see Omar. I mouthed "thank you" to the kind woman who helped me. "Don't worry about the pants, you can have them!" she called after me.

Ten minutes later I was sitting next to Omar. As I told him what happened, I could see the muscles in his jaw start tensing up. At every turn our love was being tested. Why should today be different? But we let go of all the negativity, holding on to what we knew was true in this moment—us. We didn't speak of the now, which neither of us had any control over. We spoke of the future, of when he got out. The things we could do, where we could live.

"I'll write articles, and you can do a poem and illustrate them," I said, "just like what we did with that underground hip-hop magazine. Were your homies surprised that you were published?"

"What are you talkin' about?" He looked confused.

"The magazine article, remember? They published it! I sent it to you months ago!" Omar had written me a letter that captured perfectly what prison life was like on the real. I thought it would be good for young people on the outside to know what it was really like on lockdown, instead of the glamorous thug life presented in certain songs and videos. I wanted Omar's words to be a warning to those dabbling in crime to get out before everything was taken away.

Omar had a look of hatred on his face.

"They never gave it to me. Now I know what the notice was," he said in a low voice. "I got a notice saying they had confiscated my mail because it contained 'material unsuitable for an inmate.' When I asked if I could at least know who the sender was, they laughed in my face, fuckin' pigs." Omar started squeezing both of his hands into fists, opening and closing them. "They don't want me to accomplish nothin'," he continued. "Them guards want me to think I can't do nothin' but be locked up. They even try and get me outta my college program, tellin' me I gotta work the day shift for seven cents an hour instead of gettin' an education so I can make something of myself." Omar's jaw clenched up again. Our visit was slowly dissolving into despair.

I remembered back when we were driving to Carmen's party, and we were talking about our dreams and our future. Things seemed so hard back then, but they were nothing compared to this. Who would've known we'd be sitting here, years later, talking about the same thing, but in a totally different world. I knew I needed to lift his mood, take his mind off of his current reality and get him dreaming again.

I glanced around to see where the guards were, and when the one closest to us turned his back for a moment, I grabbed Omar's face and put my lips to his, urgently swirling my tongue with his. I rubbed my hand up his inner thigh to his dick, trying to give him a moment of pleasure.

The shrill whistle made me jump, "No touching!" The guard was quickly approaching as I pulled away from Omar.

"Shit," I said. "Is he gonna make me leave?"

"Hold up, baby, let me talk to him, I know this guard," he said as he stood up, making an adjustment to his pants. The guard approached us, talking into his walkie-talkie. Other visitors and inmates were quietly watching us now, waiting to see what would happen.

"What the hell is going on here? You've been here long enough to know the rules. Tell your little friend here good-bye." The guard looked around, noticing that he was being watched.

"Excuse me, sir. I'd really appreciate it if you give me another chance. Maybe you recall the favor I did for you last week? This is a perfect time for you to repay that favor, we can call it even." Omar stared at the guard, who started fiddling with his walkie-talkie, looking nervous.

"Twenty minutes," he said, and walked away.

I exhaled with relief, and turned to Omar. "How'd you do that?"

"I've learned how to work the system," Omar said, looking off into the distance. "It's all about getting dirt on the guards, holding your own with the dudes in here, and trying to stay sane." He felt so far away from me right now.

"So where *do* you want to live, baby?" I asked lightly. "Do you wanna come to Cali with me? Or we could go somewhere else."

Omar turned his attention back to me, and sat there, silent, just looking at me. I smiled at him, it took everything I had to resist touching him again.

"I will go wherever you want to. All I care is that I'm with you, Amber. Get a good job, get you pregnant so you can raise our babies, and chill. That's all I'm looking for," he said. Then he started getting excited, telling me about how he was progressing with his poetry and art, and how he was finishing up his college degree, no matter what.

"Baby, I'm gonna take care of you when I get out, I promise. I'm working toward our future," he said, taking my hand.

A loudspeaker crackled, announcing the end of the visiting time. I got a desperate feeling in my heart. There were a million thoughts pushing through my mind, all the things I still wanted to say to this man. But now the same guard was walking toward us, and all the other visitors were saying good-bye and heading to the exit.

"Let's go," the guard said, and waited for Omar to come with him.

"Omar, take care of yourself."

"I will, baby. Just please, try and hold on."

He looked down. I knew how hard this was for him, with his life and his freedom in the hands of people who had a general disdain for everyone in this prison. I knew this from his letters, which spoke of court hearing after court hearing, new court appointed lawyers promising to get him out, all to no avail. We never talked about that night, that night that changed both his life and mine forever.

"Let's go!" The guard's voice became louder. Omar got up and said good-bye, while the guard put his hand on his arm, leading him away.

I left in a haze. It wasn't until I was driving away that the tears started. I felt so cheated. I had lost more than an hour dealing with the dress-code drama, which meant we'd only had forty-five minutes with each other. There was so much yet to be said between us.

All I had was another memory to hold on to.

Thirty-Three

My last weekend in Denver before going back to LA, Lil D called.

"Party? I don't know about all that, Lil D," I said over the phone. "I want to see some people, but I don't need to see everyone." The truth was that things had changed for me. My life was so different now. Plus, less and less people knew who I was. I didn't trust them and they didn't trust me.

"Come on, cuzz, I been waitin' to see you! Just come through for a minute. You and I can chill out in your car, talk 'n shit, and then you can bounce."

"Okay, Lil D. I'll come through, but I ain't gonna hang out long," I warned him. I had to see my little bro before I bounced back to Cali. I'd tried to hook up with him earlier in my visit, but it hadn't worked out. I wanted to tell him things about me and my new life. I wanted to tell him he had to get out.

I called Juan up. "Yo, homie, come with me to the hood for

a Crip reunion." I halfway joked. "I just got off the phone with Lil D and I'ma head down there to say what's up."

"Are you fuckin' crazy, Amber?" Juan asked. "Hell no I ain't going! I got a job, man, a life. We just talked about this in my crib the other night, remember?"

"All right Juan, you don't hafta come."

"And you shouldn't go. Don't you get it? Your Crip pass done been revoked. You can't go back—who's gonna protect you?"

"Lil D is there, and I'm sure I'll know some other folks. I just want to see Lil D."

"Plus a whole bunch of Crips that ain't never seen you before. Now how's that gonna look, a blond white girl walkin' up to a Crip party with *nobody*? That's just insane. You been in the sun too much out there, girl."

"Brunette, Juan, I don't have blond hair! I'm just gonna go down there, drink a beer, say what's up, and then I'm out!" In my head I knew Juan was right, but I didn't want to admit it. "Listen, Juan, I don't want Lil D to think that just 'cause I went to college I'm not cool with him anymore. I don't want him to think I'm acting like I'm too good for him now."

"Girl, nobody's worried about you! You are not that important to them," he said.

"I—"

"No, Amber, *listen*! You have got to move on! This is not your world anymore. I don't even think it was *ever* your world."

"What the fuck is that supposed to mean?"

Juan exhaled. "Amber, you know what I mean. If I hadn't brought you into that whole life you woulda been a regular-ass white girl."

"Dude, that's fucked up."

"I don't even know why we're arguing right now. I don't want to get into this with you—"

"You the one who brought it up, Juan."

"Look, Amber, I just don't want you to go. That's it, okay? It's not a good idea."

"Juan, I appreciate that but I don't need a mentor anymore." I hung up. *Fuck that!* I can't believe he just said all that shit to me!

I went into my room and started getting dressed. I was pissed now, all these feelings coming up about the past, about who I was. Juan was calling into question everything I had been and done all the years we kicked it together in Denver. What right did he have to talk to me like that? My head was just filled with this intense buzzing.

Ten minutes later I was out the door.

Halfway there I started getting nervous, replaying my phone conversation with Juan in my head. But then I focused on Lil D. I really wanted to see my little bro and I knew he would never let anything happen to me.

I got to the block where Lil D had told me to go. I spotted the house immediately because there were a lot of people hanging out on the front porch, and loud music. I parked the car and sat there, my eyes searching for Lil D. As I scanned the crowd I realized that I didn't recognize a single person. Maybe this *was* a mistake.

"Amber!" I jumped, scared shitless. Lil D was tapping on the window of the car, laughing.

"Shit, Lil D, you freaked me out!" I said, catching my breath.

He walked around to my side. "Come on, let's go inside and get a drink, sis!" I could tell that Lil D was drunk; he was slurring and stumbling all over the place. "Follow me."

I walked with Lil D up to the house and across the crowded porch. Everyone was getting their party on, dancing and drinking. I caught some glances as I walked in, but Lil D was holding my arm, pulling me forward. My gut was telling me to turn around and go home.

"Rodney and T-Dog are here somewhere, but I ain't seen them for a minute," he said. "Yo, cuzz, get me some of the Night Train," he yelled at a young kid standing by the kitchen counter. There were liquor bottles everywhere.

I started hittin' the Night Train, talking with Lil D as we reminisced about old times—robberies, parties, cops. We were both laughing when he turned to me, and put his hand on my shoulder. "Amber, sis, I know I'm a little drunk, but I want you to know, you the closest thing I've ever had to a sister." He grabbed me and pulled me tight. He wasn't really little anymore. He was a big good-looking guy. I remembered back to the night of my initiation, when his sweet thirteen-year-old self stopped Ray-Ray and T-Dog from fighting. He was always trying to protect people in his crew. That was his only family. I started getting emotional, and while he was hugging me I looked up, trying to keep my tears from spilling out.

"Lil D—"

"*Slobs! Slobs!* Get your gats, y'all, come on!"

Lil D pulled away as someone in the front of the house started yelling. Some girls started screaming and there was crazy commotion. Lil D was running toward the door and I was grabbing him, trying to hold on.

"Don't go, Lil D, don't go out there!" He kept moving and slipped away, leaving me with only his jacket in my hands.

Then I heard shots.

Shots and screams. Everyone running every which way. I stood there, a bottle of Night Train in one hand, Lil D's coat in another.

"Yo! They shot 'em, they shot 'em!" someone yelled. I heard the screech of car wheels spinning out, and then more shots.

My heart pounded as I ran to the door. People were all over the place, hollering. I heard sirens in the distance, their sound moving toward us. There was a crowd by the street. I pushed my way through. It took me a minute to see who was lying bloody and still on the ground. When I finally saw the smooth, young face, my heart cracked wide open.

I don't remember the drive home. When I got there, I went to the basement so that my mom couldn't hear me and called Juan.

"You were right, Juan. You were right," I sobbed. "They got Lil D. He's dead." I cried on the phone with him for hours. It was as if I was grieving not just for Lil D, but for everything. For the magnitude of loss for us all: loss of time with Juan locked up, loss of the potential of all things with Omar; mourning the years of my damaged relationship with my family; and Lil D. *Lil D.* My little bro. Why was he born into a life full of pain, without the foundation that he needed? Who was to say what could have become of him? Juan tried long and hard that night, but his words of comfort had no place to land in my body.

I had to leave the very next day for LA.

Thirty-Four

The first couple of weeks I was in a fog. Then shock turned to devastation. The image of Lil D's bloody body kept replaying in my mind, and at night in my dreams. His last words to me echoed in my ears.

Slowly, I began to realize why I wanted so badly to hang on to my relationship with the Crips, even after moving to LA. I had claimed Rollin' 30s as part of me, part of my identity. Just like my graffiti crew, which in many ways was lost to me when Juan got locked up. And who was I, really, without my crews?

That's what I needed to find out, and I hadn't wanted to.

When I got home from work, Sasha was on the phone cursing out her boyfriend. "You ain't gonna see your daughter, you sorry-ass excuse of a man!" Sasha was planning on taking me out for dinner that night to try to cheer me up. Instead, we commiserated the rest of the night together.

The next morning I woke up to loud voices arguing. I got

up and went into the living room. Terrance was standing in the room with Macala in his arms. I could tell he just got off the night shift at the gas station because he still had his work shirt on.

"Put down the baby, Terrance," Sasha said.

"This is my daughter too, and you ain't gonna keep her from me, if that's what you're thinking. You're just tryin' to get back at me." He opened the door and began to walk out. Sasha, in her pajamas, started toward him.

"Give me my baby, motherfucker. Give her to me now! I'll call the police!" She was grabbing his arm, but he kept walking toward the elevator.

I ran after both of them.

Macala had started crying, but Terrance didn't care. "Stop it y'all, you're scaring the baby." He got to the elevator and pushed the button and Sasha went crazy. She started pulling the baby from Terrance, but he wouldn't let go of her. Macala was screaming her lungs out.

"You guys are going to hurt the baby!" I yelled. "Give me the baby now. You need to settle this without her. Look what you're doing!"

But they weren't listening to me.

"I'm going to call the police right now!" I said.

"Chill out, just chill the fuck out!" Terrance yelled at us.

"Just give Amber the baby, Terrance!" I could hear the desperation in Sasha's voice. She backed away a little, to give him space. Terrance handed the crying baby over to me and I ran back to our apartment, before anyone could change their minds.

When I got back in, I cuddled with Macala, and gave her the pacifier. She finally calmed down and fell asleep, exhausted from her morning ordeal. Sasha didn't come back for a while.

I wasn't worried about her, because their arguments lasted a while. When she did come back, she took the baby from me.

"I just need to be alone for a while, to think," she said, and went into her room and closed the door.

We didn't talk about it for days. My mind was still preoccupied with Lil D, and she didn't bring the incident up. I walked in the house one day and found Terrance there, with Sasha on his lap. They were laughing and flirting, obviously back together.

I mumbled, "What's up," and went into my room and shut the door. How the fuck could she do this? After he left that afternoon, she came into my room.

"What's your problem?" she demanded.

"I can't believe you're back together with him. What's it gonna take for you to see he's ruining your life?"

"You know what, Amber, we love each other. We have a baby together, and we want to make this work! You have no right to tell me who I should and shouldn't be with! You don't know what it's like to have a daughter with someone. We are connected—forever!"

"But you guys fight every fucking week! What kind of love is that?"

"Obviously a kind you just can't understand!" She walked out and slammed the door behind her.

A silent tension swept over our house. Terrance would come and go. I kept myself busier than usual, picking up extra shifts at the shelter so I wouldn't have to come home, hanging out more at Empress and Ajaya's. Sasha didn't even keep her ritual of making us go grocery shopping every Sunday afternoon, which we had been doing for the past four years. I was miserable, and felt like my life was crumbling around me.

I talked to Empress about it and she told me I needed to let Sasha live her life. I knew she was right, but it was eating me up inside. The last time they fought it was because of another "possible" infidelity of Terrance's. How could Sasha put up with that? And all he put her through during her pregnancy, night after night alone, crying, fighting over the phone. I just couldn't be cool with it. I loved her too much.

One afternoon we just started talking about how we were both feeling.

"I just can't go on like this anymore, Sasha," I said. "I feel like I'm watching you throw your life away on this relationship. How many times are you going to break up and get back together with this guy?"

"You don't know the love that he and I have, and you can't feel what I feel. I need to live *my* life, not the one you want me to live!"

"You're my sister—I can't sit by and watch this happen. I feel like you're a dope fiend, and Terrance is the crack." Silence filled the room. The phone rang, but neither of us got up to get it. "I can't watch you become a crackhead, I just can't."

"Well, I'm gonna move in with Terrance's family."

"Cool. I'll get my own spot," and from there the divorce proceedings began. Furniture, pots and pans, sheets. We had been together for so long. There was serious history to separate. I felt like I was losing a soul mate.

I found a place in downtown LA not far from where we had been living. Yvette came up from San Diego to help me move. Amara called when she found out what happened. We hadn't seen much of each other since we graduated. She was busy with her new job at a talent agency.

Desperation was ruling me. Living by myself for the first time ever, with nothing to cling to except horrible memories and letters from a man I might never get to be with. I knew I needed to focus on K'Arma, which was so instrumental in helping kids, but even that brought me despair. How was it that I could help kids in LA get out of gangs, but watch my own brother, Lil D, perish from bangin'? I never felt so discouraged in all my life.

Just when my world was falling apart, Prophet called. He invited me to his house in San Jose for the weekend to view some new material he'd received.

Driving to his house, I knew it was critical to lift myself out of my depression. I wasn't doing anything positive; Prof. Brown's words came into my mind: "If you're not part of the solution, you're part of the problem."

When I arrived, Prophet greeted me with a beautiful bouquet of flowers.

"This is in recognition of all your hard work and dedication to this organization."

"Wow, thank you, Prophet, that is so nice of you," I said, breathing in the fragrance.

"Come on, we have a lot of work to do."

I followed him into his house and put my bags in the guest room. After unpacking, I started looking through the bookcase and noticed a volume on the Black Panthers. It reminded me of my boss at the youth organization, Mr. Jeffreys, who used to be a member. He was an elder who understood and respected the power of hip-hop culture. He experienced firsthand how this culture was able to bring people together for a common vision. Empress and I were working toward starting a hip-hop community center, and he was helping us navigate the nonprofit world.

And now here I was, studying under another incredible leader. I am so lucky, I thought. I closed my eyes for a moment, breathing in deeply. I'm gonna be okay.

"Come on, let's eat dinner before we start working," Prophet yelled to me.

I gotta be okay, 'cause I got work to do.

The first night we stayed up late, reviewing footage of documentaries covering everything from microchips implanted into inmates to the role of government in sanctioning covert operations destabilizing the Civil Rights movement.

"The reason this is critical, Corazón, is so we can learn from the techniques used in other movements in order to ascertain the possible tactics against freedom-fighting people today," he explained. "We must understand the enemy in order to destroy them."

The next day was spent running around, checking on specific chapters, meeting with other Originals to discuss progress, and speaking on a radio show. Even though he was the star guest on the show, he gave me an opportunity to talk about what was happening with hip-hop. My first time on the radio! I left feeling important, like what I was doing *mattered*.

When we finally got home, Prophet suggested that I relax while he cooked me dinner. "You can play with my record collection, or watch TV, or read. You can even take a bath, whatever you'd like," he said as he walked into the kitchen.

"Cool, thanks, Prophet. Today was so incredible, I love coming up here; building, learning, working. It feels really good."

Prophet came out of the kitchen, holding a pan in his hand. "Sis, you can come up here as much as you'd like. Consider this your home." He stood there for a while, watching me.

"Thank you, seriously. You don't know how much that means to me right now." I went upstairs to shower and change clothes.

I came down an hour later, feeling refreshed and happy. Whatever he was cooking smelled delicious. He had set the dining room table, complete with candles and the flowers he had bought me in a vase. It looked beautiful, and, actually, a little romantic. This must be what it's like to be with an older man.

"Dinner is served," Prophet announced. He poured me a glass of white wine and served me chicken marsala, risotto, and salad. We talked about K'Arma, and the movement, and who my favorite artists were. At one point he asked me how I was doing.

"I'm fine," I replied, trying to shake free Lil D's image that popped in my head.

"No, Corazón, how are you *really* doing? I could tell you were unhappy when I spoke to you last. That's one of the reasons I asked you to come up. I was concerned."

"I've just been going through some hard times, Prophet. Things haven't been easy for me lately." I finished off my first glass of wine, and he poured me another.

"Come on, Corazón, let's go into the living room." We took our wine and sat down on the beige leather couch. "Now, back to our conversation. Can you share with me what triggered this?" he asked, and I found myself opening up, telling him everything. About Lil D, my realizations, my emptiness.

He listened for a long time before he responded. He began philosophizing about racism and violence in our communities. He talked about the rise in gangs, and how that was the very reason he felt called to this work, to this organization.

"Ultimately, Corazón, it's about bringing people together. Can you imagine what that unity—black, brown, and white, all together, serving one purpose—could accomplish in this country, in this world?"

"It's what I've always dreamed of," I murmured, thinking about my attempts to bring people together in Denver; even my decision to get down with the Crips.

"We are the future—it is *our* destiny to ensure its success."

Yes, I thought. K'Arma can make this happen, and I will be part of it; I will be part of the solution! My body was tingling, and I was caught up in his charisma.

"Our role as leaders is to model new possibilities through our life examples. We need to show our people that love can exist between black and white," he said. His words resonated as truth. After all, it was my story.

The times I felt most at peace was when I was with people who had plenty of differences, but one great commonality: their ability to see beyond the surface, beyond black and white. The place where I experienced that peace was in the hip-hop community—where our love of hip-hop superseded societal barriers. That's why I was so drawn to K'Arma and its principles, its power to unite.

I thought back to our park jams, our events with thousands of young people showing up, with nothing but love and respect. White kids, Mexicans, Filipinos, black kids—all together—dancing, freestylin', DJin', just hanging out appreciating the art and culture of them, of us, of hip-hop.

"Which is why it is so critical for you to be *my* queen. Together, Corazón, my heart, we will make history."

I thought that maybe I heard wrong, but he continued on. "We are meant to be together, beautiful one. Our relationship will reflect the peace and harmony that we are all striving for. Our partnership will create unity between the races."

I started shaking my head, trying to make sense of exactly what he was asking of me. "I don't know what to say." He resumed, saying together we could change things, and even keep people like Lil D from dying.

He said it was our ultimate purpose.

He kept talking. Then he touched my arm. He kept talking. Then he touched my face. He kept talking.

I shook my head no, no, no. Not like this! Not through manipulation of the most precious thing in my life right now—my life calling.

My mind began flipping through my history with men, the deception, the pain, the betrayals—from Jamal, and the cops who made me feel wrong for loving; to Drew, who betrayed the memories of our love; even to Omar. Deep down I blamed him for not being able to get out before it was too late, before he was lost to me.

Prophet put his hand on my waist and pulled me closer. I cried, silently.

"Shhh," he whispered in my ear, "it's what's right." He put his lips to mine. Soft. He parted my lips with his tongue. I tasted the salt from my tears, I felt his tongue, gently, gently, in my mouth. I felt his body next to mine. My mind flashed to the radio show today, all the leaders I met, all the things that could be possible if I gave in, if I just submitted.

His hand traveled from my waist to underneath my shirt, caressing me as he continued kissing me. No. This is not what I want. No. This is not who I want. I put my hands to his chest and firmly pushed him away. I turned my face away, so he couldn't kiss me anymore.

"Yes, let's not do this here. Let's go to my bedroom," he said.

"I can't do this," I said quietly. "I just can't."

"Why? What are you afraid of?" He leaned back in, kissing me, kissing me.

"No, Prophet, please. Stop."

He pulled back, and looked at me. "Do you need more time?" he asked. "We can take it slow." His placed his hand on my leg, moving it slowly to my inner thigh.

"No, I don't need more time. What I need is a mentor, which is what I thought you were!" I got up from the couch. "I don't want this, Prophet."

"So why did you come here for the weekend? You spend all this time with me on the phone, at my place, talking to me about personal things. Come on, I felt you respond when we kissed. Your body doesn't lie, Corazón. You might, but your body doesn't."

How could he turn this on me, like I was the one initiating this? "I'm going upstairs," I said.

"Don't go. We need to talk."

I hesitated, and he began talking, but his voice was different, authoritative; similar to the voice I heard earlier that day when he reprimanded an Original for how he handled a situation.

"There could be serious consequences to your decision."

"What do you mean?"

He was silent.

I felt sick to my stomach. I felt ill equipped to deal with what was happening, and so very, very alone.

"What say you?" he asked.

He knew from the look on my face that I wouldn't even consider it.

I got my stuff together and left that night. Driving in the dark to my lonely house, I thought about how my life had changed so unexpectedly once again. I knew that my role in K'Arma would never be the same, but I had no idea what Prophet was about to set in motion.

The impact was sinister and immediate. My pager was blowin' up with 911 calls the following day. An emergency meeting was called.

"Corazón, you have some explaining to do," Slim said, while Scientific and the others eyed me suspiciously. We were at fellow member and friend KOS's loft downtown. It seemed like yesterday that we'd held one of our first meetings here, with graff pieces on the walls, KOS djing, mc ciphers flowing. Now the only thing going down was my trial. Anger kept my mouth from opening.

"We've been told you were runnin' your mouth about many members of this chapter. And on top of that, we heard that you're fattening your pockets from all of our events." Slim was pacing back and forth, making me uneasy. I remembered the first time I met him, and what he had threatened to do if we hurt K'Arma.

"Look," I said, "everything that you are hearing is a lie. You know I love this chapter. I've dedicated my life to it. What about the K'Arma youth chapter? What about the fund-raisers? The park jams? Come on man, all I do is work for this chapter. Don't believe the hype; it's all a lie."

"And why would O.G.s be lying to us? Why?" Slim asked.

I shut my mouth. The truth, at this point, was not an option.

Scientific had been quiet the whole time. "We are going to review your seat on the Council. We need answers. This is causing a lot of division." He glanced at me with a pained look. "We took a chance on you, Corazón, when everything was against you."

Even though he didn't say it, I knew what he was talking about. I wasn't a native of LA, I was a woman, and I was white. I wondered if I could get through this and still be part of K'Arma.

I left the meeting depleted and unsure of my next move.

"We'll get through this, Amber," Empress said. "They can't do this to you, we'll prove them wrong." All of my girls were behind me, and vowed to support me.

But the deadliest rumor was yet to come.

I got the call the following week.

"You must leave the organization at once," Slim said over the phone. "I should have known it all along. You had us fooled, Corazón, but now the truth has come out."

"About what, exactly? Making money off of y'all? That's just bullshit!"

"I don't even care about that anymore," he said. And then he told me what was being circulated about me.

"So what do you have to say for yourself?"

"I am not FBI," I answered. But in that moment, I knew that nothing I said to him would make him believe me.

When I got off the phone, I drove over to Empress's house, feeling frantic. She was at home, cooking dinner.

"What's wrong, Amber?" she asked immediately.

I sat down on her couch. "You got anything to drink?" I asked. "Like, something hard."

"Of course, baby, I got some Southern Comfort. Lemme get you a shot." She walked into the kitchen, returning with my drink. I grabbed it and threw it back, slamming the shot glass on the coffee table. Empress sat next to me and put her hand on my leg.

"Things were bad before this, but now"—I looked at her, tears of anger beginning to pool in my eyes—"it's fuckin' over, man. I'm done."

"What happened? Did Slim call another meeting?"

"No. It's way worse. Somebody is accusing me of being FBI, an undercover agent, out to destroy K'Arma." Empress held me and just let me cry.

"Fuck that man," she said, "our peeps *will not* believe that bullshit!"

"Empress, look where we're at—everybody is questioning us, me. And now this? No, for real, it's over." Up until this point I hadn't told Empress about Prophet. I didn't tell anybody about that, partly because I felt stupid, like I walked into a trap, and partly because I *had* felt so special, like the chosen one. I realized how all these years I really suffered from thinking I was not good enough for anyone—not my dad, not the

292   Love

Crips, not to be Juan's protégée or Jamal's girl. The feeling had gotten even stronger in college, and then I just kinda got used to it. And always, underneath everything, I felt a kind of homelessness, somewhere between black and white, not quite belonging anywhere.

I knew that the rumor was able to stick because of my white skin and the history behind it. I understood, really understood, that no matter what I did with my life, I would always be white.

Finally I told Empress what happened the weekend at Prophet's.

We talked for a long time about what to do. As we talked, Empress's phone started ringing. She took calls in her bedroom, and I could tell it was all about me and the lie. I heard her arguing for me with different people, and I was grateful for that, even though I knew my fate with K'Arma was sealed.

When Empress came back to sit with me, she was upset. "I'm worried, girl. The rumor, it's spread—people are out of control, man. They feel betrayed, and they want to do something about it. I think you should stay here tonight. Maybe even for a while."

I went back to my place to get some clothes. I ran in, quickly got out my suitcase, and packed as much shit as I could. I locked up my apartment and went to stay with Empress.

Thirty-Five

The next week I spent at Empress's, trying to figure out what to do. In the midst of all the drama, I ran into Sasha at a work meeting for the youth organization. We hadn't spoken since I had moved out months before. I asked about Macala. We spoke for about ten minutes and decided to schedule a lunch date that week.

I had mixed feelings as I walked into the diner to meet Sasha. But we immediately got down to business, which is one of the things I admire about her. Beating around the bush was never her style.

"Amber, I can't go on living my life for other people. I am trying to have a family, and I can't say if everything is going to work out or not, but I have to try. I need you to understand that."

"I hear you, Sasha, and I know that I don't have a baby, so some of the things that you're going through I can't fully understand. But it was too hard to watch you get hurt over and over again; I just couldn't take it anymore. It was like we could talk about everything *except* what was most important, which was your relationship."

"'Cause you can't understand what goes on between us, and this isn't about you, Amber. It's about *me.*"

I felt like a bomb had been dropped on me. Was I being selfish? Judgmental? All this time I felt like I was trying to be a real friend to Sasha, but maybe what being a real friend means is letting go. Being supportive, but at the same time allowing her to go through her own process and come out with her own conclusions. What other situations was I trying to be a savior in?

"I'm sorry, Sasha." My eyes filled with tears, and I looked down.

"You know you're my soul sister, right?" Sasha reached across the table and grabbed my hands. When I looked up she was crying too.

"So are we gonna get back together?" We both started cracking up. "I mean, look at us, we look like a couple—all cryin' and shit, holding hands." We always joked we were secretly married, because Sasha always acted like my man.

The laughter helped. We both released the pain and sorrow we had been carrying around since we separated. It felt good to understand what had happened between us, and how we could change our friendship to one that was healthier. We talked about so much that day; she filled me in on being a mother, I told her I was done with K'Arma. We parted drained but happy, knowing that our friendship would steadily grow and flourish once again.

The reconciliation with Sasha brought some grounding into my life, but also raised a lot of questions for me about *me.* I began reviewing my relationships through a new lens, seeing a part of me that I hadn't wanted to see. It reminded me of a time during one of my Africana Studies classes when an argument had erupted; I tried to clear up something between a black student and a white student, and the black student turned to me and said, "Oh, so you're the great white hope now?" The signs of my own privilege had been there all along, I had not been ready to accept them. It was tied too much to my identity for me to see it.

For the next two weeks, everywhere I went I had to defend myself. I felt labeled for life. It became reminiscent of past struggles I was trying to put behind me.

LA could hold me no longer.

I had to evolve into the activist I knew I could be. My history here wasn't going to allow for that.

Once I decided it was time to go, I wasn't quite sure where to go and how to make it happen. Luckily, it developed organically.

The same week I decided it was time for me to go, I shared my plans with my boss at the shelter, Mr. Jeffreys. He planted a seed in my head about moving to New York. But with no real money, no place to stay out there, and, of course, no job, I didn't know if that was realistic.

The following week, he asked me to accompany him to a meeting about homelessness. I thought it odd because it was for directors, so I asked him why. "I want you to meet some really important folks. Don't worry, you'll understand."

I trusted him. That night changed my life forever.

He introduced me as Corazón, which surprised me, given that it was a "professional" meeting. That night I met the founders of a school in Brooklyn that focused on social justice, and even used hip-hop in the classroom. After talking with the founder, a former Young Lord, and Diego, a young poet and teacher, they told me that a spot was waiting for someone like me. "Call us when you arrive. You will have a new home to do your work." I was walking on air.

Ajaya and Empress took me in, so I gave up my apartment and moved all my stuff there and slept on the couch.

I was still working with young people and my homeboy hooked me up with a second job, working the door at a hip-hop club. I worked all day, ran home, showered, put on my heels and lipstick, and off to work at the club.

Sometimes I doubted myself. When I left Denver for Cali, I was running away from all my problems, but this time was different. I wasn't starting over; I was starting better.

When the time came, saying good-bye was hard.

"Girl, I ain't even worried about it. We'll be together again soon, the universe will see to that. We have something too good to be broken by distance," Ajaya said, hugging me tight. My favorite girls were all there to see me off. Yvette even drove up from San Diego to say good-bye.

"Who knows, maybe we'll follow you to New York," Empress said with a teary smile. "Fo' real, girl, I'm gonna miss you. We've known each other since we was like two or somethin', I know that our friendship can withstand it all. But I'm still sad to see you go. Shit ain't gonna be the same around here without you. I love you, my ghetto queen."

"You'll always be my soul sister," Sasha said.

My last stop before New York was to see Omar. It had been years since our last visit. The prison system moved him to different states constantly, making it really hard to remain connected.

I was nervous as I endured the two-hour process to get through the security screening. Finally Omar was standing in front of me. We were both grinning, speechless for a minute. He grabbed me and held me tight. I got lost in his essence, in our history, but was brought back by the shrill sound of a whistle. The CO approached.

"No touching. I'm being nice by giving a warning. Next time the visit's up." He walked away and the reality of Omar's world hit me hard all over again.

We talked for hours. Looking in each other's eyes, taking in all the words that had been exchanged between us through our letters for the last seven years.

"Amber, one thing I've learned about you is that when you say you're gonna do something, you do it and you do it well. You're not only gonna succeed in New York, you're gonna blow up." He paused and looked down. "I just wish I could be there with you, by your side."

I cherished the time we spent together, but I had learned to be realistic about Omar's release date. He still had nine more years to do. I didn't know when I would see him again.

We parted, changed people.

Thirty-Six

was looking forward to my solo road trip. I had saved up enough money to stay in motels and visit some friends along the way. My mom also gave me some going away money. So did my dad, surprisingly.

What I was most excited about was the whole musical journey I had planned. By this point I had collected more than two hundred cassette tapes with music dating from my Denver days, to all the DJs I had met in Cali who made mix tapes for me on the regular. My goal was to listen to every single tape I owned on my way to New York.

It was sunny as I began my trip. I opened my sunroof, rolled down the windows, and let my hair blow in the wind. It felt good just to drive, allowing each song to bring back memories, and to let my emotions do what they wanted.

Soul II Soul came on and I could picture Lil D doing the Crip walk.

I thought about the Crips, and my high school days. Deep down, even back then, my choices didn't sit well in my heart. I fought against what I knew, driven by my desire to be down. Darnell knew. Juan knew. In my quest for self, I sought for others to define me. It was only God looking out for me and my white skin that saved me from my demise.

But even so, part of me was still thankful for my experiences. If not for the Crips, I never would have met Omar or Lil D. I never may have truly understood the struggle of young black men to survive. I would not understand loss, and therefore I would not be able to appreciate love.

Driving through city after city, I mourned.

I mourned all the important relationships that were brought to an end: love lost, friendships dissolved, loss of innocence, death. I sang along with each song as tears fell freely down my face.

After that first long day of driving, I decided to stop to get some rest. I got a cheap room at a motel near the highway. I was both physically and emotionally exhausted, and fell asleep the minute I laid on the bed.

The next morning I got a cup of coffee and hit the road bright and early. I felt lighter. The music blared out of my speakers, and I rhymed right along with each song, and found myself laughing hysterically as I listened to the lyrics, from Public Enemy to Eric B. and Rakim to MC Lyte and Boogie Down Productions—it was the soundtrack of my life.

Unlike day one, day two was filled with happiness, healing, and hope. I thought about how lucky I was that I'd remained friends with people I grew up with. I'd known Carmen since I was four years old, Keisha since elementary school, Juan since middle school. Not to mention my homies from California: Yvette, Sasha, Amara. And then there was my family: my mother who always stood by me, even during the hardest times;

my brother, who, although we battled hard, I knew deep down somewhere he cared—even though he couldn't show it. And my dad, who was finally beginning to try. I had to say that felt good.

Community had always been important to me, and I had been in search of my tribe for so long, often ending up in places people didn't want me. What made me think I needed to force my way in? My pride wanted me to stand my ground, like at the meeting in college where I was called a devil. Did my presence there help or hurt that day? I got sad and discouraged for a minute, and then realized that maybe I was asking the wrong question. Did I stand for justice that day in that room? Let that be what I critique myself on.

Digable Planets came on. Whatever happened to them? I wondered. That was the lesson. As I stand in my life mission, who do I want to stand with? People who love me or people who hate me? It took so much more energy fighting to be, as opposed to working together to be.

I felt so lucky at that moment, so affirmed. No matter what happened out in New York, I knew, unconditionally, that my community would be there for me. Forever.

After five days of driving, I finally made it to New York at 5:30 in the morning. I was exhausted both from the long drive and from processing my life. My map took over the passenger seat, as I tried to figure out the way to Brooklyn. Unlike California's beautiful highways lined with flowers and greenery, the drive into New York was full of gray. Cement buildings and roadways surrounded me. There was no nature in sight.

But something about the way the sun gently showered the skyline with warm hues of orange was beautiful too. And I could almost feel the energy of the city in the air. Something told me I was in the right place; and for once, I decided to listen.

Epilogue

My twenty-fifth birthday arrived. I'd been in New York two years, and felt very grounded.

The first thing I did when I got home from work at the high school was play my messages. Just as I thought, my mom, Keisha, and Carmen had already called me. Their messages filled me with happiness.

To get me in the mood for the evening, I lit some incense, grabbed a Presidente beer from the fridge, and put on old-school Pete Rock and CL Smooth. As I started getting dressed, I glanced in the mirror to admire the new outfit I caught on sale at Mandee's. I was feeling so sexy, so alive.

"When I reminisce over you," serenaded me. My gaze fell to the wooden box on my dresser where I kept all my letters. Some of those letters I could practically recite by heart. I lifted the letter Omar sent to me shortly after our final visit and began reading it.

Salutations,

I don't know when I'll see you again, but I'm guessing it won't be for a while. The many topics that we addressed during our visit have provided my dreams with a new flavor and direction. I don't know whether I should describe the lingering effects of your presence as a tantalizing taste of the future or a tormenting reminder of the present. In either case, you have reaffirmed my affinity for you.

There are a million ways for me to communicate the depth of my love, and each one is pleading for a place in this note. As a result I cannot concentrate on any other event, nothing else matters. I love you and want to be with you. I never let myself absorb the totality of that truth until I watched you walk away. I watched you from my window. I watched you disappear into the horizon, and then I watched as the trail of dust left in your path settled. All I could think of then is all that I can think of now. I love you. So this is not good-bye, but good luck as you move to the next phase of your life.

Yours Forever, Omar

I closed my eyes and pictured Omar before prison, before the ugly orange jumpsuit, before the horrifying stories of being locked in a cold, dark, cement box for protecting himself. Before all the pain and death that surrounded him this last decade.

I remembered his smile, his poetry, his art, and the pencil always behind his ear. Why had it turned out this way?

The phone interrupts my thoughts. "Hello?"

"Corazón, happy birthday, girl! We got the whole crew here!" It was Empress, and in the background I heard Ajaya and Sasha yelling happy birthday.

"I miss you guys! When are y'all coming to visit?" I asked.

"Well, we need to talk," Empress started. "Ajaya has this whole 'escape America' plan that we need to discuss with you pronto, 'cause shit is so crazy now, we 'bout to save all our money and move to an island together, fuck the bullshit." Empress and I started cracking up, and I heard Ajaya in the background saying, "The islands are calling!"

"I hear you, sis. Y'all gotta save me a seat on that plane, fo' real," I said. We bullshitted for a while. I got to say hi to all my girls before we hung up.

I walked back into my room and picked up Omar's letter, folding it carefully and putting it back in the box. I wish you well, dearest Omar, I wish you well.

I still had some time before Diego was due to arrive, so I sat on the couch to relax. Outside the streets were bumpin' the latest Fat Joe joint. As I sipped my beer, I saw my journal peering out beneath the latest hip-hop novel I was reading. A birthday is a good time to reflect, so I got lost in its words.

As I read, I understood that I might not have all the answers to the questions I've asked myself and others over my lifetime, but I believed I found a partner who would walk with me as I grappled with the complexities of race and continued to confront my own white privilege.

I would never stop walking the path I was on. It was something I had to do.

I owed it not just to myself but to everybody who had been part of my life. To Juan, Omar, Lil D, the Crips, my homies from Denver to Cali, my family, even the white DJ, Max, who had beef with me. I knew now what I didn't know then—it will be a lifelong process.

As I looked through my journal, I came across the first card Diego ever gave to me, shortly after we began dating. After hearing him read a poem at the high school, I told him how much it moved me and so he wrote out a copy for me and put it in a card. It's a poem about his mother.

> *En La Factoria*
> *my mother fashions her American dream*
> *only to be awakened by the daily bruises of her*
> *   reality*
> *En la Factoria si si se habla fluent exploitation*
> *All non-English speakers need apply*
> *En la factoria no one's safe from inflation or subju-*
> *   gation at the cost of sub minimum wage workers*
> *   lost.*
> *En la factoria pins and needles needles and pins*
> *   become her eternal damnation in her quest for*
> *   salvation*
> *En la factoria my mother tries to make a dollar out*
> *   of the 50 cents she gets paid per dress*
> *En la factoria Ralph Lauren, Tommy Hilfiger, and*
> *   Calvin Klein become the executioners of her*
> *   hopes*
> *En la factoria en la factoria en la factoria*
> *My mother struggles every day, to be a woman.*

This is a good thing I have with him. The doorbell rings. I put my journal away, and open the door. Diego hands me a rose and kisses me on my cheek.

"*Hola, querida,*" he says. "Let's go celebrate your life."

Acknowledgments

To my gentle warrior and beloved husband Hector, you are my foundation, my hope, and my dream come true! To my children, my heart never knew this kind of love. I am in awe watching your spirits dance.

I am grateful to all my friends and family spread across the country. To my mom, for all that you are and continue to be in my life—you are my hero! R.D. welcome to our family. For my father, I am so thankful that our relationship has blossomed, and I am so moved by your undying support of my process and this book. To Pete, your clarity and honesty helped me tremendously. Shannon, Millie and Natasha—thanks for the laughter and the joy you bring. For John, I look forward to the day when your brilliance can shine to the world.

Gracias por todo mi familia en NYC, Hector, Nina, Quico, Carmen, Jose, Alma, Ana Lucia, and the entire Fernandez family. To my circle of sisters—my foundation, my rock—I am so blessed to have you in my life! Marti, Lalania, Anda, Asia, Joanna, Kim, Vania, Wanda, Brandy, and Rha Goddess. Shout out to the people who make this world beautiful: Rosa Clemente, Julia Grob, Kahlil Almustafa, Corey, Baba, Dawn, Todd, Herbie, Beth, Alli, the whole We Got Issues! Crew—Fly, Jen, Kelly, Allison, Kamilah, Chelsea, Marla, Adeeba, Moni, Stephanie, Phakiso, Kibibi, Rosa, Michele, Onome, and Jennette. Thanks to all the courageous women who shared their voices in the *We Got Issues!* book. Much love and respect to my entire El Puente family, especially Frances and Luis, and all my former students—K'Arma souljahs where ya at? This book is for you! Youth Ministries for Peace and Justice, Aroosha Rana, Ben Synder, Kris Diaz, Teresa Basilo, Danny Hoch, WAAAK-One and the whole Breaks Kru, Daphne Farganis, Angela Hardison, Tim Wise, DJ Kuttin' Kandi and my REACHip-Hop peoples, Queen God-Is, Maribel and Clyde, KET, Eli Ceballos, Rocky, Chuck D, Afrika Bambaataa, Lathan Hodgemi, Christie and Fabel, Peter Miranda, Dominic Colon, Adam Mansbach, Jeff Chang, Lemon, Davey D, April Silver, Melanie Bush, Rhea Vedro, Ashara, Jeff Campbell, Faatma, Karma Café, Basheba Earth, Steve, Lola, Piper Anderson, Inga Musico, Chris Alvardo, Andrea Thome, Ninoska, Noelia, Jessica, Josephina and Nicholas, Rosa Baergas and family, Julz, Kahlil and Eli, Kevin Coval, Oscar, Fidel and Sol, Rafael Planten, Yako and Bambi, Kate, Chino and the whole PMP crew, Hectah, Jeremy Glick, E-Fierce, Patty Dukes, WBAI, Doze, Phyzek, Donald D, Just I, DXT, and the heads in Denver, SD, LA and the Bay who have shared their life with me, you are not forgotten. RIP to the lost soldiers. Extra special shout out to Dennis, Jay, and Sam.

Thanks to my peoples who read drafts of this book in all its forms! Your insights were invaluable.

To my mentors: Dr. Hayes and Dr. Weber—you may never know what an impact your strength had on my life. Thank you for the gift of questioning and discernment.

To Nan Satter, thank you for your insight and guidance in sharing my story.

Special thanks to: Sofia Quintero, Cathy Wilkerson, Suheir Hammad, Johanna Castillo—without you, this book would not be!

My fabulous agent, Jennifer Cayea, who patiently listened and supported me through my process; my editor Krishan Trotman, thank you for all you have done for this book!

To all the activists I have had the pleasure of working with— forward ever, backward never.

264731BV00001B/8/P

9 780743 287814